# ALEXIA'S SECRETS

# ALEXIA'S SECRETS

## Una-Mary Parker

This first world edition published in Great Britain 2008 by
SEVERN HOUSE PUBLISHERS LTD of
9–15 High Street, Sutton, Surrey SM1 1DF.
This first world edition published in the USA 2008 by
SEVERN HOUSE PUBLISHERS INC of
595 Madison Avenue, New York, N.Y. 10022.

British Library Cataloguing in Publication Data

Parker, Una-Mary
   Alexia's secrets
   1. Debutantes - Fiction 2. Social classes - Fiction 3. Love
   stories
   I. Title
   823.9'14[F]


   ISBN-13: 978-0-7278-6616-5   (cased)
   ISBN-13: 978-1-84751-055-6   (trade paper)

*All Severn House titles are printed on acid-free paper.*


Typeset by Palimpsest Book Production Ltd.,
Grangemouth, Stirlingshire, Scotland.
Printed and bound in Great Britain by
MPG Books Ltd., Bodmin, Cornwall.

Dedicated to the memory of Sonia Marks, a remarkable
and inspirational woman, and to her husband Louis Marks,
whose talents have won him so many awards and whose
kindness is beyond words.

# Prologue

An eighteen-year-old girl with dark hair, a heart-shaped face and intelligent brown eyes is getting into a first class carriage at Paddington Station. She is travelling to Oxford as the guest of Lord and Lady Clifton, who are giving the first grand debutante ball of the season for their daughter Virginia and their son Simon, who is celebrating his twenty-fifth birthday. This is her first time away from home, but that does not explain how uneasy she feels at the prospect of staying with a family she has never even met.

Driving up from his home in Cornwall in a shabby Alfa Romeo, a man in his late twenties, with a strong profile and great presence, views the coming weekend with mixed feelings. He is a distant cousin of the Clifton family and has recently been demobbed from the army, having served in Northern France. It's years since he's stayed at Marley Court and he wonders if the Great War will have changed the lavish hospitality for which the hosts were renowned.

With the blushing skin and blond hair of a typical Englishman, the rider gallops his new hunter up the steep incline, urging the mare forward with wild, excited bursts of laughter until he reaches the top. From here he can look down on Marley Court, which has been in the family since Henry VIII gave it to one of his ancestors in 1544. Built of honey-coloured Kentish stone, with battlements, turrets, gables and elegantly slim chimney stacks, its one hundred and twenty rooms contain a treasure trove of exquisite antiques and paintings.

One day the young man will inherit everything that lies before him.

The girl and the two young men are moving inextricably towards each other, but only the girl has a sense of destiny and destruction from which there is no escape.

In fact, for all of them the point of no return has already been passed.

# One

The place was enormous; more a palace than a house. Alexia's eyes widened with amazement as Marley Court emerged through the trees at the end of a long drive, as pale as a sandcastle and as ornate as icing on a wedding cake. Surrounded by formal gardens and parkland, it stood facing a sloping lawn that led down to a lake, beyond which lay distant woodlands and hills.

'Heavens,' she said under her breath, smoothing her new grey suede gloves. A car had been sent to meet them at the station and now, sitting in the back with her appointed chaperone Lady Goodwin and her daughter Jane, Alexia's apprehension increased as they drove out of the shady tunnel of oak trees into the brilliant afternoon sunshine.

Marley Court. The family seat of the immensely rich Earl and Countess of Clifton. A world away from the dingy Kensington flat and the lack of money which was the only home she knew.

Lady Goodwin, a plump matronly figure with a warm smile which disguised her desperately ambitious marital plans for Jane, had been very chatty on the train journey, asking all sorts of questions about her family.

Alexia had answered carefully and guardedly, wondering how she was supposed to make the leap from being a naïve schoolgirl to a grown-up young lady. Jane was obviously being guided every step of the way by her mother in the art of social behaviour, but all that Alexia's mother, Margaret, had said to her was that it was a pity she had such bad breath, and if she couldn't say anything intelligent, it was better not to say anything. Above all, Alexia was told, never let on that you're poor.

Alexia's great fear was that she'd forget and reveal giveaway details – that they had no servants, for instance, or that her grandmother made most of her clothes.

The car rolled relentlessly on towards the house, the chauffeur looking inscrutably ahead while Miss Green, Lady Goodwin's lady's maid, sat beside him clutching her employer's jewel case as if it was a bomb that might explode at any moment.

'Aren't we lucky with the weather?' Lady Goodwin observed, craning her neck to get a better look at the beautifully kept grounds. 'Look, Jane! Just look at those horse chestnuts. Have you ever seen such glorious trees?'

Jane, small, pale and plain, looked unimpressed and said calmly, 'Umm. Lovely.'

Alexia wished she felt as calm; instead, a mounting sense of doom was making her heart pound. After all, she'd only been invited to stay for three days. Before she knew it she'd be home again, regaling her granny with excited accounts of her visit.

They'd reached the main entrance and the car tyres crunched noisily on the evenly raked gravel that resembled sugar crystals. A butler and two footmen in dark green livery stood in the open doorway, their expressions as impassive as if they were expecting a delivery of coal.

Lady Goodwin and Jane stepped elegantly out of the car but Alexia found herself hampered by her tight mid-calf skirt. Her movements were gawky, like a young colt. At that moment a gust of wind swept across the lawns, and her coat flapped open as her long narrow scarf streamed from her neck like a banner.

'Oh, *crikey!*' she exclaimed loudly, clutching her hat before it blew off.

Lady Goodwin gave her a withering glance. Miserably she followed them into a huge dark hall. It seemed as big as a tennis court. They were immediately greeted by the housekeeper, Mrs Abbey, who led them up a heavily carved Jacobean staircase and along a wide gallery hung with tapestries. Off this there were smaller corridors, and it was several minutes before they arrived at their rooms.

'The bathroom is further along,' Mrs Abbey informed them. 'Tea will be in the red salon at five o'clock. If there's anything you want, just ring the bell.'

The only thing I'll need is a map so I can find my way back to the hall, Alexia reflected, panicking at the thought that Lady Goodwin and Jane might go ahead, leaving her to find her own way downstairs again.

No one had told her it would be like this. She'd expected to be welcomed by Lord and Lady Clifton themselves. She'd thought there'd be lots of other guests of her own age milling around, an atmosphere of anticipation before the ball. Instead, the empty silence of the place made her feel as if she was stuck in a museum after closing time.

A moment later the footman arrived with her cases. Alexia straightened her shoulders and raised her chin. She would not let anyone see how overwhelmed she felt.

'Thank you,' she said, as if she were used to servants waiting on her, and he departed, closing the door quietly behind him. She'd been warned not to attempt to do her own unpacking. Her grandmother had told her, 'A maid will do that and she'll press your clothes, lay them out for you and run your bath. When you come home, don't forget to leave a shilling on the dressing table.'

Alexia looked around curiously. The four-poster bed was hung with pale green silk. An over-stuffed sofa faced a crackling fire although it was May, and a table and chair stood in the window. On the table was a rack of writing paper headed with an earl's coronet above the address, and a pen and silver inkwell. She looked at herself in the full-length mirror and realized that beside the beautifully dressed Jane, she looked like a servant in her cheap overcoat.

Taking it off, she threw it on to a chair, wondering how she was going to get through the next few days without giving the game away. They only had to look at her to realize her family was penniless and she had no business coming to a place like this.

The sound of car engines below her window attracted her attention.

Flinging down her hat, she opened the lead-latticed window carefully and leaned out. From here she could see the magnificent formal garden, but it was the sight of several cars, all arriving at the same time, that interested her. A beautifully dressed couple, accompanied by their two daughters, got out of the first Rolls-Royce, which was quickly followed by a second car in which were presumably the lady's maid and valet, with eight trunks.

Alexia glanced at her father's battered leather suitcases with a sinking heart. Her attention was drawn back to the drive. Three more cars had arrived, the chauffeurs eyeing each other's vehicles with critical appraisal while footmen scurried to and fro, dealing with yet more luggage. Then came a very old-fashioned horse-drawn carriage clip-clopping up the drive, and out stepped an elderly couple who looked as if they hadn't changed their style of clothes since 1910. Finally, bringing up the rear was a mud-splattered open-top Alfa Romeo, driven by a young man wearing goggles and a tweed peaked cap.

Alexia leaned further out of the window to see better. The Alfa Romeo had drawn up with a flourish and a swish of spitting gravel outside the front entrance but instead of its driver being welcomed by the butler, a blond-haired young man came charging out of the house, shouting delightedly.

'Rodders, old chap! Good to see you!'

The driver climbed out of the car, nonchalantly taking off his gauntlet gloves. 'Hello there, Simon.' His tone was casual as he stretched out to shake hands, but the young man flung his arms around him in a bear hug.

'I thought you'd never arrive, Rodders,'

'God, it's such a drive from Penhalt,' he said wearily as he disentangled himself, and removed his cap and goggles. 'Would you believe I set off at cock's crow this morning?' He was tall with broad shoulders, and his light brown hair flipped like silk in the strong breeze. Tossing it carelessly out of his eyes he said, 'Happy birthday, by the way.'

'Thanks. Come on in. The family are longing to see you again.'

*So that's Simon Stanhope*, Alexia reflected thoughtfully as the two men disappeared back into the house. Viscount Stanhope, heir to the Earl of Clifton and one of the most eligible bachelors in the country.

Having washed her hands and sponged her face, she found to her dismay that her worst fears had been realized. By spending such a long time watching people arrive, she'd been left behind by Lady Goodwin and Jane, who had already gone down to tea.

Setting off along the corridor she remembered there was a turning which led to a wide gallery. She passed several closed doors until she came to a T-junction. There she paused, wondering which way to go. She didn't even remember coming this way half an hour ago.

'Hello there! Can I help you?'

Alexia spun round. A young man with untidy golden hair, a tall wiry frame, dazzling blue eyes and an engaging smile, met her gaze. It was Simon.

'Hello. I'm Alexandra Erskine,' she explained, flushing with embarrassment. 'I've lost my way. Can you tell me how to get to the red salon?'

'I'll take you there myself.' He came forward eagerly and for a strange instant it seemed as if a cloud of tiny flies were blotting out her view of his face. She blinked. His head and shoulders were momentarily obliterated and, thinking she'd been dazzled by the sun streaming through one of the windows, she paused before thanking him. A moment later her vision cleared and she found herself looking into the palest blue eyes she'd ever seen. So pale that the pupils looked like black holes drilled into his skull. He was gazing at her with a curious expression.

'So *you're* Alexandra Erskine? I heard you were coming to stay. Do you know Virginia? She's a deb too, this year.'

'I'm not really a deb,' Alexia said hurriedly, not wanting to give the wrong impression. Maybe he thought her parents were going to give a ball or something and then he'd expect to be invited.

'Oh! I thought you looked about the right age.'

'I am eighteen, but we live in London, you know . . .' Her voice trailed off uncertainly and she felt stupid.

Simon grinned and, slipping his hand through her arm in an intimate fashion, led her along corridors and passages until they reached the top of the main staircase.

'I thought London was where it all happens?' He dropped his voice as if he were confiding a great secret. 'Virginia's *furious* that since the war there've been no presentations at Buckingham Palace. What are the King and Queen thinking of? There's not much point in being a deb if you can't get presented at Court, is there?'

She blinked, baffled. 'No. I suppose not.'

'You haven't been here before, have you? How do you know us?'

His outspoken manner and the excited way he expressed himself intrigued her.

'My father was at Oxford with your father; they were friends. Then your mother bumped into Daddy in Bond Street the other day and she said she'd invite me to stay.'

'Have you any brothers or sisters?'

'I'm an only child.'

His pale eyes sparked with approval. 'Lucky old you!'

They'd reached the hall and he led her to the far side, through double doors and into a room which was predominantly decorated and furnished in ruby red damask, embellished with gilt. A dozen or so people were sitting around, sipping tea from dainty cups, amongst them a smug-looking Lady Goodwin, with Jane beside her. They were talking to a young man with the expression of a whipped dog.

'Mama! Pa! Look who I found wandering around the Great Gallery like a lost sheep!' Simon shouted jovially. 'It's . . . it's . . .' He turned to Alexia in agitation. 'What did you say your name was?'

Alexia couldn't be sure whether he was joking or not. 'I'm Alexandra Erskine. How do you do?' She looked at the grim-faced man who stood with his back to the fireplace. A once beautiful woman rose from a chair and came forward, hand outstretched.

'How do you do, my dear? I'm so glad you were able to come. And really, Simon – ' she turned to her son and spoke with mock severity – 'do try and be more polite. The poor girl will think she's entered a madhouse if you go on like that.'

Simon turned his hot blue eyes on Alexia. 'She's a good egg, and can take care of herself! I could see that right away. You can, can't you?' he urged mischievously.

Alexia couldn't help laughing, liking him a lot. 'I'm obviously going to have to!' she retorted. She found his boyish manner very disarming and she looked forward to getting to know him better.

'So you're Malcolm Erskine's gel, then?' Lord Clifton enquired grumpily, his florid complexion gleaming with fine sweat, his portly body tightly encased in brown tweed. 'Humph! Haven't seen your father for years. What's he doing with himself these days? Still losing money on the gee-gees?'

'Daddy doesn't back horses any more,' she said in a small voice, suddenly wishing she were anywhere else but here. Everyone was looking at her. The other guests, cups poised, were watching her with silent curiosity.

'*Such* a nice-looking girl! Pity about the father, though,' she heard someone whisper.

Lord Clifton continued loudly, 'Can't afford to now, eh? Blown all the family lolly I suppose?'

'Really, Ian,' protested Lady Clifton. 'That's quite unnecessary.'

He looked at his wife coldly, his eyes embedded in the flesh of his face like polished grey marbles. 'What's the point of beating about the bush? Everyone knows Malcolm Erskine's a waster who lost all his money betting. It's not the girl's fault.'

Alexia stood biting her bottom lip, sudden tears threatening to rise to the surface.

'My father's a wonderful man,' she blurted out vehemently. 'Everyone likes him and he's never hurt a soul in his life.'

'What? Even those he's borrowed money from?' Lord Clifton looked down at her with disdain, but something flickered in his eyes as if she'd touched a raw nerve. 'Well, you're his daughter. You would think that, wouldn't you?' he conceded grudgingly.

Ignoring him, his wife came over and slipped her arm around Alexia's shoulders. 'Pay no attention to him, my dear, come and have some tea,' she said in a no-nonsense voice, as she led the way to a low round table covered in a snowy lace cloth, on which stood a Crown Derby tea set on a silver tray.

At that moment more guests arrived and soon a lively tea party was in full swing. Alexia found herself being introduced to the couple with the two daughters she'd seen arriving, but she was finding it hard to concentrate as they proceeded to indulge in what her grandmother called 'banal small-talk'.

Lord Clifton's disparaging words had wounded her deeply, making her wish she'd never come, and making her wonder if other people held her father in such disregard. She loved him more than anyone in the world, in spite of her mother's continual talk of how rotten he was, such a waster who had ruined her life and how much better they'd be without him.

Fighting to control her emotions, she looked around the room. Simon had vanished and everyone seemed to be ignoring her now and talking amongst themselves. Even the girls of her age didn't seem to want to be friendly. Then up came a pert looking girl with insolent eyes and a mass of chestnut brown hair that tumbled unfashionably down her back.

'So, you're Alexandra Erskine?'

'Yes, but everyone calls me Alexia. And you are . . .?'

'Virginia Stanhope, of course.' She looked Alexia up and down from her black lace-up shoes to the collar of her simple white blouse, with undisguised disdain.

Taken aback, Alexia blurted out gauchely, 'Oh! So you're Simon's sister!'

Virginia stared malevolently at Alexia, pinning her to the place where she wanted her to be and where she intended to keep her. 'Why were you invited to my party? I don't think we know you, do we?'

'Our fathers were friends at university, as I explained to Simon earlier . . . I was lost, and didn't know how to find the red salon . . .'

'*Lost?*' Virginia repeated. 'I've never heard anything so ludicrous as someone being lost *indoors*.'

Alexia flushed a deeper shade of red. 'You do have a rather large house.' This was turning out to be the most dreadful day. Beside Virginia, in her expensive and fashionable after-noon dress and long amber necklace, she was feeling horribly inferior.

At that moment Simon zoomed back into the room, full of excitement. 'I've just seen the ballroom!' he exclaimed breathlessly to the assembled company. 'Rodders and I had a dekko. It's *divine!*'

Then he spotted Alexia, looking glum. '*Darling*, you must come and see it!' He grabbed her hand and started pulling

her towards the door, to the surprise of those enjoying a
sedate cup of lapsang souchong. 'And I want you to meet
Rodders! He's a sort of distant cousin and a great chap.'

Out of the corner of her eye she could see Virginia's furious
expression, while Lady Goodwin was prodding Jane to go
with them, but the girl shook her head, refusing.

Roderick Davenport was standing in the middle of the
hall, gazing up at a painting of a dead stag.

Simon waved his arms around. 'This is Roderick
Davenport. Rodders, meet Alexandra Erskine. Alexandra,
meet Rodders.'

Looking up into his face Alexia knew instantly that this
was someone she could trust. His features were strong, his
olive skin smooth, and his dark eyes looked kind. His mouth
curved into a slow smile as he returned her gaze.

'Hello, Alexandra,' he said in a deep quiet voice.

'Hello. I'm usually called Alexia.'

His smile deepened. 'And *I'm* usually called Rod.'

'Not by me you're not, old thing,' Simon said impatiently,
linking arms with both of them. Then he turned conversa-
tionally to Alexia as if he'd forgotten Roderick's presence.
'The ballroom was built in the fifteenth century, but one of
the ancestors decided to do it up in the seventeenth. It's a
bit big and scary, so don't get a fright.'

Roderick looked incredulous. 'For heaven's sake, why
should she get a fright?'

Simon shrugged theatrically. 'You know, it's so *imposing*!
So over*powering*!'

'So is the whole of Marley Court, if it comes to that,'
Roderick observed dryly.

Simon stepped in front of them and, with a flourish, flung
open large double doors. 'There! What do you think? Pukka,
isn't it?'

Alexia reflected that it was certainly the most ornate room
she'd ever seen. There seemed to be no end to the rich carv-
ings, the decorative plasterwork embellished with gold leaf.
A fireplace of variously coloured marbles reached up to the
moulded ceiling, and there were Ionic columns with capi-
tals and scroll-like ornaments in the four corners. The polished
floor stretched for eighty feet like a honey-coloured ice rink

and there was a profusion of flowers everywhere: wound around the pillars, in great vases on every surface, and garlanding the French windows on to the terrace. Enriching this already over-gilded expanse was a plethora of little gilt chairs, side tables, damask hangings, family portraits and objets d'art.

Alexia felt Roderick's eyes on her and she glanced quickly at him. His expression was one of amusement, as if he wondered whether she'd be as impressed as Simon wanted her to be.

'Will there be enough room for dancing?' she asked doubtfully.

Simon looked crushed. 'Of course there will,' he retorted crossly. 'People will want to sit and talk as well as dance. Don't you think it looks marvellous?'

'It's beautiful,' she agreed, aware Roderick was still watching her. 'And the flowers are lovely.'

Crestfallen, Simon turned away. 'Well, I think the ball will be the talk of the county for the next three months.'

'No doubt about that,' Rod remarked quietly.

'Let's have a drink! Let's celebrate! It is my birthday, after all.' Simon turned to a hovering footman. 'Bring us some champagne, Belmont. And three glasses.'

'I don't . . .' Alexia began.

'Of course you do,' Simon retorted, cheered up again. 'Just a little glass, darling. To drink my health?'

She smiled weakly. 'All right.' It seemed rude to refuse under the circumstances and she couldn't help feeling a quickening sensation every time he called her 'darling'. No one had ever called her that before and it made her feel thrillingly flattered and grown-up.

Simon sprawled on one of the gilt chairs. 'Take a perch. Let's enjoy this room before the masses arrive. Did I tell you we've got a jazz band playing tonight?'

Half an hour and two glasses of chilled champagne later, Alexia was making a desperate attempt to find her way back to her room. God, how many corridors and galleries were there?

Panic set in once again when she realized she'd twice passed a painting of cows standing in a meadow. Light-headed with

alcohol, never having been allowed to have even a sip of wine
before, she wondered if she dared knock on someone's door
to ask them to ring for a maid, who would then show her the
way.

At that moment she heard voices. It was Mrs Abbey,
showing some late arrivals to their quarters.

'I'm afraid I'm lost,' she told the housekeeper.

Mrs Abbey smiled brightly. 'Everyone gets lost at first.
We had one guest who left a trail of white cotton thread in
order to find her way to the bathroom and back.'

The relief she felt at being back in her room was immense.
The maid had unpacked her clothes and stored them in
cupboards lined with flowered chintz. Her pale blue evening
dress had been laid out with her matching satin shoes and
long white gloves, and her underclothes had been folded on
a chair, ready for her to put on with the white silk stockings
with clocks, bought for her by her grandmother. The fire
glowed comfortingly, and there was a tray with biscuits and
a jug of water on the side. By her bed were several recently
published books and magazines.

Suddenly a new sense of self-confidence, mostly caused
by the champagne, swept through her, making her feel she
was capable of going anywhere and doing anything.

There was a tap on the door. 'I've run your bath, miss,'
said a bright young voice.

Alexia could have hugged the little maid, she felt so happy.
This was heaven. The life she wanted. The life she intended
to have, away from quarrels, away from the lack of money,
away from her miserable childhood. Tonight was the turning
point; nothing was going to stop her now from enjoying
herself.

That evening passed in such a dazzling swirl of glamorous
impressions that Alexia could only remember snatches the
next day. After a dinner party for the fifty house-guests,
seated at a table which shimmered with gold plate, crystal,
white orchids and candles, and at which a first course of
consommé was followed by whiting in a cream sauce, roast
lamb, cabinet pudding and finally a savoury, *Bouchées de
Caviar*, three hundred further guests arrived for the ball.

They filled all the main ground floor rooms and hall with chattering voices and laughter, while footmen bearing trays of champagne skimmed to and fro in a silent frenzy, making sure everyone had their glasses refilled the moment they were empty.

To Alexia all the women seemed beautiful, in satin and chiffon, glittering with jewels as they batted their ostrich-feather fans seductively, while the men were dashing and flirtatious as they whirled their partners around the candlelit ballroom. Even the snatches of conversation she heard dazzled with wit and aphoristic repartee.

Observing it all, and drinking in every moment of the atmosphere, Alexia became even more determined that this was the life she wanted. She'd never known such fun existed. Never seen such a lavish display of spending on pure pleasure. Never observed such mutual happiness between people.

Then Simon brought up a very tall man in his late twenties to meet her.

'You must meet Baggers, or rather Benjamin Mortimer-Smythe,' he announced. 'I was his fag at Eton and lived to tell the tale!'

'Call me Baggers, everyone does,' he exclaimed jovially. 'And you are?'

'Alexandra Erskine.' She sensed an aura of decadence about him.

'And you're called . . . what? Alex? Ali? Al?' he asked as he slipped his arm around her waist.

Her tone was cool. 'Alexia.'

'Al-lex-zeeia!' he drawled. 'Oh, very Anna Karenina. Are you a romantic young lady?'

'I don't think so,' she retorted.

Baggers gazed myopically into her face. 'You don't think so? Dear child, I think we should find out whether you are or not, don't you?'

Roderick appeared at that moment. 'Baggers, behave yourself,' he said firmly. 'I know your tricks of old.'

Alexia looked at Roderick in surprise. 'Were you in the army together?'

Both men smiled and then burst out laughing.

'In the army?' Baggers repeated. 'Dear girl, the army

wouldn't have me with my bad eyesight even if the Germans were landing on the beach at Dover. Come along, let's dance.' And he whirled her away before she could stop him, as the band played a hot number and the Clifton ancestors looked down from their golden frames at the assembled company with silent disapproval.

In fact Alexia found there were a lot of men like him at the ball; all friends of Simon's, all flirtatious, flippant and utterly insincere. They all had ridiculous nicknames too, like 'Hoots' McVean, 'Porgie' Hargreaves-Webb, 'Plummy' Pearson – no doubt because of the way he talked – and 'Snuggle' Sinclair. She never did find out what any of their real names were and she didn't really care. She was having fun and she wondered why, whenever one of them started flirting with her, Roderick hove into view like a protective guardian angel.

'Are you all right, Alexia?' he kept asking.

'I'm perfectly all right, thank you,' she replied briskly, accepting another glass of champagne from a passing footman. At one point Simon also rushed up, looking inquiringly into Alexia's face and asking, 'Are you OK?'

'Of *course* I'm OK.'

Why were they worried about her? Did they feel sorry for her because of her father? Because her evening dress was homemade? And because she was not a debutante like the others?

'I'm absolutely fine,' she asserted firmly. 'I'm having a wonderful time.'

'Let's dance then.' Simon swept her on to the floor, leaving Roderick standing looking after them as they romped around to the brittle, bright sound of jazz music played on saxophones. She smiled into his face. Tonight was more wonderful than she could ever have imagined and he looked so handsome, in a touchingly youthful way, in his white tie and tails, his ruffled hair golden in the light of a hundred candles, a white gardenia pinned to his lapel.

'Isn't this the most wonderful night?' she breathed.

His face lit up attractively, pale blue eyes drilling hers as he grinned at her. 'It's the ticket, isn't it? Ma and Pa have really pushed the boat out tonight.'

'I think this house is marvellous.'

He raised blond eyebrows. 'It looks good tonight,' he agreed. 'You must come and stay again.'

'Oh, I'd *love* to.'

'Then we'll fix it.'

Her expression was dreamy. 'You're so lucky to live here.'

Simon looked at her askance. 'Think so?'

'Oh, goodness, yes!'

His mouth tightened and his expression darkened. 'Things are not always what they seem, you know. It's all smoke and mirrors.'

'Really?' she asked, puzzled.

'Who the hell cares, though? Damn the lot of 'em! Life is for living, that's what I say. Let's get out of here; it's too bloody hot.'

She allowed herself to be led quite forcefully through the French windows on to the terrace. The moon hung brightly like a round Chinese lantern against a black sky, and the strong perfume of the white jasmine flowers that grew up the side of the house was sickly sweet.

'What are your family like?' he asked abruptly, taking a gold cigarette case out of his breast pocket and offering her one.

'*My* family? Well, fairly ordinary I suppose. No thanks, I don't smoke. My parents aren't rich like yours, and we're not at all grand.'

'I don't care about all that. I mean what are they *like*? Jolly? Morose? Kind? Cruel? Are they nice to you, for instance?' He took a long drag of his Senior Service cigarette.

Alexia gave a careful sigh, playing for time, not wanting to answer his questions. 'I expect, like all families, they're a bit of everything,' she replied vaguely.

'My mother never once came up to the nursery to kiss us goodnight.' He looked at her with mournful eyes, reminding her of a sad puppy. 'Pa used to whip me with a riding crop. *Bang! Bang! Bang!*' He thumped the stone balustrade that surrounded the terrace with his clenched fist.

That was when Alexia realized he was very drunk. He swayed for a moment and then sat down suddenly on a nearby bench.

'Were you ever beaten, Alexia?' he asked, his voice angry.
'I don't think girls get beaten.' She felt slightly scared.
Simon had grabbed her arm and pulled her down beside him.
His breath smelled of brandy.

'I only want to know what love is,' he said, his voice
suddenly low and soft. 'Do you know what love is?'

She sat rigid, not answering, feeling both frightened and
embarrassed. Turning her head away, she pretended she hadn't
heard him.

'I *ache* to be loved,' he continued, snatching her hand and
placing it over his crotch. He moved closer, his mouth half
open, his glazed eyes half shut. He lurched towards her. 'Can
you love me, darling? I do so want you to love me.'

Alexia jumped to her feet in alarm, pulling her hand away.
This was exactly the behaviour her grandmother had warned
her about. Young men getting drunk and trying to take advantage of a girl. Her reputation could already be in jeopardy
if anyone had seen her sitting in the garden alone with him
in the middle of the night. And if she let him kiss her, goodness only knew what would happen or where it might lead.

'I m-must go back indoors,' she stammered.

'Don't leave me, darling,' he wailed. 'I only want to . . .'

She turned away and as she was scurrying back towards
the house she saw Roderick silhouetted in the open French
window. He was standing still, watching her as she came
towards him.

Angry for having allowed herself to get into a compro-
mising situation, she forced a smile to her face, half expecting
him to ask her once more if she was all right.

Instead he smiled warmly and said gently, 'I was looking
for you. Would you like to dance?'

'I'd love to.' She hoped she didn't sound too grateful. At
least no one else seemed to have seen what had happened.

It was two o'clock in the morning before she got to bed.
The maid had left a tray with a plate of dainty sandwiches
and a glass of milk on a side table, her bed had been turned
down, her nightdress laid out ready for her to slip into, and
a fireguard placed before the burning coals for safety.

Tonight had been a revelation, imbued with magic and
romance, transforming her from a gauche schoolgirl into a

young lady. Unable to sleep she hung out of her window, breathing in the warm scented air and watching as four night-watchmen patrolled the grounds around the house, aware that the ladies staying would have brought thousands of pounds' worth of jewellery with them.

'I do apologize,' Simon whispered the next morning as everyone gathered in the breakfast room. 'It was unforgivable of me to behave like that. The trouble is, I was too excited to eat any dinner, so a couple of glasses of champagne . . . and wham! I was as high as a kite! Will you ever forgive me?'

Alexia looked into his anxious eyes and relented. After all, she'd been a little tipsy herself.

'Really, it's all right.'

'Are you *sure*?' His tone was earnest, his brow furrowed.

'Absolutely sure.' She giggled nervously, horrified that with hindsight his behaviour had secretly excited her.

'Did you enjoy yourself? Did you have a good time?' He shook his head dolefully. 'I don't really remember anything after you skedaddled back to the house.'

She spoke with sincerity. 'Actually, I had the most marvellous time ever.'

Virginia, helping herself to scrambled egg from the side-board, overheard her. 'You certainly *did*,' she said cattily. 'You danced every dance, didn't you? And you're not even a bona fide debutante!'

Simon glared at his sister. 'That's really rude, Virginia. Just because she had more dance partners than you doesn't mean you can act like a spoilt brat! Alexia is a good egg and I've invited her to stay again, so there!'

'It's not up to you who stays here, Simon.' Virginia's eyes shone with malice. 'You haven't inherited this place *yet*.'

Lady Clifton, looking pale and sipping black coffee, glanced over at them from where she sat at one end of the breakfast table. 'When will you two grow up, for heaven's sake? Please forgive their bad manners, Alexia. Help yourself to breakfast and then come and join us all.'

Deeply embarrassed, Alexia ignored the array of silver

chafing dishes under which little methylated spirit heaters kept the food hot, and helped herself instead to coffee.

'Aren't you hungry?' Simon asked, loading up his own plate with eggs and bacon.

Sick with misery at Virginia's nastiness, she said curtly, 'No thanks.'

'You're still angry with me, aren't you?'

'Not in the least.'

'Will you play croquet with me later?'

She nodded politely, but a sudden sense of foreboding made her wish she could leave straight away. The magic and glamour of last night had vanished. The enormous house might be run on the lines of a grand luxurious hotel but there were dark undercurrents she didn't understand; was this what Simon had referred to as 'all smoke and mirrors'?

'And a game of tennis, too?' Simon cajoled.

'I'm afraid I don't play tennis.'

He stared at her blankly. 'Then what do you do with your tennis court?'

'We don't *have* a tennis court.' To her mortification she realized he had no knowledge of the vast differences that lay between them. He probably wouldn't want to have anything to do with her anyway, once he knew how stultifyingly ordinary and poverty-stricken her life was, compared to his. 'Houses in London rarely have tennis courts,' she added haughtily, as if she thought him stupid.

He grinned, unperturbed. 'I was forgetting you live in town. I'm going up to London myself next week. Can I call on you? I suppose your family wouldn't let me take you out to dinner? Do you have chaperones like that boring Lady Goodwin you came down with? Poor you,' he continued without waiting for an answer, 'it must be dreadful being a girl.'

'I'm quite used to it by now,' she mocked airily as she sat down at the long mahogany table, praying Lady Goodwin hadn't overheard him.

Simon's laughter ricocheted from wall to wall of the room, startling the hung-over and those who took eating breakfast seriously.

'You're quite used to it . . .!' he repeated, chortling.

'Darling, you *are* a one! God, I'm mad about you! Come and stay next weekend. No, better still, don't go home at all. Stay here! Your chauffeur could bring down some more clothes if you need them, couldn't he? Oh, do say you'll stay!'

Everyone was looking at her, especially Lady Goodwin, whose expression was piqued as if she thought her charge was pushing herself forward in an un-ladylike way, quite overshadowing poor Jane.

Alexia blushed, feeling hot in her ugly hand-knitted jumper, conscious that all the other girls were wearing pure silk blouses and pearls with their tweeds. 'Sorry, but I've got things to do – in town.'

'But surely you could—?'

'For God's sake *shut up*, Simon,' Lord Clifton bellowed, staggering into the dining room at that moment. He looked bloated and liverish, as he surveyed the sideboard. 'Where are the sausages? You know I like sausages for breakfast. Why the hell are there no sausages?' he added, aggrieved.

The butler, looking pained, scurried from the room.

'Why not have something else for a change?' Lady Clifton suggested tightly.

'And why don't you bloody shut up!' her husband roared, giving her a baleful look.

Shocked, Alexia sipped her tea and studiously looked at the butter, which had an imprint of the Clifton crest on its smooth yellow surface. So her parents weren't the only un-happily married couple? Not that they ever shouted at each other. Theirs was a cold, remote unhappiness, where the silences between them were long and painful, overlaid with brooding regret and disappointment.

Lady Clifton turned to Alexia. 'Tell me, my dear, how is your father? When he was at Oxford he was the most hand-some man of his generation, you know.'

'Daddy? Really?' Alexia's eyes widened with delight. She tried to imagine her father as a young man, laughing and happy, going to parties and being attractive to girls.

'Please give him my best wishes.' Lady Clifton gazed out of the window at the grounds beyond with a wistful expres-sion. 'What fun we all had, when we were young.'

After breakfast, Alexia wandered into the orangery, where the older guests had sat the previous night, away from the noise of the band. She wandered over to the far side and looked through the glass to the lake, at the black swans gliding smoothly to and fro. It all looked so peaceful, and she wondered what it would be like to live here.

Had she seen Marley through a champagne haze last night? Had the sheer enchantment of the ball imbued her with the spirit of ecstasy, so that she'd floated around in a fantasy, feeling like a princess in a palace and wishing the feeling would last for ever?

'You're Malcolm Erskine's gel, aren't you?'

Startled, Alexia turned to see a short plump man in his fifties watching her with sly hazel eyes. He had an ingratiating smile on his pale, slightly sweaty face and his hair, greying at the temples, was carefully combed over a balding head with brilliantine.

'Yes, I am,' Alexia replied guardedly. She'd noticed him the previous evening, taking lots of photographs and sidling unctuously up to the richest looking guests, flattering the women and being charming to the men.

He clapped his hands with glee. 'I thought so!' he said triumphantly. 'Your mother is Margaret Erskine, isn't she? Used to be a dancer, under the soubriquet of Mademoiselle Zeni?'

Alexia was appalled. How did this man know so much? Her mother never talked about her past, hid in a suitcase under her bed all the photographs of herself, in different costumes and poses, taken when she'd been on the stage. Respectable girls didn't go on the stage or become ballet dancers unless they were like Anna Pavlova.

'That was a long time ago,' she hedged nervously.

He settled himself in a chair opposite her. 'My name's Kenneth Ponsonby, by the way. I knew your father at Oxford, and Ian Clifton was my best friend. We go back a long way.' He gave a knowing laugh that was almost a sneer.

'I see,' she said politely, feeling uneasy. Who was this oily creature to whom she'd taken an instant dislike?

'The party last night was good, don't you think, Alexia?'

'Yes, very good.'

'You're obviously a hit with Simon.' He clasped his hands across his pouter pigeon chest.

The colour rose furiously to her cheeks. 'I don't know about that.'

'Oh, but I do! And he's so eligible, too! The family trust fund has let him have over a million pounds; when he inherits this place he'll be really very wealthy. I'm sure your mother would like you to make just such a match,' he added slyly.

'I'm sure my mother's thinking no such thing. I'm much too young,' she said, rising quickly, anxious to get away.

'The last time I saw your father,' Kenneth continued, 'he was in great debt. Has he managed to pay back all the people he borrowed money from? I suggested he declare himself bankrupt; so much easier than grovelling around trying to scrape together the pennies, don't you think?'

Alexia spoke mutinously, her dark eyes flashing. 'I don't wish to discuss my father with you, Mr Ponsonby.'

Kenneth shrank back offended, withdrawing into his shell like an oyster squirted with lemon. 'Dear me, I seem to have upset you,' he retorted huffily.

Alexia stood her ground. 'I didn't mean to be rude but I don't like people gossiping about my father.'

'Of course you don't. I remember him as a young man. He was sweet on Leonora, you know. I think he'd have proposed but her parents, Sir Richard and Lady Willoughby, would never have allowed her to marry him.'

'Leonora?' She frowned, puzzled.

His eyes danced with glee. 'Leonora Clifton of course! Your hostess, my dear. Didn't you know? She was a great beauty and her parents were determined that she would make a good match. And let's face it, there weren't any catches bigger than Ian Clifton . . . except perhaps for the Duke of Westminster, who was also attracted to her.'

'I see.' Her mind was spinning at this revelation.

'Perhaps history is about to repeat itself?' He gave a cunning smirk. 'Now that would be something, wouldn't it?'

She turned away abruptly and at that moment Simon sauntered into the orangery. He halted abruptly when he saw Kenneth Ponsonby.

'What are you doing?' he asked coldly.

'Having a little chat, dear boy.'

Simon glowered. 'Come on, Alexia. I want to show you the horses.'

Kenneth watched her as she left. Like a toad watching a fly, he relished her discomfort. Little did she know how much sway he held with the Cliftons. And a bit of matchmaking would be sure to cause a storm in a teacup, when it concerned the precious son and heir. How amusing that would be!

He unfolded his copy of *The Times*, to see who had died recently.

'I was looking for you everywhere, Alexia,' Simon said as they crossed the hall to the front door.

'I thought you were playing tennis?'

'I got bored. I want to show you my new hunter. A birthday present from Ma and Pa. Come on.'

'Who is Mr Ponsonby?'

'A loathsome creature and I hate him. He's always here, sponging off us, and creeping around the place. Mad about photography.'

'He told me he used to know my father.'

'He seems to know everyone's father. For some reason Papa feels sorry for him because he's always broke, but I'd ban him from the house if I could; he's a real mischief maker. Now come on, this way.' Simon strode off in the direction of the stable yard and Alexia almost had to run to keep up with him.

Her only experience of horses was watching them trotting around Rotten Row in Hyde Park. Although she admired them from afar, she was nervous of being too close to them.

'Here we are,' Simon continued as they rounded the corner of the house that led to a cobbled space surrounded by loose boxes on three sides. A dozen beautifully groomed horses were looking over the top of their stable doors, and she felt a stab of fear at how big they were.

A groom came forward with a metal dish filled with scrubbed carrots, which he offered to them.

'Thanks.' Simon grabbed a handful. 'Help yourself, darling.' He went over to a dappled grey that was looking expectantly towards him.

'Here's my beauty! This is Prancer. Isn't she top-hole?'

Prancer arched her neck elegantly and with a dainty gesture took the carrot from his hand. She had a thick silvery mane and a fringe that fell to her dark intelligent eyes.

'She *is* beautiful,' Alexia admitted.

'You can ride her if you want,' Simon offered generously, as Prancer nuzzled him and he laid his cheek against hers.

Alexia shot him an agonized look. 'Oh, I don't think so! I've never ridden in my life.'

'Never ridden?' he repeated incredulously. 'Then I'll teach you.' He was fondling the mare's ears as if she were a pet cat or dog. 'Next time you come to stay bring riding clothes with you. You'll love it. There's nothing as thrilling as galloping across the downs and jumping the fences on the back of a strong powerful creature like Prancer. It's the most exhilarating feeling in the world.' He threw back his head and the wind ruffled his golden hair as he closed his eyes for a moment, recalling the glorious sensation of riding.

Alexia felt quite sick with fear but she knew that if she wanted to keep coming back to Marley Court, which she suddenly did now that Simon was by her side again, she'd have to adapt to their ways.

In spite of her earlier misgivings the place had woven a spell around her, seducing her with its magnificent grandeur and luxury. Last night hadn't been just an illusion showing her a way of life she hadn't known existed two days ago, it had made her realize what she really wanted.

Marley Court, with its turrets and gables and hundreds of glittering windows, was breathtakingly beautiful, a jewel set in lush English countryside, an historic gem where dreams could become reality and fantasy a way of life.

With sudden clarity she knew she was destined to claim this place as her own. A great wave of elation swept over her; she *would* get to see her dreams become a reality. There were no doubts in her mind now.

'All right,' she agreed readily, smiling at him. 'You can teach me how to ride.'

A clatter of hooves striking cobblestones made her turn. Her eyes widened when she saw it was Roderick, mounted on an enormous, powerfully built black stallion with a gleaming coat and a thick, wild mane and tail. He tossed his head impatiently, jingling the harness as Roderick reined him in, and Alexia stepped back instinctively.

'Hello there, Rodders. Good ride?' Simon asked, grinning.

With a swift, assured grace Roderick slid from the saddle, throwing the reins to a groom before sauntering over to where they stood.

'Great, thanks.'

'I'd have come with you but Ma insisted I stay and play tennis with those ghastly Williams sisters. Imagine! I thought I'd *expire* from boredom until I found Alexia. She'd been hiding away in the orangery.'

Roderick shot Alexia a deep steady look. 'Hiding away?' he mocked gently. 'I can't believe that.'

She looked back at him, wondering if he'd be here next time she came to Marley, already knowing she'd be disappointed if he wasn't.

# Two

*When I was sixteen I made myself a promise. I vowed
that as soon as I was grown up I would take control
of my life, and I'd never, ever let anyone push me around
again. I loved my father and I loved Granny but I feared
my mischief-making mother who always tried to make
me side with her in every family quarrel.*

*My life would be my own. I would never let anyone
make me do things I believed no child should be made
to do. And I would stop feeling the need to apologize for
having been born. I would try to forget that when I was
small my mother had called me Incubus . . . I'd thought
it was a pet nickname until I looked it up in the dictionary.
And I would banish the guilt that made me believe I'd
ruined both my parents' lives.*

*I will never break that promise to myself.*

*Today, as the car taking me to the station left Marley
Court, I looked back and made myself another promise.*

*I swear I will come back. It will become my home,
my haven, my life, no matter what. I've no idea how
I'm going to do this but I promise I will make it happen.
Someday. Somehow.*

*I have to. I must. I have to get away from that
bleak flat where there is never enough money and the
atmosphere is imbued with the sickening shadow of
bitterness, the stifling claustrophobia of desperate
regret and disappointment.*

There was a confident glow about Alexia when she arrived
home that her family had never seen before. Her eyes
sparkled as she told them about her visit and how wonderful
it had been.

'I'm so glad you enjoyed yourself, my dear,' her father said warmly. 'I thought you'd find the Cliftons kind and friendly.'

Alexia looked away. How could she tell him that Lord Clifton had been insulting about him?

'I liked Lady Clifton,' she said carefully.

Her father's face lit up. 'Isn't she sweet? And so beautiful.'

'She said you were the handsomest young man around, when she first knew you.'

Malcolm turned crimson. 'I don't know about that,' he protested gruffly. 'Anyway, I'm glad that my seeing her again led to you being invited to their party.'

'She's still quite beautiful in an elderly way.'

'Elderly?' He sounded shocked. Then he smiled. 'I suppose nearly fifty is very elderly to you. How did you get on with the younger ones?'

'Virginia and Simon? I liked Simon very much. He's amusing and full of fun, and very good looking. He made a great fuss of me, which was nice.'

'And Virginia? She's about the same age as you, isn't she?'

Alexia nodded. 'I'm afraid I didn't care for her, Daddy. She's quite catty and we didn't really hit it off. They've asked me to stay again, though, and Simon is coming up to London next week. He said he'd telephone.'

'Perhaps we could invite him to tea or something.'

'Here?' Her expression was doubtful. 'I don't think we could ask him here, do you?' She saw the look of hurt in his eyes and felt dreadful. 'Not that it's your fault, Daddy,' she added hurriedly. 'It's just that Marley . . .'

'But it is my fault,' Malcolm admitted. 'And I'm terribly sorry about it all. I'd give anything to turn the clock back. Gambling is a mug's game and I was an utter fool.'

'There are worse things than gambling and worse things than being poor,' she pointed out stoutly.

'Not when you come face to face with your old friends who are rich, and they despise you for losing all your money.'

He sounded so wretched that she reached out and laid her slender hand on his arm. 'Daddy, I bet if Lord Clifton hadn't inherited everything he's got, he'd be destitute by now! He's not at all clever, is he? Like you?'

Malcolm patted her shoulder affectionately. 'Thank you for your loyalty, sweetheart. It means a great deal to me. But I was stupid. He was the clever one to hang on to all his money and land.'

Returning to the shabbiness of the flat, even after only three days, was a shock. She'd had a taste of wealth and all it could provide and now her home seemed colder, darker and more dilapidated than she'd remembered.

Instinctively she refrained from telling her mother what a wonderful time she'd had because all she'd get in response were bitter and jealous remarks about rich people, but she couldn't resist pouring out her experiences to her grandmother.

'You've never seen so much food and it was all exquisite,' she confided with childish delight when they were alone. 'We had three courses for luncheon every day, and four or five for dinner, and there was such a variety of dishes! And so many servants like cooks and maids and footmen and a butler and a housekeeper. There's even someone whose job it is to arrange the flowers every day. Granny, do you know they've even got their own household fire brigade with an engine and everything? And apart from the indoor staff they've got eighteen woodmen working in the grounds, and twenty-three under-gardeners and even a rabbit catcher! Lady Clifton has a lady's maid of course, and a proper seamstress who makes all her and Virginia's clothes. Then there are the stables . . .' Alexia rattled on excitedly, describing every moment of her stay before eventually adding, 'I can't tell you how I'm longing to go back.'

Helen McNaughten listened with indulgent amusement laced with mild concern. Alexia had obviously had a wonderful time but she feared it was going to be difficult for her granddaughter to return to the reality of living in a small flat where the annual income was less than two hundred pounds a year.

The day after her return, Alexia started going through all her clothes, rashly throwing away what she knew was no longer suitable for the new life she was sure was about to begin.

'Granny, can you help me make a silk blouse?' she asked.

'And a long narrow tweed skirt?' Artificial pearls she'd get from Woolworths. And if there was any money left over from the two shillings a week pocket money her father gave her, she'd buy a length of soft woollen fabric in crushed raspberry and make herself an afternoon dress, like Virginia had worn at teatime.

She washed and pressed the clothes she'd decided to keep, while her grandmother dug into her savings so she could buy jodhpurs and a hacking jacket and the right boots for riding. She was now ready for when the Cliftons' next invitation arrived.

Would Simon drop in unexpectedly when he was in London? Would he phone? Or would there be a letter in the post from his mother?

Restless, she kept checking to see that the dingy drawing room looked tidy and that the bunch of flowers she'd bought for twopence hadn't wilted.

Tuesday passed and nothing happened. Wednesday was the same. There was nothing in the post and the telephone remained broodingly silent.

'I'll hear from them tomorrow,' she told herself determinedly as she sat sewing a long white tennis skirt at the kitchen table, having had an advance of pocket money from her father. They'd *said* she must come and stay again. Simon had promised to get in touch when he came to London.

By Thursday a shaft of panic slid into her mind. Had something happened to him? Had Lady Clifton changed her mind about having her to stay? Even her grandmother was looking anxious.

Malcolm looked at her with concern when he returned the next evening from his badly paid job in the accounts department of the London County Council.

'Dearest, I hope you didn't take the Cliftons too literally? People like them, kind though they are, make promises which they plan to keep but then they get distracted and forget all about it. Were any definite arrangements made for you to visit again?'

Alexia's pale, heart-shaped face froze with disappointment. 'No. They just said "You must come and stay again," and

Simon said he'd see me when he was in town this week. But now it's Friday and he's not going to come, is he?'

Malcolm sighed. 'I'm afraid it's typical of people who have a busy social life. Their intentions are good, dearest, but remarks are made on the spur of the moment and then forgotten. The number of times people used to say to me "You must come to the shoot," or "Let's get together for dinner," and then I'd never hear from them again. Sometimes it's like a form of saying goodbye in a nice way, by letting you down gently.'

Tears swam in Alexia's dark eyes. 'That's horrid,' she burst out, shocked.

'Oh, I'm sure they meant it at the time,' he countered swiftly, seeing how upset she looked, 'and I'm sure they *will* ask you again, but not necessarily next week, or even next month.'

> *How long can I wait? Every day is an agony as time passes and nothing happens.*
>
> *What is Simon doing? Is he thinking about me? Does he even remember me? I know from the* Daily Mail *that the Season has started. There are parties and balls every night and he and Virginia are bound to have been invited to them. They're probably at their London house in Belgrave Square right now, changing to go to a grand dinner party. Simon will be meeting pretty girls, girls with money who are his equal socially and who are clever and witty, and he'll forget he ever met me and I'll be stuck here for ever and I don't think I can bear it.*

'You're a liar! A bloody liar!'

In her bedroom next to her parents' room, Alexia could hear her mother screeching at her father. His replies were almost inaudible.

'You're a complete *waster*!' Margaret continued loudly. 'Don't tell me you haven't stolen my camera and sold it so you could gamble, you lying bastard.'

There was a murmur and the slamming of wardrobe doors and drawers being shut and then her father's voice, low and angry.

'There's your blessed camera! Why didn't you look for it before accusing me?'

After more murmuring she heard her mother say some-thing about 'bills to pay'.

Then her father's voice again. 'The child must have—'

'That's all you care about!' her mother's voice shrilled. 'Alexia always comes first with you! Christ, I've wasted my life being bloody married to you, and all you do is side with her all the time!'

'It's not her fault.'

Alexia lay curled up on her bed, sick with misery, wishing the flat had thicker walls. She'd overheard this sort of conver-sation over and over since she'd been small and she didn't know how much longer she could stand it.

Her mother was off again, shouting, 'It's never her bloody fault, is it?'

'For God's sake, leave the child out of it.'

'It's all very well for you, but I'm stuck here with no money. We don't want you here, can't you understand that? Why don't you get the hell out of it? You're useless, you're a disgrace, and you've brought shame on us all.'

'That's enough, Margaret.'

'Oh, go to hell!' Their bedroom door slammed, and Alexia heard her mother hurrying to the front door. A moment later it too banged shut and a deathly cold quiet filled the flat.

*'We'd be happier without Daddy, wouldn't we, Alexia? I'm leaving Daddy, and you're coming with me . . . Daddy's rotten to the core and you don't want to see him again, do you?'*

Alexia held her hands over her ears as if to blot out the ugly things her mother had said to her when she'd been small. And now she remembered, to her undying shame, that she'd been so frightened of her mother's temper at the time that she'd nodded, agreeing with her. *'But I love Daddy. I want Daddy to stay . . .'*

Tears gathered in her eyes as she buried her face in the pillow, the desire to get away overwhelming her.

A week later the front door bell rang in the late afternoon. Her mother was out and her father was at work. She looked at her grandmother questioningly.

'Why don't you go and see who it is?' her grandmother suggested.

Alexia had had a strange feeling all day that Simon might call, and she'd even put on her new crushed raspberry afternoon dress and taken care to put her long hair up into a fashionable bun at the nape of her neck.

Hurrying out of the room, her heart thudding thickly in her ribcage, her cheeks pink with excitement, she flew along the narrow corridor to the small square hall, where she opened the front door with a flourish.

'Oh! What are *you* doing here?' she blurted out, shocked.

Roderick Davenport stood looking down at her with a smile, and his dark eyes glinted with amusement. Elegant in a dark blue suit, with a white shirt and a silk tie, he bowed theatrically as he placed his homburg hat to his heart.

'Shall I go away again then?' There was laughter in his voice.

Recovering herself and trying to hide her disappointment, she opened the door wider. 'Sorry! I was just surprised to see you. Come in.'

'Were you expecting someone else?'

'Yes. I mean no. Not exactly. How are you?' As she spoke she led the way into the drawing room, which she realized smelled musty and un-lived-in. 'Would you like some tea?'

He looked swiftly around the room with interest. 'Please don't go to any trouble. I was just passing, and I wondered if you'd like to come to the private view of my exhibition tomorrow evening? It's being held at the Sloane Gallery.'

'Your exhibition . . .? I thought you were in the army.'

His smile deepened. 'I was for a while, but now I've gone back to painting portraits. I'm hoping this show will get me some commissions.'

Alexia sat on one of the stiff armchairs, which was covered with cretonne patterned with blue flowers on a cream background. Roderick dropped on to the hard sofa facing her.

'I didn't know you were a painter,' she said.

'That could be because I didn't tell you,' he teased.

She noticed the way his mouth curved down at the corners when he smiled, revealing attractive teeth.

'So who have you painted, Roderick? Anyone famous?'

'Not famous but interesting. Mostly men. And several of the soldiers who were in my battalion in France. I like doing rugged realistic portraits. I'm afraid you won't find any pretty society beauties in my exhibition . . . That is, if you can come?'

'I'd love to.' She was thinking fast. Granny could go with her. In fact she'd ask her right away, otherwise her mother would expect to chaperone her instead and she didn't want that. 'Will you wait a moment, please?' she asked, rising. 'I'd better check with my grandmother.'

She could feel Roderick's eyes on her as she hurried out of the room.

When she returned a minute later she was smiling broadly.

'That's all right, and Granny wonders if you'd like a glass of sherry.'

Roderick stayed for over an hour, and when he rose to leave she felt unexpectedly bereft. He was like the older brother she'd always wanted; someone to talk to and laugh with, someone with whom she could feel relaxed and easy.

Then, casually, as if it wasn't of any great importance, he remarked as he bade her goodbye, 'Simon and Virginia will be there tomorrow night, so it should be quite fun.'

The gallery was packed when they arrived, and the echoing din of raised voices in the low-ceilinged, uncarpeted room was deafening. Waiters struggled to get through to serve people, balancing trays of drinks at shoulder height. Alexia couldn't even see Roderick in the melee, though strictly speaking it wasn't him she was looking for.

Accepting a glass of orange juice, she gazed at the life-size canvases hung on the white walls.

'Oh, they're magnificent,' she heard her grandmother say in awe-struck tones.

'What are?'

'The paintings! Just look at them!' Helen pointed to one particular study. 'I've never seen such vitality in a portrait. Look at the expression of that soldier; you can almost feel his suffering, can't you? And this one – you just know he's had a terrible time.'

Alexia studied the powerful paintings. There was something raw and savage about Roderick's work that almost embarrassed her, as if she'd seen something she wasn't supposed to see. His subjects – weary, shell-shocked, scarred soldiers straight off the battlefield in their crumpled and mud-stained uniforms – spoke volumes about the horror of the rat-infested trenches. Some were mere boys who looked as if they'd just left school, their eyes filled with pain and fear, their soft vulnerable mouths tightened in an effort at self-control.

'He was there himself. In France,' Alexia explained in a small voice, shaken by what she'd seen.

Helen nodded, obviously moved.

Roderick was pushing his way towards them through the crowd now, his eyes fixed on Alexia's face.

'Hello. What do you think?' he demanded as if her opinion was important to him.

'I think they're marvellous.'

'Really?' He didn't sound convinced. Gazing at a canvas depicting a Tommy, turning to look over his shoulder as if he were being pursued, Roderick continued, 'I tried to get the feel of movement and action and danger in this painting . . .' His voice drifted off with dissatisfaction. A moment later he was encircled by more admirers who swept him away on ripples of praise.

'What a fine young man,' Helen observed approvingly. But Alexia was looking around the gallery with a sinking heart. There was still no sign of Simon and his family.

'We ought to be going now,' her grandmother pointed out when they'd looked at all the pictures once more.

'Can't we stay another few minutes, Granny?'

'But we've spoken to your friend and looked at his work. Don't you think it's time we left?'

'Roderick said the Cliftons were coming tonight.' Alexia still scanned the room anxiously.

'It's getting quite late. I doubt if they'll come now. People are starting to leave.'

Alexia's heart plummeted, leaving her feeling cold. 'All right.'

As they waited for a number seventy-four bus, tears of

despair welled up in her eyes. Her dreams were shattered. She'd probably never see Simon again.

At that moment there was a screech of brakes, and a large open-topped car swerved to a standstill in the middle of Knightsbridge. A young man in a pale grey suit, with a flushed face and smooth blond hair, waved his hand and shouted, 'Alexia!'

She gave an excited little shriek. 'Simon! Granny, it's Simon Stanhope.'

Making a swift and rather dashing U-turn, Simon pulled up right beside the bus stop and jumped out, leaving the engine running. His appearance was all bronze and gold in the rosy evening light and his pale blue eyes blazed with delight.

'*Alexia!* How wonderful to see you! I've been meaning to get in touch. Why haven't you been back to stay with us?' Without giving her a chance to reply, he turned to his mother, who had also stepped out of the car. 'Ma? Why haven't you invited Alexia to stay again?'

Lady Clifton, elegant in pale grey with long ropes of pearls and a chic little cloche hat, shook Alexia warmly by the hand.

'How are you, my dear? It's very nice to see you again.'

Simon was practically hopping about with enthusiasm. 'You've got to come and stay. I promised to teach you to ride, didn't I? What are you doing at the end of this week?'

Helen McNaughten and Lady Clifton looked at each other, smiling indulgently at the enthusiastic impetuosity of youth. Alexia, thankful her mother wasn't with her, proudly introduced her grandmother instead.

'Why don't you join us for a few days, Alexia?' Lady Clifton suggested. 'We're driving down tomorrow evening and you could come with us. Would that be all right, Mrs McNaughten? I'll take good care of Alexia!'

'How kind, Lady Clifton. That would be perfectly all right,' she replied, seeing Alexia's ecstatic expression.

'Good egg!' chortled Simon.

'That's settled then. We'll pick you up after tea and I hope you can stay for several days. Virginia has a bunch of her friends staying, so there'll be lots going on.'

Speechless with delight, Alexia watched as they drove off,
and Simon gave a farewell tootle on the horn.

'Why did you agree to let her go?' Margaret Erskine asked
her mother angrily. 'I should have been consulted. You are
not the girl's mother. Lady Clifton should have sought my
permission.'

Helen remained silent, not wanting to cause another row
by reminding her daughter that she'd never cared for Alexia,
had never looked after her and had even rejected her at birth.
'Take care of her for me, will you?' she'd said. 'And don't
let her call me "Mummy". I'll get no more jobs as a dancer
if people know I'm old enough to have a child.' At the time
she'd been twenty-seven.

'I knew you wouldn't object to her going,' Helen said at
last.

'But they might have invited me to stay as well, if I'd
had the chance to meet Lady Clifton,' Margaret continued
sourly.

'What was I supposed to say?' Helen protested. 'They're
old friends of Malcolm's; I had no reason to refuse to let
Alexia go.'

Margaret's jealousy of Alexia had always driven Helen
crazy, and it had become worse in the last few years. Now
she openly resented that a new life was opening up for her
daughter, but not for her.

'Anyway,' Helen continued with spirit, 'it's time she had
some friends of her own age. And the Cliftons seem to be
a very nice family . . .'

'And very rich,' Margaret noted bitterly.

'Yes, and they can give Alexia a lovely time in the country
and it will do her the world of good.'

'I suppose you've told Malcolm?'

'He's not back from work yet.'

'Oh, he'll be pleased. I bet he wishes the Cliftons had
kept up with him, but he didn't have to ruin my life as well
as his own!'

Helen's voice was low. 'He didn't ruin your life,
Margaret.'

'You think making me pregnant didn't ruin my life? You

think being forced to marry him didn't ruin my life? My career was in tatters after she was born. They've *both* ruined my life, him and Alexia.' Margaret started sobbing loudly.

'What is past is past. Now it's time for Alexia to have a chance of finding happiness.'

'A chance she stole from me!'

Neither of them saw a shadow fall across the doorway as Alexia crept away and, going to her room, shut the door behind her. She'd heard nothing new, but the resentment in her mother's voice made her feel more unwanted than ever.

The moment Alexia saw Marley Court rising through the lush greenness of trees and parkland, she *knew* her future lay here and she felt a surge of joy. Although it was an overcast evening, the building seemed bathed in a golden glow and the leaves on the trees had never looked greener. From the battlements the flag bearing the Clifton coat of arms fluttered in the breeze, and her heart echoed the flutter as Simon pressed down hard on the accelerator and with mounting excitement she felt the car surge forward.

'Tonight we're dining *en famille*,' Lady Clifton announced, as the car swished to a halt by the front door, 'and tomorrow some friends are arriving and there's a large dinner party at night.'

'Oh *God*, how boring,' Virginia groaned, getting out of the car. 'They're all old people, I suppose? My friends and I hate it when old people come to stay.'

'Darling, we had a house full of your friends last week,' her mother remarked mildly. 'Your father and I do like to see our own friends, you know.'

'Anyway,' Simon piped up, switching off the engine, 'your friends are a bunch of silly debs who clutter up the place and giggle inanely all the time.'

Virginia looked enraged. 'That's not what you said the other night. You were all over Patricia Baillie, and Belinda Milne said you tried to kiss her at the Metcalfs' party!'

Alexia felt the blood drain from her face. As she feared, he'd been meeting lots of other girls at all these parties.

'Bollocks!' Simon exclaimed, scarlet in the face. 'Your friends are enormously silly creatures, trying to draw attention to themselves. I wouldn't want to touch any of them with a barge pole.'

'Simon, please do not talk like that,' his mother remonstrated.

'But she's lying, Ma! She's just jealous because none of the young men fancy her.'

'I can have any young man I want,' Virginia said scathingly.

'Like hell you can! Because old Baggers made eyes at you, you think you're a *femme fatale*! Actually Baggers told me you were as thick as two short planks.'

Lady Clifton groaned and, looking at Alexia, cast her eyes to heaven. 'Aren't you glad you're an only child, my dear? These two have scrapped like cats and dogs since they were born.' She turned to them. 'Now stop it at once, or I'll get your father to sort you out, once and for all. You exhaust me with your bickering.'

At that moment a second car drew up behind them with all their luggage and some special provisions from Fortnum & Mason.

*Who wouldn't want to live at Marley?* Alexia thought, as the butler stood in the entrance doorway and several footmen stepped forward to look after the luggage. She was back in paradise once more.

They were having breakfast the next morning when Lord Clifton blustered into the dining room.

'There'll be an extra one for dinner tonight,' he bellowed to no one in particular.

Thompson murmured, 'Very well, m'lord.'

'Who is it?' Leonora asked, looking up sharply.

'Kenneth.'

'For God's sake . . .!' Simon groaned. 'Why the hell is he here all the time?'

His father's eyes flashed balefully, and his hands shook with anger as he piled sausages, cold grouse, ham and devilled kidneys on to his plate.

'Don't you dare talk to me like that, boy,' he thundered peevishly. 'I'll bloody well ask who I like to my house.'

'But the man's a creep! He sponges off us, he borrows money, he brings his lodgers to stay and we have to feed them as well, and does he contribute anything? No, he smokes your cigars and helps himself to your wine, and I bet he never tips the servants. He's a leech, Father, and if I had my way I'd have Thompson eject him the next time he appears.'

'It'll be you who is kicked out if you speak to me like that, Simon. You're getting above yourself. I should have stopped the trustees letting you have all that money. It's gone to your head. You'll be polite to my guests or by God, you're not too old to be horsewhipped!'

Simon glared defiantly at his father, a slender figure with his chin raised arrogantly, while Alexia sat very still feeling scared and embarrassed.

'I don't understand why you invite him, Father.'

'He's had a hard life, not that it's got anything to do with you. You've had it too cushy, Simon. There are others who are not so fortunate.'

'Ian,' Leonora protested in a weak voice.

He turned on her. 'Shut up,' he said nastily. 'We don't need your pennyworth.'

Simon eyed his father's plate with disgust. 'At the rate you're going, I'll probably inherit everything sooner than you think. And then you can be sure Kenneth Ponsonby will be barred from this house.'

'That's enough, Simon,' his mother warned. She gave Alexia a tight smile that never reached her eyes. 'I'm sorry about this, my dear. This family is famous for being ill-tempered at breakfast.'

Simon flashed Alexia a brilliant smile as if nothing had happened. 'Are you ready to go riding? I've ordered Smith to saddle up Silver Stream for you.'

A shot of terror flashed through Alexia. The very name Silver Stream sounded fast and dangerous.

'Right,' she replied, managing to keep her voice steady. 'I'll nip upstairs after breakfast and change.'

'Are you riding Prancer?' his mother asked.

He shook his head. 'Not today. I'm taking Redowa. Prancer is too lively, and as this is the first time Alexia has ridden I want to be on a steady horse.'

'Will you be all right, Alexia?'

'Yes, of course. I'm looking forward to it,' Alexia replied brightly although her legs felt suddenly weak.

'Simon, you'll put Silver Stream on a leading rein, won't you?'

He grinned. 'Mama, Alexia isn't the first person I've taught to ride. We'll have a quiet little jog around the estate, and you'll love it, won't you, darling?'

Virginia raised her dark eyebrows cynically. 'Of course she's going to say that, you idiot. Alexia's no fool.'

Ian grunted. 'At least she doesn't talk about "horse riding",' he remarked grudgingly, as he helped himself to toast. 'Remember that ghastly common girl you invited for a weekend, Simon? All she could talk about was "horse riding". What were we supposed to think she normally rode? Donkeys? Zebras? Elephants?' He chortled at his own wit.

Alexia hurried up the stairs to go and change, her morning already spoilt at the mention of other girls in Simon's life. Had they meant anything to him? Was he already in love with someone else?

'G'morning, Smith,' Simon greeted the head groom when they arrived at the stables. 'Are we ready to go?'

'Good morning, sir. Good morning, miss. Yes, Silver Stream and Redowa are all saddled and bridled.' As he spoke, two younger grooms led the horses out of their loose boxes.

Alexia's heart was hammering as the pale grey gelding was brought to where she stood.

'He's ever such a gentle horse, miss. He's got a very soft mouth. You'll have no trouble with him,' Smith assured her.

Simon showed her how to mount, and suddenly there she was, sitting astride the beautiful animal, holding the reins. A moment later, Simon was mounted on Redowa, a neat-looking chestnut horse with a coat like shiny satin. He took Silver Stream's leading rein and they moved off.

To her surprise Alexia felt comfortable almost immediately at the gentle rocking motion as they walked out of the stable yard, and turning left, followed a wide grassy path that led to the open countryside.

'Hello there!' Ian Clifton called out. He was marching along followed by his six Great Danes, whose bodies rippled with muscles as they walked to heel. 'I'm going for my morning constitutional. Take care of that gel, Simon. She looks as if she's got a good seat.'

'She's going to be brilliant,' Simon shouted back. They walked on a bit further, the horses shoulder to shoulder, snorting with delight at being out of the stables.

'There's nothing to it, is there?' Simon observed encouragingly.

Feeling quite flushed with excitement, Alexia grinned. 'No, it's fine.'

'Let's have a little trot now. Try and catch the rhythm of the horse, or you'll bounce around on the saddle like a sack of potatoes.'

When the trotting started Alexia felt as if the breath was being jarred out of her body as she kept missing the beat. The saddle bumped hard underneath her and she was jogged about uncontrollably.

'Rise up in the stirrups and then fall, Alexia. Rise and fall. Rise and fall. Good. Use your legs. Bend and straighten. Keep going. Keep going. You're getting it. That's the way,' Simon urged.

Out of the corner of her eye she saw Simon's movements, so graceful and effortless that it seemed he were one with the horse as they trotted elegantly together.

Then, suddenly, just when she thought the hammering up her spine would never stop, she and Silver Stream were moving in unison, smoothly and comfortably.

'You've got it!' Simon shouted triumphantly. 'Well done, darling!' He drew the horses back to a walking pace and she met his smile of approval with a broad grin.

'This is good fun,' she said, pleased with herself.

'Fancy a bit of a canter?'

She hesitated. 'How fast is a canter?'

'It's easier than trotting. You don't have to move at all. Come on! You've got to do it! It's a three-beat movement! Sit deep in the saddle and grip with your knees. OK?'

'I don't . . .'

But it was too late. With a double click of his tongue, Simon lightly tapped his crop on the base of Redowa's neck, and the horse sprang forward, taking Silver Stream with him on the leading rein. Their pace lengthened, going faster and faster, as they cantered side by side, their manes flying.

Alexia clung on, clutching the pummel with both hands. They seemed to be going faster than ever now, and the ground slipped past beneath her horse's hooves, speedy as running water. She crouched forward, desperately trying to keep her seat, determined not to be thrown.

Then Silver Stream strained forward, outstripping Redowa, tearing up the slope of a hill, ears pricked forward, hooves thundering; he was determined to beat Simon's horse to the top. At that moment she was filled with terror and yet at the same time an extraordinary sense of exhilaration.

Gradually the gelding dropped speed and began to slow down, and then Simon was pulling back on the reins of both horses and shouting 'Woah!'

When they drew to a standstill she saw the landscape, green and lush, spread out before them as far as she could see. It was bathed in bright sunshine.

Simon turned to her, his eyes blazing with approval. 'Good show!' he exclaimed. 'That was magnificent.' He leaned out of his saddle and, throwing his arm around her shoulders, pulled her towards him and kissed her passionately on the mouth.

'I'm so proud of you, darling!'

Alexia felt so jangled she didn't know whether to laugh or cry. The excitement and the fear, her achievement and then Simon's kiss was almost too much to bear. 'Oh, my God!' she whispered, her head spinning.

'You're a natural, darling! And you're so brave.' His voice was filled with sincerity. 'No one *ever* gallops on their first ride!'

Her voice wobbled. 'I thought we were cantering?'

Simon threw back his head and laughed, so loudly that the horses jiggled nervously. 'You thought we were . . .' But he was guffawing so much he couldn't continue. 'You're amazing,' he spluttered eventually. 'Marry me, darling. You're the most top-hole girl I've ever met. Wait until I tell Ma and Pa what you've just done.'

She found herself the centre of attention when they got back to Marley.

'She'll be jumping five-barred gates before long,' Simon said exultantly, as excited as if the triumph had been his. He looked at her fondly. 'I'll teach you to ride side-saddle, too. Then you can come hunting with us.'

She smiled, dazed, hardly taking in what he was saying because her mind was elsewhere. Something he'd said kept buzzing in her brain like a persistent fly.

Had he been entirely joking when he'd exclaimed 'Marry me' as they reached the summit of the hill? He must have thought, if only for a moment, that it was a good idea.

That was when she realized she adored him. Passionately. Obsessively. Unconditionally. He was the first person to make her feel important, and . . . and womanly, she reflected, blushing. Something tugged deep within her as she looked at him, standing in the hall in his cream riding breeches and shining black boots. Startled, she felt a strange feeling of wanting something that she'd never felt before. She longed to touch his windswept blond hair and stroke his flushed cheek. And the sight of his broad shoulders and long legs filled her with an even deeper longing.

In bed that night, all she could think about was Simon. She loved his lazy, hazy blue eyes, which could be dreamy one moment and piercing and sparkling the next. She loved his strong hands and the way he'd handled the horses with gentle strength. Most of all she kept remembering how he'd kissed her on the mouth with lips that seemed to do more than kiss; they seemed to penetrate her soul, and in so doing to give her a part of himself.

He was also her *open sesame* to staying at Marley Court for ever.

# Three

In the weeks that followed, Alexia found herself swept along at a breathtaking pace as the Clifton family stayed in London for the Season, only returning to Marley Court at weekends. As it was the summer of Virginia's debut, Leonora Clifton suggested Alexia join in some of the activities, so by mid-June she was chaperoning both girls to parties every night, while Ian Clifton met his old cronies at Boodles where they played cards and drank port.

'But I'm not a debutante,' Alexia protested, embarrassed at being treated like one.

'You are now, whether you like it or not,' Simon quipped, with a mischievous grin. 'When Mama takes someone under her wing she makes sure they're properly looked after. Come on! I was dreading this summer, and having to meet all Virginia's ghastly friends and go to boring parties, but now you're on board, it's going to be fun! We're going to paint the town red, my girl, so don't let me down.'

Alexia giggled, liking the way he called her 'my girl'.

'You're good for Simon,' Leonora Clifton told Alexia one day when they were alone. 'He can be so tiresome if he gets bored, but you seem to know how to keep him entertained.'

To be swept up in the Cliftons' world was an adventure that never, in her wildest dreams, had Alexia thought she'd ever experience.

Through it all Margaret Erskine watched her daughter's comings and goings with sullen jealousy. Helen had pawned her few items of jewellery in order to buy different fabrics to make up into party dresses, ball gowns and smart daywear so Alexia wouldn't feel out of place, an extravagance that Margaret viewed with deep bitterness.

'It's a terrible waste of money,' she pointed out, as Alexia stood rigidly while Helen pinned a shoulder seam so it fitted to perfection. 'The Cliftons are only inviting Alexia to parties because they feel sorry for her.'

'That's not true,' Helen observed, frowning at her daughter.

Alexia refused to get upset by her mother's words. 'They're my friends and they're just being very kind.'

'But what happens when the Season ends? They're not going to want you hanging around for ever. Mark my words, they'll drop you like a hot brick come August.'

'Well, if they do, they do,' Alexia replied airily. 'I'm meeting lots of other people and making masses of new friends, so I'll be fine.'

'I hope so,' Margaret retorted darkly. 'At the moment you've got all your eggs in one basket.'

*It's almost as if my mother is willing me to fail. Tonight I'm going to a ball at Lansdowne House which is set in an acre of garden near Piccadilly Circus and I can't wait for Simon to see me in my new evening dress, which is made of shot silk in pink and gold. I've also had my hair bobbed and Marcel waved. I shall soon be so fashionable I won't be able to recognize myself!*

*I'd no idea there were such grand houses in London! Or that so many people were so rich! I've been to Grosvenor House and Devonshire House and they're full of marvellous works of art and furniture and the Dukes of Grosvenor and Devonshire were so charming to me. But I'm sure that's because they look upon me as Lady Clifton's protégée, and maybe my mother's right when she says they're only being nice because they're sorry for me. Perhaps they're sorry for me for being poor but I don't believe they're sorry for me because they don't like Daddy.*

*I hope Simon dances with me tonight. He's supposed to do 'duty dances' with the hostess's daughter and all the other girls at the dinner party he went to before, but he's usually able to twirl me around the floor for a few minutes. I find it such a strain keeping my eyes on him all evening, watching who he's talking to and*

*dancing with, and all the time I'm praying he won't
find the other girls more attractive than me.*

Alexia wasn't sure why but when she awoke in the mornings, especially when she was staying at Marley Court, she
felt such a rush of excitement she could hardly wait to get
out of bed. For the first time in her life she had something
to look forward to. New people to meet, new places to go.
And every moment permeated with pleasure and surprised
delight at discovering how the rich occupied themselves.
London dazzled with gaiety and even the shortage of young
men as a result of the Great War didn't seem to blight the
frenetic round of socializing.

Then, at the end of the week, she would join the family
in the country, where the air had never smelled sweeter and
where she went riding every morning and learned to play
tennis, croquet and boules.

High with excited anticipation, she barely ate anything
and sleep was fitful, yet she never felt hungry or tired. The
gaiety and the good time she was having, coupled with her
adoration of Simon, seemed enough to sustain her because
she was sure her wildest dreams were about to come true.

'We get on so well we'll just have to marry!' Simon had
joshed one night at a ball at Londonderry House, as they stood
on a balcony overlooking Hyde Park which was bathed in the
misty pink light of dawn. His blue eyes had sparked with
amusement and, champagne glass in hand, he'd grinned
mischievously. 'What a lark that would be!'

Alexia had laughed at the silliness of the suggestion, but
her laughter had been false. It wasn't a jape as far as she
was concerned. She longed to hear those words spoken seriously. She longed for him to take her in his arms and kiss
her. And she longed to settle down at Marley Court for the
rest of her life.

But when? It was already mid-July. The older generation
were drifting back to their country seats and the younger set
were heading for fashionable resorts like Deauville and
Biarritz. In a week or so no one who mattered would be seen
dead in town.

Alexia didn't need anyone to tell her that her future, and

that of the other girls of her age, lay in making a good marriage. It was an accepted fact and she felt a deep pang of sorrow for the young women whose boyfriends and fiancés had been killed in the war, leaving them condemned to spinsterhood for the rest of their lives.

Simon was her passport to love and security, and she refused even to contemplate the dreadful thought that he might drop her when the summer came to an end.

Then one morning she bumped into Roderick Davenport in the Brompton Road.

'How are you?' she asked, pleased to see him again. In the whirl and exhilaration of the past three months she'd forgotten how attractive he was.

He stood looking down at her with a steady, focused gaze. 'I'm fine. More to the point, Alexia, how are you?' He spoke as if she'd been ill.

'I'm extremely well,' she replied, surprised.

He looked up at Harrods. 'Are you in a rush? Have you time for a cup of coffee?'

'Yes, I'd love that.'

They entered the store and made their way to the extravagantly tiled café on the ground floor, which was set with small round tables and chairs.

'How is your work going? Was your exhibition a success?' she asked, as she sat down and took off her beige gloves.

He nodded. 'I got several commissions. I've got a studio in Chelsea now.'

'Are you still specializing in portraits of men?'

'Mostly.' He smiled, taking in her delicate features and the tilt of her head with the discerning eye of an artist.

When he'd ordered their coffee he leaned towards her, his elbows on the table, his hands clasped under his chin. 'So, what have you been doing with yourself? You've been seeing a lot of the Cliftons, I gather?'

'Yes.' She sensed from his tone that he didn't approve. 'They've been terrifically kind to me,' she continued stoutly, 'and although I'm not a deb they've got me invited to all the best parties. I've been having a wonderful time.'

He raised his dark, wing-shaped eyebrows. 'With Simon?'

'Yes.' She met his gaze defiantly.

Roderick looked away for a moment, frowning. Then he turned back to her, his expression troubled. 'You won't take him seriously, will you Alexia?'

'What do you mean?'

'He flirts with all the girls he meets. He likes a good time, you know, and he's not always as sincere as he appears.'

Alexia drew back, shocked. 'I think he's perfectly sincere.'

'I believe he means to be, but then he gets distracted. I don't want to be disloyal but he hasn't got a very good reputation, you know. He's still very immature and Leonora has always spoilt him.'

'He's no younger than any of the other men I meet and he's a great deal more amusing.'

Roderick's smile was almost weary, as if he'd heard it all before. 'He's certainly fun to be with, I grant you that. But I'd hate to see you hurt. You don't want to believe all he says. He's very spontaneous and impulsive but he can blow hot and cold.'

Alexia gave an exaggerated shrug. 'You needn't worry about me.' She sounded bright and brittle. 'I don't take him seriously anyway. I've no intention of taking *anyone* seriously just yet.' She looked at her wristwatch. 'Gosh! Is that the time? I'd no idea it was so late.' She pushed back her chair and rose, gathering up her gloves and handbag. 'I promised my grandmother I'd be back by noon, so I'm afraid I can't stay for coffee. I'm so sorry. Lovely to see you! Goodbye.'

She scurried away, out into the street, and started walking back to Kensington, thankful she'd got away before the tears started streaming down her cheeks.

Helen looked at her granddaughter's red and swollen eyes. 'What's happened?'

Alexia sank into a chair and covered her face with her hands. Between sobs, she repeated what Roderick had said.

'Are you sure you can trust this Roderick Davenport?'

Alexia nodded decisively. 'Yes. He's utterly trustworthy, of that I'm certain. He's always been protective of me, but he wouldn't make mischief between Simon and me just for the fun of it.'

'Is it possible he likes you a lot himself?'

'No. I'm much too young for him; he must be at least twenty-nine or thirty.' She wiped her eyes and blew her nose. 'They're all off to Marley at the end of the week and they haven't mentioned my going to stay this time.'

'Don't be too hasty, dearest. After all, you've only known Simon for three months. It's very early days yet.'

Alexia leaned forward and spoke in a hushed voice. 'Is Mummy out?'

'Yes. Why?'

'Please do the cards for me, Granny. I must know what's going to happen.'

Helen stiffened nervously. 'You know your father doesn't approve, Alexia.'

'I know, but he needn't find out. You're so good at reading them. You can always tell what's going to happen.'

'You know I would get into trouble over the Tarot cards, don't you? If it ever gets out . . .'

'I *promise* you I'll never breathe a word!'

'Very well.' Helen left the room to fetch the pack of seventy-eight cards with their symbolic signs, which she kept hidden under a loose floorboard in her bedroom. When she returned Alexia had cleared a space on the kitchen table.

They sat facing each other, Alexia's heart starting to pound as she recognized the beautifully illustrated figures, each with their own meaning. When she'd been small she'd discovered the cards and had played with them for quite a while before the grown-ups had noticed. Malcolm immediately ordered Helen to burn them, while Margaret had accused her mother of teaching Alexia witchcraft.

Now, as Alexia spotted the naked figure of The World, then The Fool skipping merrily along, followed by Judgement, The Moon and ominously, Death, she felt the thrill of recognition. Even at the age of six, she'd somehow known and understood what these symbols meant.

Helen shuffled the cards before placing the pack on the table. 'Cut them twice,' she said quietly. 'Then choose one pile and shuffle those, too.'

With shaking hands Alexia did as she was told. When

she'd finished her grandmother spread them on the table into the triads of the Tree of Life.

'Well . . .?' Alexia asked, urgently. She knew that the symbols on their own did not tell the future, it was the way they lay in conjunction with each other that told the whole story. 'What do you see, Granny?'

'This is very interesting.' Helen's tone was perplexed. 'There's a lot going on here.' She pointed with her finger. 'See how Understanding and Wisdom lie side by side? And Victory and Splendour are linked? And in the centre Wealth predominates?'

'Yes, yes,' Alexia said impatiently, 'but what does it mean?'

After a pause, Helen looked up at her. 'It means,' she said slowly, 'that you seek to control your life. You will make your dreams come true . . . but when they do, you won't want them.'

Alexia clasped her hands together excitedly. 'Oh, but I *will*,' she said fervently. 'No matter what, I will.'

Alexia decided to forget all about her meeting with Roderick. So what if Simon was a flirt? It was only natural that a good-looking and highly eligible young man would be popular with girls; and wasn't she guilty of a little harmless flirting herself?

To her relief, Leonora invited her to spend the summer with them and she set off in high spirits with several suit-cases and even her father's old school trunk, packed to the brim with clothes.

If she'd found the London season a whirl of gaiety, life at Marley Court during August and September was even more eventful. There was a constant stream of house guests. Some were friends of Leonora and Ian Clifton, others were fellow debutantes and young men referred to as 'debs' delights', while Simon had a string of Old Etonians to stay. And while they all came and went, there seemed to be two fixtures on the guest list: Kenneth Ponsonby and Baggers Mortimer-Smythe. Although the latter was several years older than Simon, he seemed to be as prominent in his life as Kenneth Ponsonby was in Lord Clifton's.

Alexia didn't like either of them and felt uneasy when

they were around, poisoning the atmosphere with a certain malice disguised as bonhomie. Each in his own way wielded a malevolent power over the father and son who were their hosts, and she wondered why they put up with it.

In the meantime the days and nights were filled with activity. Time was not to be wasted. The Cliftons were a family who did not like people lounging around.

In fine weather they were out of doors all day long, riding, taking the Great Danes for walks, playing tennis or golf or having picnics. In bad weather they played endless games of billiards, ping-pong, and racing demon or *vingt-et-un*.

On 12th August the shooting season started, and she followed the guns with the other women, fighting tears of grief and horror as beautiful pheasants dropped dead at her feet from out of the sky. She simply couldn't understand the mentality of someone who wanted to kill such beautiful creatures. In the evenings, dancing in the ballroom or a game of charades followed a formal dinner, and if one of the guests happened to be musical, there might be a recital in the orangery.

Alexia realized that if she was going to be 'one of us', as Lord Clifton called it, she was going to have to join in with whatever was happening. It was a revelation to learn how the aristocracy lived.

Meanwhile, she stayed close to Simon, watching him adoringly all the time, loving his quicksilver movements, his muscular strength when he rode and his expression when he turned to look at her, his pale blue eyes blazing with enthusiasm and his mouth curved into a mischievous grin.

His unpredictability excited her, too. She never knew what he was going to do next.

One day, when she was sitting in the orangery talking to Virginia, he came bounding into the room, waving his arms excitedly.

'Come and see what I've bought! It's just been delivered and it's divine!'

They jumped up and followed him across the hall.

'Spending all your inheritance, Simon?' his sister joked.

'I haven't even *started*! This is just the first of *lots* of things on my shopping list.'

Ian Clifton came out of the library at that moment. 'I hope

that's not true, Simon.' His tone was sharp. He had the implacably unfriendly stare of a tiger, about to pounce on his prey. 'You're supposed to invest that money, not squander it on extravagances. You should be buying more land. What about the ten-acre wood that's up for sale in Langley? It's only a mile away and timber is such a good investment.'

'Blow that!' Simon retorted carelessly, as he dashed past his father and shot out through the front door. 'There's not much fun to be had in a few planks of wood, compared to what I've just bought.'

They followed him into the drive.

Alexia and Virginia stood mouths agape, looking at a dashing bright red one-seater open sports car. It had a snub nose, and down either side of the bonnet were four silver cylinders that resembled great fat snakes.

'Isn't it pukka?' Simon beamed in the same way as when he'd shown off Prancer. 'It's two hundred horsepower and has three speeds,' he added proudly.

'Three speeds with which to kill yourself,' Ian Clifton stormed. 'You're a bloody fool, boy! What the hell made you go and buy a thing like this?'

Virginia asked, 'What sort of car is it?'

Simon leapt into the seat. 'It's a 1912 Benz and they're not going to make any more, so I was lucky to get it.' He turned on the engine, and with a spluttering roar the car sprang to life, scattering gravel as he headed off down the drive at breakneck speed.

'If he wanted to have a car why hasn't he bought a nice saloon or something?' Virginia grumbled.

Alexia nodded sadly. Having bought a one-seater, he'd never be able to take her out for a drive.

The car wasn't the only extravagance Simon indulged in during the long hot summer. Two dozen handmade shirts and six bespoke suits were delivered to Marley Court from Savile Row, alongside a dozen pairs of silk pyjamas, dressing gowns, cashmere socks and shoes for every occasion, together with hats, scarves, gloves, and jewellery in the form of cufflinks and shirt studs set with sapphires and pearls. His extravagance shocked Alexia, who had never realized anyone could spend so much money on themselves.

Then one day after they'd had breakfast he said, 'Darling, I think it's time I taught you how to drive.'

'Me?' She had visions of trying to grapple with his parents' Rolls-Royce.

'Why not? Your chariot awaits you in the drive, madam,' he grinned, catching her hand and dragging her outside.

A charming little blue two-seater coupé was parked invitingly at the bottom of the front door steps. The top had been folded back, revealing a double seat fashioned like a deep-buttoned brown leather sofa.

'Oh, how sweet!' she exclaimed. 'Look at the pretty headlamps!'

He laughed uproariously. 'You are killing! I've never heard anyone refer to a car as "sweet" or "pretty"! Never mind, it's yours, and I'm glad you like it.'

'What do you mean . . . mine?'

'It's a present, darling. From me to you.' He flung an arm excitedly around her shoulders and hugged her. 'Isn't it grand?'

'You can't give me a valuable present like that!'

'Well, I have, darling. It's called a Stellite, and it only cost two hundred and eighty-five pounds, so it's not what I'd call valuable.'

Simon might not think it was a lot of money, she thought, but it represented two and a half years' rent on her parents' flat.

'But . . .' she began, flustered, 'the only presents I'm allowed to receive from young men are flowers, chocolates or a good book.'

'Not a bad book? Not a wicked book?' he teased, his eyes sparkling with amusement. 'I tell you what. I'll teach you to drive, and you can keep the car here, instead of taking it back to London. Then your parents need never know.'

Words of warning from her grandmother, like *compromised*, *obligated* and *reputation*, swept through her mind. She had to be pure, whiter than white and without a 'past', or no decent young man, including Simon, would want to marry her.

'Oh, I can't do that!' she said, on the brink of tears. It was such a sweet gesture on Simon's part but at the same time she felt upset because if he'd really respected her, he'd never have risked ruining her reputation.

'Come on, darling,' he coaxed, slipping his arm around her waist, making her fear his intentions even more. 'Don't be like that. This is me you're talking to.'

She looked into his eyes. That was the trouble. It *was* him she was talking to and she was so in love with him, she would have done anything to please him. But not this. This would have been the quickest way to lose him.

'I can't accept the car,' she said regretfully. 'It wouldn't be right.'

'You're such a good girl, aren't you, darling?' he said tenderly. He kissed her gently on the cheek. 'Let's say then that I've bought this little runaround for myself, but I'll teach you how to drive it, because knowing how to drive is very useful. How about that?'

She nodded, not trusting herself to speak.

'Good. Come along. Hop in, and let's get started.'

The long summer of 1919 finally came to an end and it was time to return to London. The Little Season was under way and the Cliftons brought Virginia up to their town house in Belgrave Square to continue the round of parties that would go on until Christmas.

For some of the debutantes who had come out in May, it was a case of once seen, never seen again. For others, like Virginia, the serious task of consolidating friendships, especially with young men, began in earnest.

Back once more in the Kensington flat, amid an atmosphere of unresolved issues that were never talked about, life continued for Alexia's parents and grandmother as if nothing had changed. Only Alexia had moved on, and having moved, now found herself with nowhere to go.

Baggers Mortimer-Smythe had invited Simon to join him and a group of friends on his yacht for a trip around the Greek islands. 'How long will you be away?' Alexia had asked in a small voice when she bade him goodbye.

Simon shrugged. 'Six weeks, maybe more. Dashed decent of him to ask me.' He sounded thrilled at the prospect.

'Who else is going?'

'Hoots, Boysie, Plummy, you know, the usual lot.'

At least there'd be no girls, she thought. 'I suppose you'll be back in time for Christmas?'

'I imagine so.'

No 'I shall miss you' or 'See you when I get back'. Just a cheery 'Goodbye' and he was gone.

As the weeks passed Alexia realized with a growing sense of despair just how desperately she missed him. And always at the back of her mind was the fear that her mother had been right all along; the Cliftons would drop her when the Season ended.

She was invited to several parties but it wasn't the same without him. None of the other young men had the energy and vitality to sweep her off her feet like Simon, and in fact she found them all boring by comparison.

'You must cultivate the other friends you've made so far,' her grandmother suggested.

'You mean before I sink back into obscurity, penniless and friendless once again?' Alexia asked bitterly, feeling that she'd failed to live up to the promises she'd made to herself.

'That's not going to happen, darling. The world doesn't begin and end with the Clifton family. Make lots of girl-friends. You never know, they might have lovely brothers.'

As a result, though, Alexia flung herself into having a good time at every party she went to, collecting telephone numbers, exchanging addresses and forming new friendships along the way. Several eligible young men even pursued her with flattery and flowers.

Virginia, she noticed with gratification, was watching her with amazed jealousy, especially when she saw Alexia dancing several times at one ball with the heir to the Duke of Rothbury.

I hope she tells Simon, Alexia thought, flashing her a radiant smile as she foxtrotted past. As her self-confidence grew so did her allure; so much so that people began to talk about 'the Erskine girl'.

Photographers took her picture at parties now, and the results appeared in the October and November issues of the *Tatler* and the *Bystander*. In her own way, through sheer determin-ation, she'd arrived and made her mark on society. Dowagers, sitting watching the young people at various parties, gossiped and whispered that no doubt she'd forgotten all about the head-strong young Viscount Stanhope. Without doubt she had bigger fish to fry. It looked as if she might even be the Duchess of Rothbury one day.

He saw her before she saw him.

Gliding into Claridge's for a pre-Christmas party, Alexia, looking exquisite in jade green, with a matching velvet coat, cuffed and collared in white fur, turned to greet a group of friends and was chatting to them when a figure came hurtling towards her through the crowds.

'Alexia! Alexia!'

She spun round and found herself staring straight into the smiling face of Simon.

'Darling darling,' he exclaimed, throwing his arms around her. 'I've missed you so much.'

'Have you?' she laughed, pure delight washing over her, leaving her weak with relief.

Taking her in his arms Simon held her close as he rocked her from side to side and turned her around and around, his cheek pressed against hers, oblivious of everyone else clustered in the foyer.

'Darling love, I was afraid you'd forget me,' he whispered, kissing her neck.

'Were you?' Alexia wondered if she was dreaming. Simon in her arms, saying he'd missed her and kissing her now; it was all that she'd fantasized about for the past three months.

He straightened up and gazed piercingly into her eyes. His tone was pleading. 'Virginia said you were getting proposals. You haven't found anyone else while I've been away, have you?'

Alexia had never felt so powerful or in control as this in her whole life. 'Did Virginia say that?' she parried, raising her eyebrows archly.

Simon nodded, as if his throat were clogged up. 'Say you'll marry me, darling. Please say you'll marry me. I can't bear the thought of being without you ever again.'

Nothing could stop a rapturous smile spreading across her face, which he took as her acceptance.

'Oh, darling darling! You *will*? You'll really marry me?' he breathed, before kissing her passionately on the mouth. She kissed him back, and they stood kissing and kissing and kissing until they suddenly became aware they were surrounded by clapping and laughing friends, and shouts of 'Good show!' and 'Steady on, old boy!'

It was, she reflected the next morning, the most public announcement of an engagement anyone in high society had ever had.

Afterwards, Alexia could barely remember what had happened during the following days, so stunned did she feel at the swiftness of the turn of events. Her father's eyes had welled up with tears as he'd told her how happy he was for her, how proud he felt. Her mother had been cool and formal and said she supposed there'd be a big wedding and who the hell was going to pay for it? Her grandmother had wept with mixed emotions, thrilled at the brilliant marriage her granddaughter was making yet grief-stricken at the thought of her leaving home.

The next few days became a blur of activity; her parents meeting the Cliftons for dinner in Belgrave Square, Simon asking Malcolm Erskine formally for her hand in marriage, endless discussions about the forthcoming nuptials. She couldn't sleep and she lost her appetite. Her wildest dreams had come true.

Then it all became official as the engagement between Viscount Stanhope, only son of the Earl and Countess of Clifton, and Miss Alexandra Faith Erskine, daughter of Mr and Mrs Malcolm Erskine, was announced in the Court Circular of the *Times* and *Telegraph*.

To confirm her position she now sported a large emerald and diamond ring which Simon had bought from Asprey's in Bond Street, although, as his mother had groaned, there were '*boxes* of family rings deposited in the bank vaults' which he could easily have given her.

But Alexia was happy, so deeply happy that all her former anxieties flowed away, leaving her feeling warm and content, safe in the knowledge that Simon loved her as much as she loved him.

Why, she vaguely wondered, had the Tarot cards said she

wouldn't want her dreams when they came true? She was
getting everything she'd ever wanted and she was relishing
every moment of her new-found happiness.

Now that he was getting married, Simon's extravagance knew
no bounds. Alexia found herself the proud owner of a beautiful seventeen-hand chestnut mare, whom he insisted on
calling Dancer, to go with his horse, Prancer. One day she
even found an exquisite sable coat lying on her four-poster
bed at Marley and in one of the pockets was a priceless
diamond necklace.

'Simon!' she protested laughingly, but she felt slightly
scared, worried that his parents might think she'd put him
up to buying her these expensive gifts.

'Nothing is too good for you, darling darling,' Simon
quipped, sweeping her up in his arms. 'I just want us to be
married so I can love you even more,' he whispered, pressing
himself against her. 'Couldn't we . . .?'

'No!' she said firmly. She was determined to keep him
out of her bed until their wedding night. That was the way
she'd been brought up.

'Just once, darling,' he kept begging. 'I'm in hell, longing
for you. I don't think I can wait until May.'

'We must both wait,' she told him gently.

The next time she stayed at Marley Court, Simon was out
hunting when she arrived, but she found a note from him on
the hall table.

*Darling adorable one,*
    *To help you through the long lonely nights until we can
be together, you will find a little beating heart awaiting
you in your room. May he give you the comfort and company
I long to give you. My love forever, S.*

Alexia raced up the carved staircase and along the galleries
and corridors until she came to her room. Flinging open the
door, she ran to the bed and found a small dachshund, curled
up on a velvet cushion. Beside her was another note.

*My name is Shadow, because I will be your shadow wher-*
*ever you may go for the rest of my life. I am dedicated to*
*being devoted to you and I will love you with all my heart,*
*forever.*

Eyes stinging with tears of emotion, she gathered up the
puppy and held her close. She had a warm baby smell and
her dark eyes gazed up into Alexia's with confident friend-
liness.

'Oh, you're so sweet,' she breathed, kissing the top of
Shadow's head. She'd never had a dog before, although she'd
always longed for one, and she felt deeply touched by Simon's
gesture.

Carrying Shadow down the stairs she had reached the hall
when a booming voice from the library doorway startled her.

'No dogs allowed in the house!' Ian Clifton bellowed.
'Take that thing to the kennels where the other dogs are
kept.'

'This is a present from Simon,' Alexia replied, sounding
braver than she felt. She knew it was vital she make a stand.
Hadn't she sworn never to let anyone push her around again,
once she was grown up?

'I don't care who it's from, you're not to keep it indoors.'

'That would upset Simon very much,' she countered evenly,
meeting his angry, bloodshot eyes. 'I'll look after Shadow
myself and she'll be no trouble.'

Without another word she turned towards the front door
and carried the little dog out into the garden. Her legs were
shaking, but she'd stood up to her future father-in-law and
nothing was going to make her back down now.

As the day of the wedding drew near it struck Alexia that
in all the months she'd known Simon, they'd never had the
opportunity of spending time on their own, apart from when
they went riding.

The very shallowness of their lives now made her wonder
what it was going to be like on their honeymoon. What were
they going to talk about?

Most couples made plans for the future. In their case
they were told that they were to have their own apartments

and staff in the north wing of Marley Court. A young girl called Lily had been appointed as her lady's maid and a man called Clark was to act as Simon's valet. Simon was also financially responsible for the running and upkeep of their quarters, and Alexia would be given a generous monthly dress allowance.

So far she had taken all these arrangements in her stride, as if they were happening to someone else. Now, in a moment of fearful clarity, she realized her life had been completely taken over without her being consulted. If she was escaping the claustrophobia of her home, she was at the same time walking into another sort of prison, where other people still made all the decisions. She was handing over the freedom she'd promised herself since she was sixteen to a man she loved but hardly knew.

Picking up Shadow and cuddling her, Alexia placed the puppy on her lap and sat, deep in thought. Everything had been arranged and over a thousand people were attending the wedding. She knew she was desperately in love with Simon, but . . . but . . . had the Tarot cards been right after all? Now that her dreams were coming true, was she having doubts that this was what she wanted, after all?

The wedding day dawned sunny and warm and St Margaret's, Westminster was crowded with the rich, the aristocratic, the fashionable, the jealous and the plain curious. Everyone was agog to see Alexandra Erskine, the rank outsider who hadn't even been a debutante, make her vows as she married one of the most eligible young men in England.

Those who hadn't met her questioned the Cliftons' wisdom in allowing Simon to marry someone from such a doubtful background. And those who knew Simon only too well, marvelled that he'd married such a well-adjusted and spirited girl.

Outside, the crowds gathered in the street to watch the proceedings. When Alexia arrived with her father a great cheer went up, while photographers stood on ladders to make sure they got a good picture. To the people in the street she was a princess, a breathtakingly young and beautiful girl with dark vulnerable eyes who smiled back at them, slender and fragile looking, in a straight ankle-length ivory satin dress, embroidered with tiny pearls around the neck and wrists. Low on her forehead, the diamonds of the Clifton family tiara – designed on the lines of an ancient Greek warrior's helmet – glittered in the sunlight.

To the guests inside the church, standing in judgement, she was a nobody who had done well for herself. A most unsuitable bride for Simon Stanhope, seeing as her mother had been a dancer. Such a shame, really. There were so many sweet young girls he could have married.

But to one of the ushers, watching in the shadows, she was inspirational: fresh and unspoilt, beautiful and kind, and crazy in his opinion to take on Simon as a husband. He'd warned her but she wouldn't listen and now it was too late. Heavy hearted with regret, he stepped forward as she entered the church. When she saw him she smiled.

'Hello, Roderick.'

He looked at her and for a long moment gazed deeply into her eyes. 'Good luck.'

She smiled back at him. And then, as the organ trumpeted 'Lead us heavenly Father, lead us' and the music swelled in glorious harmony, she looked up the long, red-carpeted aisle to where Simon stood with his best man, Baggers Mortimer-Smythe.

For a moment Simon's face seemed obliterated by a woolly darkness, and she remembered the same thing happening the first time she'd met him, recalled having thought then that she'd been temporarily blinded by the sunlight streaming through a window. Now she knew she'd inherited her grandmother's gift of Sight. It hadn't been a blaze of sunshine that had dazzled her, but the black aura around Simon that had predicted his future.

'Are you all right, darling?' her father asked anxiously as she involuntarily pulled back.

She didn't reply at once, knowing in that moment that Simon was her destiny as well as her destruction and that with him she was also doomed; knowing too that there was nothing she could do about it, because it was meant to be.

'Yes, Daddy,' she replied quietly, 'I'm ready.'

# Four

*July 1920*

*I've come to the conclusion that marriage is like opening a Christmas present when you already know what's inside the box. I suppose I expected astonishing surprises, fanfares, rainbows, and heavenly bliss of an unimaginable kind. Not that there was anything wrong with our two-month honeymoon, and I love Simon, love him, love him more than ever. It's just that everything seems so normal and predictable whilst I was expecting the reverse.*

*We motored down to the Riviera, stayed with the Westminsters on their yacht, ate delicious food and I started drinking wine now that I'm a married lady! In Italy Simon bought me two long ropes of pearls interspersed with uncut rubies. It was all lovely and I feel very spoilt. But no different. I'm still me and that's the most surprising thing of all.*

*We're now living in the North Wing of Marley Court, with its ten bedrooms and four reception rooms and there's even a private chapel. Whenever I pass it I feel I should walk on tiptoe and whisper.*

*I'm pretending to feel grown-up but I can't say I do. How many girls of nineteen have a butler, two footmen and so many servants? I can't even arrange the flowers myself, because I'm told it would offend Miss Langley, who does all the floral arrangements in the main part of the house. I'm sure I'll get used to the strangeness in time, though. The problem is I don't have enough to do. I'm going to ask Simon if I can turn the old walled garden where they used to grow vegetables into a garden*

*for myself. I mean, a real garden where I can dig and*
*plant things and watch them grow.*

Very early every morning Alexia carried Shadow from the
bedroom down to the paved courtyard at the side of the North
Wing, where she scampered about, tail wagging, alert to
every sound and sight. The dog was her loyal friend now,
an intuitive comforter and devoted companion. And that, she
thought with a flicker of amusement, was rather an odd thing
for a newly married young woman to feel.

'Can I get you anything, m'lady?'

She turned and saw Spencer, their new butler, standing in
the doorway. He was a stout red-faced man, balding, with
glasses and a head that jutted forward on his shoulders like
a bird of prey.

'No thank you.'

'Very well, m'lady.' He paused, his head cocked on one
side, gazing past her as if it would be unseemly to look at
her in her dressing gown. 'Would you like me to get one of
the maids to take your little dog out in the mornings in future?'

'No, I like to do it myself,' Alexia replied quickly. She
liked the fact that looking after Shadow gave her days some
structure.

Spencer turned back into the house, leaving Alexia to
wander round the courtyard, breathing in the sweet air. It
was a beautiful summer morning and the sun filtered through
the leaves of the trees that shimmered restlessly in a light
warm breeze.

At that moment Shadow started barking furiously, and the
loud clanging of the wrought-iron gate that led to the main
gardens startled Alexia. Glancing up she saw a wizened-looking
old woman glaring at her. Her long grey hair straggled greasily
to her shoulders and although her clothes did not look cheap
they were dirty and crumpled. Her eyes shone with glowering
rage.

'They can't buy my silence for ever,' she shouted in a
hectoring tone. 'Why should I keep quiet?'

'Excuse me, are you lost?'

The old crone obviously wasn't a servant, nor did she look
like one of the farmers' wives.

'Why should I be lost?' she retorted menacingly.

Alexia pulled her dressing gown tighter around her waist. 'Then who are you looking for?'

The woman stepped closer, her fist raised. 'Don't pretend you don't know. There's only one person who's guilty!'

'I'm afraid I can't help you,' Alexia said firmly. Then she picked up Shadow, who was still yelping, and turned and walked hurriedly back inside the house.

'Spencer?'

The butler came looming through the green baize door. 'M'lady?'

'Can you get rid of the old woman in the courtyard, please? I don't know who she is or what she wants but I think she must be a bit mad. Tell her we can't help her.'

Alexia hurried up to the bedroom again, where Simon was still in bed, reclining against the pillows, smoking a cigarette.

'You've been ages.'

She told him what had happened.

He chuckled indulgently, his pale blue eyes filled with amusement. 'Oh, darling,' he chortled, 'how can you be scared of old Mrs Quinn! She lives in that cottage on the other side of the woods. She's a harmless old biddy, a bit senile, perhaps. She doesn't usually come up to the house. What did she want?'

'Retribution, I'd say,' Alexia retorted, crisply. 'She was raging. She said, "There's only one person who's guilty." What did she mean?'

Simon shrugged. 'Haven't the faintest, darling. She's lived on the estate for years and years and she's always been a bit odd.'

'Odd isn't the word for it. Did her husband work here?'

'My grandfather might have employed him, I suppose. I don't know. Nor,' he added, grabbing her hand and pulling her towards him, 'do I care. Put that damned dog down and come back to bed and make me happy.'

Later that day, as they lunched with his parents in the main house, Alexia brought up the story of her encounter with Mrs Quinn.

'She gave me such a fright,' she said, laughing about it now. 'Popping up in the courtyard like a jack-in-the-box, and there was I, still in my dressing gown.'

Ian Clifton turned scarlet and shot her a quick haunted look. 'What the hell did she want?' he blustered.

'I'm not really sure, but she kept on about no one could buy her silence. She seemed really angry about something.'

He swore under his breath. 'Pay no attention to her and for God's sake don't talk to her. She's as mad as a bag of snakes. In fact she ought to be locked away!'

Leonora Clifton spoke irritably. 'Are we never going to be rid of her? Did your father *really* give her that cottage for life? It doesn't seem fair that we're saddled with her. And what Alexia says is true, she can be quite scary.'

'My father put her up in that cottage and that's that. There's no use going on about it,' he snapped, enraged.

'I wasn't going on about it, I was merely saying . . .'

'Anyway it's none of your bloody business, so just shut up.'

'But Pa . . .' Simon cut in, equally furious now. 'Your father died yonks ago; why should we do what he says any more?'

'You don't know what you're talking about!' Ian thundered, throwing down his table napkin.

'But Simon's right,' Leonora pointed out. 'We need to find a cottage for the new waterman and his family. Couldn't you find a place in an old people's home for Mrs Quinn?'

'Go to hell!' Ian roared. Almost apoplectic, he rose so violently his chair tipped backwards, crashing to the ground. 'Or I'll find *you* a home, where you'll be locked up for ever! Bloody woman!'

Leonora also rose, her face white with anger. 'You can't talk to me like that!'

'I'll talk to you how I bloody like!'

'Stop it!' shouted Virginia, who'd remained silent up until now.

Alexia watched them all, aghast. The family were acting like angry wasps trapped in a jam jar. Simon was shouting, Virginia was shrilly telling her father what she thought of him, and Leonora kept repeating 'You can't talk to me like that.'

Ian was the first to break away. 'Fuck the lot of you!' he yelled, lurching clumsily towards the dining room door, which he then slammed behind him with such force that the house seemed to tremble with shock.

Leonora hurried after him, visibly upset. Virginia followed her.

'Well!' Simon remarked, looking at Alexia quizzically. 'Don't you just love playing happy families? Welcome to Marley Court. I'm going out. I'll be back later.' He threw down his table napkin and sauntered from the room, lighting a cigarette as he went.

Alexia decided to go back to the North Wing to fetch Shadow and take her for a walk. As she crossed the hall, past the partly open library door, she heard the low rumble of Ian's voice. He was talking to someone on the telephone.

'You'd better get down here as soon as you can,' he was saying urgently. 'We've got to get that bitch to shut up.'

Alexia paused, holding her breath.

'I don't give a damn!' Ian continued, sounding desperate. 'And I don't care what it takes!'

There was no sign of Simon when she got back from her walk so she busied herself writing more bread-and-butter letters. They'd received over fifteen hundred wedding presents and she'd been told that she, personally, must write to thank everyone.

When he returned it was early evening. As soon as he came staggering into their drawing room she could smell brandy on his breath.

'Where have you been?'

'I drove into Oxford.' He flopped on to the sofa by the fireplace, rubbing his forehead as if he was in pain.

'I was getting worried about you! What were you doing in Oxford?'

'Oh, for Christ's sake . . . stop nagging, woman!'

She froze. He'd never spoken to her like that before. She stared at him reproachfully and he glanced up at her, his expression defiant.

'What's the matter?' His eyes were like chips of ice now. 'I *told* you this place was not all it seemed to be. If you had some silly romantic notion that Marley was like fairyland, then I'm sorry to disappoint you. But you'd better get used to it.'

'Simon, what's wrong?' She rose and came over to him. 'Are you still angry with your father about Mrs Quinn?'

'I want a drink,' he announced, ignoring her. Then he rang for Spencer. 'Bring me a bottle of brandy. And a couple of glasses.'

'I don't drink brandy,' Alexia said in a low voice when they were alone again.

'I don't bloody care whether you do or not! I asked for two glasses to appease your bourgeois sense of propriety.'

She sank on to a chair opposite him, feeling defeated. 'Why did you marry me if I'm so bourgeois?'

Simon shrugged. 'Right now, I've absolutely no idea.'

Spencer returned and placed the tray with the brandy and glasses on a side table. When he'd gone, Simon got to his feet again, picked up the bottle by its neck and slammed out of the room without another word, leaving Alexia stunned and alone.

He did not appear at breakfast the next morning and she presumed he had gone to bed in one of the spare rooms, ashamed at being drunk and probably suffering from a hang-over now. But as the long morning crept past and there was no sign of him, she began to worry. Pride forbade her asking the servants if they'd seen him, but she decided that if he didn't appear by lunchtime, she'd ask his mother if she knew where he was.

Then, at noon, she heard the roar of his sports car tearing up the drive.

Determined not to show her anguish, she remained at her writing table, although her heart was pounding in her ears and her hands were shaking.

A moment later the door burst open and he bounded into the room, grinning mischievously, his blue eyes sparkling.

'Hello there, darling.' He flung his arms around her in a bear hug. 'Were you waiting for me, sweetheart?' His cheek was warm and hard against hers.

Alexia felt stunned. It was as if the row yesterday had never happened.

'Look! I've got something for you,' he crowed with childish delight as he withdrew a flat leather case from his inner breast pocket.

'Another present?'

'Just a little trinket for the most top-hole girl in the world.'

She opened the case, and there lay a lover's knot brooch, fashioned in rubies and diamonds. Her face lit up. 'Oh, Simon! It's exquisite.'

'Put it on, so we can see how it looks.'

She pinned it to the lapel of her jacket. 'I love it. Thank you, darling.' She leant forward to kiss him. 'Have you really driven all the way up to London this morning just to get this for me?'

'I left at dawn,' he replied without missing a beat. 'And now I'm starving. What's for lunch?'

'Saddle of lamb, then castle pudding.'

'My favourites! Let's have a glass of champagne first . . .' He slid his arm around her waist and pulled her close. 'And then perhaps . . . a little rest afterwards?' he added with a suggestive smile.

'What's that mark on your collar?' she asked suddenly. There was a red smear down one side, and in a heart-stopping moment she knew the answer.

'I don't know,' he retorted defensively.

'It's lipstick, isn't it?' Her heart was thudding and she felt sick.

He shrugged. 'Ma's got a new laundry maid who does the ironing. She must have brushed against it, stupid slag! I'll go and change and then we'll have that drink.'

'Ma and Pa are having a big house party at the end of the week,' Simon announced breezily the following day. 'Why don't we ask a few of our friends to stay? Then we can all combine forces for a real knees-up on Saturday evening.'

Alexia was in no mood for frivolity and yet she welcomed the thought of having other people around. She'd hardly slept the previous night, she was so overwrought with misery and suspicion, but now she decided to persuade herself the mark on his collar had been a mere accident in the laundry.

Anything else was unthinkable. Simon loved her and he'd never betray her now that they were married.

'All right,' she agreed. 'I'd like to invite Granny.'

He grabbed her hand excitedly. 'OK. And let's ask Baggers and Rodders, and maybe Boysie and Hoots? I say, this is rather pukka, isn't it? Our first house party! What about girls? We'd better ask a few to make up the numbers. What can we do to make the rooms look more cheerful? The place has been neglected for far too long.'

'Flowers? Candles?' she suggested.

'Top-hole, old girl! It'll be great, won't it?' He turned and kissed her tenderly. 'You know how much I love you, don't you?'

This was what she'd always wanted: a husband who loved her, a beautiful home and lots of good friends.

'I love you, too,' she whispered, reassured.

'So how is married life?' Roderick asked, as he sat on Alexia's right at luncheon. Their ten guests, including Helen McNaughten, had arrived during the morning. In a fever of excitement, Alexia had been up since dawn, checking all the spare rooms, going through the menus for the next three days with the cook, buying the latest magazines to place on a table in the drawing room, and supervising the floral arrangement to the annoyance of Miss Langley, who had very fixed ideas and didn't approve of mixing different types of flowers in the same vase. Alexia also instructed Spencer to keep the candles in the chapel lit all day on the Sunday.

Flushed with excitement after her busy morning, she turned to Roderick, her dark eyes looking dazed with happiness.

'Married life is marvellous. I ride Dancer every morning and then I take Shadow for walks, and it's so nice to have our own part of the house, so we have some privacy.'

Roderick smiled. With eight servants hovering around he didn't see how Alexia could enjoy any privacy. On the other hand her skin glowed with good health and the quiet shy girl he'd first met the previous year now sparkled with self-confidence and assurance. Even her clothes were different; elegant haute couture and very classical.

'You certainly look very well.' He spoke quietly, studying her face intently. 'I'm so glad you're happy, Alexia.'

'Oh, I always knew I would be,' she said with a touch of defiance. 'You should try married life yourself.' Was it her imagination or did a shadow fall across his face? 'It can't be much fun being on your own,' she added.

'It's better than being with the wrong person. And my work keeps me very busy,' he retorted, turning abruptly away to talk to an ex-debutante called Lady Zoe Middleton, who was artistic and wrote poetry.

Alexia had invited Zoe, Primrose Telford, Jennifer Halesworth and Nonie Rochester to make up the numbers, and to her delight her grandmother seemed to fit in with all their young friends, who thought she was 'marvellous and so modern for her age'.

It was obvious they were also very impressed that Alexia had managed to capture and marry such an eligible young man as Simon. From time to time she caught them watching her, as if to learn from her how she'd managed to do it. A rich, titled husband was on the top of all their secret agendas, whilst they protested they had no such plans.

After lunch, everyone went on to the terrace of the main house, so they could mingle over cups of coffee with what Alexia referred to as the grown-up house party.

'Isn't this a lark!' Simon whispered enthusiastically as he slipped his arm around her waist. Then he stopped dead, swearing as he looked angrily at one group standing at the top of the stone steps leading down to the lawns.

Alexia followed his gaze. 'What's the matter?'

'Look who Pa's invited again! Bloody hell, this really isn't on.'

Kenneth Ponsonby was swanning around as if he owned the place, a cigar in one hand and his Kodak camera in the other.

'There's nothing you can do about it,' Alexia warned.

'The man's a damned leech. Look! Now he's taking a picture of Boysie with Zoe.' He sighed deeply. 'What does he think this house is? A bed-and-breakfast hostel?' He left her side and she saw him stomping over to his mother to complain.

It wasn't long before Kenneth Ponsonby came up to her in his smarmy manner. 'So how are you getting on here?' he asked slyly.

'Very well, thank you.'

'Still mad about the boy? And even madder about Marley Court?'

She raised her eyebrows at his impudence. 'Of course I love it here,' she replied coldly.

'It's very different from what you're used to though, isn't it?' He gave a derisory laugh. 'I mean, a basement flat in Kensington is rather different from a sixteenth-century stately home, isn't it? It must be very difficult for you. You're a real-life Cinderella, aren't you?' Saliva bubbled from the corners of his sneering mouth and he leaned closer, dropping his voice to a whisper.

'I see you've invited your granny? Must be a big treat for the old dear to stay in a place like this. People are saying that Simon has married beneath him. Isn't that nasty? But you'd better make sure the pumpkin never turns up, or you'll find yourself back in a basement again. Ha! Ha!' He threw back his head and laughed loudly. 'Back in a basement again,' he repeated mirthfully in a loud voice. 'What a turn-up for the *bookies* that would be, wouldn't it? So apt as your father's downfall has been the bookies.'

Alexia drew herself up, enraged. 'I know one thing about living here,' she said haughtily, 'and that is you're not a friend of Simon's or mine and we have no need to entertain you in our part of the house.'

She strode over to where Simon and Roderick were talking to a couple of their friends. Simon was engrossed in telling them a story about being stopped by the police because he was speeding, but Roderick took one look at Alexia's face and, taking her by the elbow, led her to a quiet corner of the terrace.

'What's the matter?' he asked anxiously.

'It's that loathsome man, Kenneth Ponsonby,' she said, fighting back tears of humiliation. 'He's been so insulting about my grandmother. How I hate him.' She shook her head in disbelief. 'I've never been spoken to like that in the whole of my life.'

Roderick's face hardened. 'Let's go for a walk. Tell me what he said.'

When she'd finished he looked at her, his own face flushed with anger. 'I'll talk to Ian. That man's gone too far this time and it's disgraceful.'

'I don't think it will do any good. Simon's father seems to adore him.'

Roderick looked thoughtful as they sat down on a bench in the Elizabethan knot garden. 'Actually I think he's terrified of him,' he said bluntly. 'For some reason he doesn't seem to be able to refuse Kenneth anything.'

'But why? Is he a relative or something?'

'All I know is that Ian, Kenneth and my father were at Balliol College at the same time.'

'So was my father.'

'Have you ever asked your pa about Kenneth? Does he remember him?'

Alexia shook her head. 'He said the name was familiar but he couldn't place him.'

'Try and forget the hurtful rubbish he talked. He's an evil old man.'

She smiled sadly. 'The point is it wasn't all rubbish. I just hope Simon doesn't summon my pumpkin one day,' she added half jokingly.

'He'd better not try,' Roderick retorted angrily. 'As it is, you're far too good for this family.'

That evening Leonora and Ian gave a dinner party for all the house guests. The table in the grand dining room was extended to seat thirty-six and every member of staff from both households was on duty, serving course after course of exquisitely cooked food, with a different wine carefully selected to accompany each course.

Through the branches of the high silver candlesticks that stood on the table, interspersed with arrangements of flowers, Alexia caught Roderick's eye and smiled. Kenneth Ponsonby, face glowering like an evil gargoyle, had been seated at the far end of the table near Ian, who was looking distinctly ill at ease.

Leonora Clifton sat stiffly at the opposite end as if everything was too much to bear and she was longing for all the guests to leave. Alexia silently sympathized; she too wished everyone would go away so that she and Simon could be on their own again. She noticed he was drinking heavily and becoming loud and bawdy, telling risqué stories to Zoe, egged on by his friends.

At that moment Baggers Mortimer-Smythe noticed the ruby and diamond lover's knot that she'd pinned to the shoulder of her dark red velvet dinner dress.

'I say, old gel, that brooch is damned pretty, isn't it? I helped Simon choose it, y'know!' He guffawed.

Alexia hid her surprise and smiled politely. 'Really?'

'Least I could do! The poor old chap was legless earlier this week after our heavy night in various Soho spots, where the – er . . . ahem! – the entertainment, shall we say, was ravishing!' he added, leering suggestively. 'So I steered him into Asprey's first thing the next morning! Told him you'd need mollifying, eh?' He laughed uproariously again. 'Seems it did the trick!'

Alexia felt as if she'd had an electric shock. An icy explosion raced through her veins, nearly making her heart stop. Her face seemed paralysed, her features frozen.

'Whoops!' he exclaimed, seeing her skin bleach white as she stared back at him, her large dark eyes wide with comprehension. 'Have I said the wrong thing?' He looked around at the others, with a comic 'but-what-have-I-done?' expression.

With a tremendous effort Alexia held herself together, knowing she mustn't break down in front of all these people. She raised her chin and looked at him coldly.

'I'm surprised you can remember anything, knowing how drunk you get when you go anywhere.'

For a moment he paused, stunned, his decadent features hanging loose on his dissolute face. He attempted to joke. 'Ouch! I say, old gel, you'll give me a bad name!'

'You've got that already.'

Virginia, sitting next to Baggers, gave an amused laugh, cold like tinkling glass. 'Careful, Baggers! Alexia is very prim and proper. She won't approve of you encouraging Simon to get up to his old tricks. She's still got her granny hanging around, you know, making sure her little darling maintains her purity.'

Alexia's eyes flashed with fury. She longed to throw something at the pair of them, expose them as shallow immoral socialites.

Roderick rose and went to stand behind Baggers and Virginia, whispering angrily.

'You can't talk to me like that,' Virginia told him shrilly.

'I can and I will.' His voice rumbled like distant thunder.

Baggers laughingly tried to make another joke but Roderick silenced him with a ferocious glance. Then he went back to his own seat, but later on she saw him in deep conversation with Simon.

*Oh, God! So Simon really has been unfaithful to me and now everyone knows. My heart is breaking and I don't know what to do. Everyone's in bed and at last I'm on my own with Shadow to keep me company. I've locked the bedroom door because I don't want Simon near me tonight – but what about tomorrow night? And all the nights that will follow 'until death us do part'?*

*How could he do this to me? Not the Simon I love, with his dazzling blue eyes and quirky smile, who swore he loved me more than anything on earth! How can I face all our friends tomorrow? Roderick is the only person I can trust.*

*My promise to myself to be in control of my life hasn't changed though. I will still carve out of this mess the sort of existence I want. I'm nearly twenty now. A grown-up woman.*

*I will make it work.*

# Five

'Alexia? Darling darling? Where are you?'
Nearly five months had passed since Baggers had exposed Simon as an adulterer, and although Alexia had forgiven him, after weeks of grief and anger, their relationship had changed. The fear that it might happen again still haunted her, although he'd sworn to be faithful. At best they'd reached a sometimes uneasy truce, and it was only because she loved him and was determined their marriage would work that she'd remained at Marley Court.

'Alexia?' he called again. A moment later he came bounding out through the French windows, a broad smile on his handsome face, his blond hair windblown and his pale blue eyes blazing with excitement.

'Darling sweetheart! You'll never guess what I've got for us! It's too thrilling for words.'

Looking at him, she couldn't help once again feeling that first rush of falling in love she'd experienced when he taught her how to ride. But she was cautious these days, not yet trusting him.

Seemingly unaware that she was regarding him warily, Simon flung his arms around her and kissed her on the cheek. 'You are going to love it! It's too divine for words,' he said impulsively, before flopping on to a garden seat beside her. He looked at her expectantly.

Alexia looked back at him, suddenly filled with renewed anger. He was as chirpy as a London sparrow without a care in the world, and she'd suffered so much anguish. It didn't seem fair.

'What have you bought now?' she asked curtly.

Simon scowled like a schoolboy who'd been caught stealing sweets.

He blinked and looked hurt. 'That's a bit steep! Give a fella a chance, Alexia. I've got something marvellous to tell you and all you do is nag!'

'I'm only asking you what you've bought.'

He reached for his silver cigarette case. 'I've made a purchase that I thought would be a nice surprise for you. Now you've gone and spoilt it all,' he added childishly.

'A new car? A yacht?'

'I don't see why I should tell you now. I thought you'd be as excited as I am, but you're such a spoilsport you're no fun to be with.' He lit his cigarette and puffed exaggeratedly at it as if to blow away her ingratitude.

'I'm sure I'll be excited when I know what it is.'

His sharp eyes spiked her distrustfully. 'It'll get us away from being cooped up here all the time, driven mad with boredom.'

'I thought you loved being here!'

'This place is cursed, Alexia. Don't you realize that? My father's angry all the time and my mother's miserable. Now it's even ruining our marriage.'

Alexia frowned nervously. 'So what are you suggesting?'

His brow cleared and he brightened, like a recalcitrant boy who has been told he can have what he wants after all. 'I've solved the problem. We should have done it as soon as we got married.'

'What are you talking about, Simon?'

'I've taken a house in Grosvenor Square! It's ready to move into, furniture and all. We can come here at weekends, but we're going to be living in London in future.'

Alexia leaned back, stunned. It would mean she could see a lot of her family, but on the other hand there were temptations in London that Simon could fall prey to; Soho with its nightspots was only a ten-minute taxi drive from Mayfair.

'Well, that is a surprise.'

'But you're pleased?'

'It will be fun to be able to see all our friends,' she said carefully, 'and lovely to be near my family.'

'That's what I thought,' he said swiftly.

'How did you find it?'

'Baggers knows someone . . .' He broke off, flushing guiltily.

'And it's big, is it?' she cut in determinedly, wanting to deny the truth, even to herself, that he'd obviously been in contact with Baggers again, although he'd promised to end their friendship. By doing so she realized she was now helping him to cover his tracks, but what was the alternative? To admit failure and walk away from her marriage after a few months?

'Very big,' Simon replied quickly, looking relieved that she wasn't going to make a scene. 'Five reception rooms, ten bedrooms, staff quarters, and a garden that will please Shadow.' As he spoke he leaned over and stroked the little dog on her lap, then his hand moved to her knee. 'We could have such fun on our own, darling,' he said in a pleading voice. 'Because of my family we're never really alone here and we should be. We should still be on honeymoon,' he added softly, his hand sliding higher up her leg, 'and I love you so much. You know that, don't you, sweetheart? I love you more than anyone in the world.' His blue eyes gazed soulfully into hers, and his full-lipped mouth was soft and tender.

Alexia smiled, desperately wanting to believe him. But in her heart she knew she was signing a pact with the devil: if she continued to turn a blind eye to everything she hated and everything that hurt, then her reward would be a life of luxury, privilege, and – if she was careful – the freedom, within reason, to do as she liked.

It wasn't what she'd wanted, it wasn't her dreams of romantic happiness, but she would make it work to her advantage. And she wasn't going to let Simon ruin her life. No one was going to be allowed to do that.

They took up residence in the six-storey house two months later. As she went from room to room Alexia could hardly believe she was the mistress of this magnificent mansion. The great rooms had a regal atmosphere, with panelling in Queen Anne style, Waterford crystal chandeliers, rich velvet and silk hangings, and delicate Louis XV gilt ormolu-mounted *marqueterie* furniture.

Gobelins tapestries and fine paintings hung on the damask-covered walls, and even the sheets on her bed were made of pale pink crêpe de chine, appliquéd with satin flowers and leaves.

'Where did all this stuff come from?' she asked wonderingly, as she explored the kitchen quarters and pantry and discovered cupboards filled with silver, glass and china; enough to give a dinner party for forty guests. It was as if the occupants had just gone away for the weekend, and the house waited in readiness for their return.

Simon shrugged. 'The previous owners are getting divorced, so I bought the contents of the house from them, lock, stock and barrel.'

'Oh!' she said, shocked. It was like buying into the remainder of someone else's doomed marriage. 'I hope that's not a bad omen.'

Simon threw back his head and laughed. 'You are killing! You and your good omens and bad omens. I got it all for a song, because the Duke of Allendale wanted to get rid of everything that reminded him of his wife, who has run off and left him for a young piano teacher. I was doing them a kindness. The Duchess has got her young man, plus a handsome settlement, and the Duke can now go and live with his mistress on the Riviera, so everyone's happy. I've taken on a ninety-nine-year lease from the Grosvenor Estate so we're sitting pretty.' He was as excited as a child with a new toy. 'We're going to be London's golden couple! You'd better splash out and get lots more evening dresses, darling. And I must get you some more furs. White Arctic foxes for the evening, don't you think? And a new tiara! You must have a new tiara to go to the opera.'

Alexia didn't argue. She was living in a fantasy world and she decided she might as well enjoy herself as much as possible.

The Season of 1921 would soon be under way and within days of the announcement in the Court Circular of the *Times* and *Telegraph*, that 'Viscount and Viscountess Stanhope have taken up residence at 28, Grosvenor Square, W.1.', dozens of invitations started arriving by every post.

Alexia was soon swept up in a round of dinners, receptions,

masked balls and cocktail parties. Every night there was some kind of amusement, and Simon became more profligate than ever, thinking nothing of taking a party of ten to dine at the Ritz, where he ordered champagne and caviar for everyone as carelessly as if it were lemonade and biscuits. He filled the house with guests, insisting they entertain on a lavish scale, holding lunch, tea and dinner parties, which gave him the opportunity to show off the contents of their new residence but left Alexia exhausted.

With cynical amusement, she noticed that everyone she'd met since she'd known the Cliftons had suddenly become her best friend. Girls who had been bona fide debutantes and had hardly acknowledged her were now boasting they'd been at school with her, and in some cases had known her all their lives.

*We are indeed sitting pretty, as Simon would say. So this is the world of sophisticated high society. But am I really sophisticated enough to deny what I don't want to know, but enjoy all that surrounds me? Marley Court at least feels like my home, but this is different. Simon has taken on the existing staff who have worked here for the past twelve years, so it's like living in a hotel and I've nothing to do except change my clothes several times a day. Simon is kept fully occupied doing all the things he likes best, especially drinking champagne and brandy, but at least he stays by my side, and hasn't, thank God, gone off in the evenings without me. It is now obvious to me that whether we're in London or at Marley, he needs to be kept constantly amused. But I'm so tired. My smile is so fixed I get headaches. My mind is numbed by the social banality. Thank God I can see Granny every day.*

*I'm quite determined now to take over the old walled garden at Marley, where I can create my own little paradise.*

*If I didn't adore Simon so much I'd be tempted to run away, but I love him in spite of his terrible mood swings. Those hypnotic pale blue eyes sear my very soul when he looks at me and I'm afraid I'm his for ever.*

\*   \*   \*

At the beginning of August, when London was abandoned by the aristocracy who shut up their houses as if a siege was about to take place, Simon and Alexia returned to Marley for the shooting season. There they found that Roderick was staying with the Cliftons, who had commissioned him to paint their portraits.

In the morning room a heavy easel bearing a canvas seven feet high stood in place, whilst a matching canvas, already bearing a charcoal sketch of Ian, stood propped in readiness against the wall.

'Crikey! What's going on?' Simon demanded, barging into the room, followed by Alexia. 'Ma, you look as if you were off to Buckingham Palace!'

Leonora, wearing a vivid purple lamé evening dress with a tiara and necklace of diamonds and amethysts, remained motionless, gazing with a faraway look through the French windows to the garden beyond.

Roderick, in an open-necked shirt with an apron over his trousers, stood before the easel holding sticks of various thicknesses of charcoal. With total concentration, as if he was alone, he made bold, broad, confident strokes on the canvas, and as they watched, the image of Leonora gradually appeared.

'I say, old boy, what a jape!' Simon continued brashly. 'I didn't know you were doing the parents.'

Roderick threw him a careless glance over his shoulder. 'I don't like being disturbed when I'm working,' he said bluntly. Then he saw Alexia and his face lit up. Putting the charcoal carefully to one side, he stepped forward and kissed her on both cheeks.

'What a lovely surprise,' she exclaimed. 'I didn't know you were here!'

'This is a big commission,' he said, jokingly. 'I think I'm going to be here for the duration.'

Simon was studying the sketch more closely. 'It's awfully like you, Ma,' he said in a surprised voice.

'So I should hope,' Leonora retorted. 'Now go away, darlings. Come over for dinner tonight and then we can all get together.'

'But why are you and Papa getting painted?'

'Because all the family have their portraits done, Simon. Look at the pictures of your ancestors in the hall. You should get Roderick to paint you and Alexia, too.'

'Yes, you'd better commission me soon,' Roderick joked, picking up the sticks again. 'I shall soon be charging even more than you can afford, Simon.'

'Really?' Simon sounded impressed, not noticing the irony in Roderick's remark.

Alexia looked at Roderick and as their eyes locked a shiver swept down her spine. It was a look of such complete understanding it felt as if one of them had spoken. So complete, it was as if they knew that neither of them was on the same wavelength as the Cliftons. So complete, it was as if they both stood outside the family looking in and not liking what they saw.

Most dangerous though was that their shared look said: It is we who belong together.

Alexia blinked, flushing scarlet. She turned away quickly for fear that Simon had noticed how long they had held each other's gaze. When she got to the door she glanced back, but Roderick was so absorbed in his work that it was as if he'd never even noticed she was in the room.

'So how does it feel to see your likeness on canvas, Ian?' Kenneth Ponsonby asked, as they all sat down to dinner that night.

Ian had been in a bad mood all evening. 'Hardly a likeness, yet. Roderick has only done a rough sketch so far.'

'But it's already exactly like you,' Kenneth insisted snidely. 'It does make a change from seeing yourself in a photograph, though, doesn't it?'

'Have some more wine,' Ian snapped.

'No thanks. I'll leave that to you,' Kenneth retorted.

'Are you suggesting I'm drunk?'

'I wasn't suggesting anything. I was merely pointing out that whereas the camera can't lie, an artist's impression of how someone looks can depend on a lot of things.'

Alexia watched the two men sniping at each other like angry old warhorses, dreading that the argument would escalate.

'You know nothing about painting,' Ian said arrogantly, his eyes blazing.

Kenneth's smile was sly. 'But I know a great deal about photography, don't I?' He turned to Roderick, who looked bored by their badinage. 'I suppose you'll exhibit the portraits of Ian and Leonora at the Royal Academy next May?'

'I'll certainly submit them, but whether they're accepted is another matter.'

'I have a mind to hold an exhibition of my photographs. Maybe at one of the Duke Street galleries.'

Everyone looked at Kenneth as if he was mad.

'Your photographs?' Leonora asked incredulously. 'I know you're a keen amateur photographer, but no one holds exhibitions of photographs. Unless of course you've taken posed shots of the King and Queen and the royal family,' she added jokingly.

Kenneth looked smug. 'My pictures would be much more interesting than any royal portraits, wouldn't you say, Ian?'

Ian's face was like thunder. 'Go to hell!' he snarled, his voice rising with hysteria.

Alexia eyed Simon nervously. His father's explosive temper always had a disastrous effect upon him, and he was already gulping down his wine and signalling to the footman to refill his glass.

Kenneth's eyes glinted with malice. 'I'd call my exhibition *Memories of a Misspent Youth*. Don't you think that's a wonderful title?' His smarmy voice caressed the words almost lovingly.

'I'll see you dead first!' Ian rose from the table and rushed out of the room holding his table napkin to his mouth.

Kenneth's rosy face puckered and he stuck out his bottom lip like an elderly baby. 'Oh, dear! Poor Ian! I didn't mean to offend him, but he never could take a joke.'

Leonora looked daggers at him. 'Then why do you do it, Kenneth? You spoil weekend after weekend for us with your stupid games of trying to rile Ian. I really cannot bear it any longer. If you upset Ian, you upset all of us. Please stop it, or I really will have to ask you not to come again.'

'Oh, my dear Leonora, Ian would never allow you to do that!' He smiled smugly. 'I'll go and apologize to the poor old boy. I can't think why he gets in such a tizz. No sense of humour, I suppose.'

Simon shot his retreating figure a look of loathing. 'If that creep comes back here . . .' he began threateningly.

'That's enough, Simon.' Leonora spoke firmly. 'He's just a stupid old tease, but Papa rises like a salmon every time. It's such a pity.'

Alexia met Roderick's eyes again, and they both knew instinctively that Kenneth's taunts hadn't been teasing. Something strange was going on between the two men. And Ian looked like he was scared.

Simon got very drunk that night, and Roderick and Alexia had to help him back to the North Wing. Once in bed he lay awake, restless and almost feverish.

'Is there anything I can get you?' Alexia asked, climbing into bed and lying down beside him.

'I keep trying to remember . . . remember,' he mumbled drunkenly. 'I was small. Pa and Kenneth were fighting and I was hiding behind the sofa.'

'And . . .?'

'They were quarrelling so badly I was frightened.'

'Can you remember what it was about?'

'Not really . . .' His voice drifted off, and Alexia thought he had fallen asleep.

She lay still, so as not to disturb him. In the basket at the foot of the bed, Shadow scrabbled around in a circle and then curled up and went to sleep. The house was silent, and through a gap in the curtains a sliver of moonlight sliced through the darkness like a steel blade.

Suddenly the stillness was broken by raised voices in the garden below. She recognized Ian's distraught voice. 'Damn you, you bastard.'

The other voice was low and soft. She was sure it was Kenneth but she couldn't hear what he was saying.

Then she heard a groan and deep rasping sobs. 'Please . . . please, Kenneth.'

*I wish I knew what was going on. Several people have seen Mrs Quinn prowling around the garden lately, sometimes watching the windows as if she was spying on us, and at other times walking to and fro and muttering to herself.*

*I'm sure she and Kenneth Ponsonby are linked in some way. Simon can't remember what frightened him when he was a child, but whatever it was it's had an effect on him. Every time his father loses his temper and sounds furious – or could it be frightened? – Simon drinks more heavily than usual and seems to want to run away.*

*The next morning, we went riding and then we stayed in the North Wing for the rest of the day, to avoid having to see either his parents or Kenneth. There's an uneasy feeling in the house and for some reason I'm appre-hensive at times, wondering what's going to happen next. At times I believe Simon when he says the house is cursed; one moment it can be a glorious place to live but the next sinister shadows make the very air oppressive and the atmosphere evil.*

In early Autumn Alexia found she was pregnant. Simon, headstrong with excitement, rushed around spending money recklessly, buying enough toys for a dozen babies. He ordered two rooms in the North Wing to be decorated by a leading designer and turned into a day and a night nursery. Another designer was appointed to turn the second floor of Grosvenor Square into a nursery suite including accommodation for a nanny and a nursery maid. Then came the choosing of prams and cots, bedding and baby clothes.

'He must have everything,' he declared, 'and of the finest quality.'

Alexia was touched and amused that he'd taken over all the arrangements but she was worried at his obsessive desire for a son and heir. One weekend, when they were staying at Marley, she pointed out that the baby might well turn out to be a girl.

'Of course we're having a boy,' he retorted impatiently, as he stood and looked out of the bedroom window. 'The firstborn in this family is always a boy. We'll have him chris-tened here in our own chapel and we'll have Baggers as one of the godfathers.'

Alexia sat up in their massive four-poster bed. 'Hang on a minute, Simon. I'm certainly not having Baggers as a godparent.'

Simon turned, staring at her. 'Why the hell not?'

'Because he's not suitable. He may still be a friend of yours but I don't want him to have anything to do with the baby.'

Simon's eyes blazed with aggression. 'Baggers is eminently suitable! He's aristocratic, rich, very generous and a Protestant.'

'He's also a womanizer, a drunkard and a bad example to any child,' she countered swiftly. 'He has a bad influence over you and leads you astray and he's the most decadent person I've ever met. Honestly, Simon, he's totally unsuitable.'

Simon started pacing around the room as if powered by a clockwork mechanism. The words came spitting out of his mouth with childish fury.

'What do you know about the aristocracy? You're so bloody middle class and bourgeois. My son is going to be brought up like a gentleman and he's going to have top-drawer godparents! Baggers is my best friend and I don't give a damn what you say, he's going to be a godfather.'

Being pregnant had given Alexia a feeling of empowerment she'd never had before, and now a fierce sense of protectiveness towards her unborn baby rose to the surface.

'I have a say in who we choose as godparents, Simon. If anything were to happen to us, the godparents are responsible for the child's moral and spiritual welfare and I will not have a man like Baggers involved with my baby in any way.'

Simon stood stock still, staring at her with pure venom, his fists clenched, his jaws working uncontrollably.

'Let me tell you something, you stupid cow. I'll have who I like as a godparent, so don't think you can boss me about. I suppose you think your fucking dog is more suitable?'

He made a quick jerking movement with his foot. There was a screech of agony and a second later Shadow came hurtling across the room, landing with a thump against the skirting board, where she lay as still as a rag doll.

'Simon!' Alexia cried out in horror, jumping out of bed and running to the little dog. She gathered her up in her arms and Shadow gave a piercing howl of pain.

'My God, she's badly hurt! Go and fetch the vet,' she shouted. Her face was white with shock.

Simon looked on impassively, with detached disinterest.

'Get the vet!' Alexia sobbed in fury.

Ignoring her, he charged out of the room, slamming the door so hard the whole of the North Wing seemed to shudder.

'My darling, my poor little lamb,' Alexia whispered, grabbing a shawl and draping it over Shadow as she lay on the bed, trembling. With shaking hands she got dressed and, picking the dog up carefully, hurried down the stairs to find Spencer hovering anxiously in the hall.

'M'lady, are you all right?' he asked with concern, arms outstretched as if to take the dog from her.

'Has Lord Stanhope gone to fetch the vet?'

Spencer averted his face and shuffled his feet. 'His Lordship said he was going up to London and wouldn't be back tonight, m'lady.'

Alexia felt a body blow of shock at Simon's cruelty. He'd viciously kicked her dog and then run off, refusing to take any responsibility.

'Shadow's had – an accident,' she explained haltingly. 'She's in great pain and I must get her to the vet.'

'I'll get the car right away, m'lady. Shall I take her to the vet for you?'

'No. I'll take her myself.' Her voice broke as she struggled to control her emotions.

'Are you sure I can't . . .?' Spencer looked at Shadow, who was whimpering with pain.

'I must take her myself,' she repeated, gulping back the tears. 'I'm afraid her back may be broken.' *Oh, please God! Let Shadow be all right. Please God! Please.*

Simon finally appeared the following evening, unshaven and dishevelled and smelling of alcohol.

'Darling, I'm so, *so* sorry,' he said in a shaky voice as he came into the bedroom, and found her in bed propped up with pillows.

Alexia looked steadily at him, her expression cold.

Tears sprang to his eyes. 'Will you ever forgive me? I'll buy you another little dog. I'll . . .'

'There's no need,' she replied in a flat voice.

He looked shocked. 'Don't you want to replace Shadow? I thought you liked her?'

She swung her legs on to the floor and stood up, facing him. Though she looked thin and fragile in a cream silk negligée, her pale face was nevertheless set in stern lines.

'In spite of your brutality Shadow isn't dead,' she said stiffly. 'Her pelvis is fractured in five places, but as long as she's immobilized for six or seven weeks, the vet thinks she'll recover.'

As she spoke she walked around the bed, and there, in a cosy corner near the fire, was a small metal cage, the floor of which was lined with sheepskin. Shadow lay curled up asleep, but as Alexia dropped to her knees, the little dog woke up and looked at her with an expression of trust.

'It's all right, sweetheart,' she murmured in a low voice. 'Go back to sleep.' Then she rose and turned to Simon, who was standing like a scared little boy expecting to be chastised.

'I can't forgive you for doing this,' she said quietly. 'A man who ill-treats a defenceless dog is a man who can also ill-treat his wife and children if the mood takes him. This alters everything, Simon. I don't trust you any more. Even without drinking you turn violent if you don't get your own way. You could have killed Shadow. Who will you lash out at next? Just because you can't control your temper?'

He sank limply into a chair, looking stricken. 'It won't happen again. I promise you.'

'That's what you always say.'

He looked panicked. 'I can't help it. Something just comes over me . . . my father's the same.'

'That's no excuse. For one thing you should stop drinking.'

His mouth hardened and his eyes glinted dangerously. 'Stop drinking?' It was as if she'd told him to stop breathing. 'How can I stop drinking?'

'If you want to stay married to me you're going to have to,' she countered. 'It's for your own good. I love you, Simon. Don't throw away everything we've got for drink.'

He hung his head, his blond hair flopping over his brow. 'I feel dreadful about Shadow. Please be nice to me,' he whined.

'Be *nice* to you!' she said incredulously. 'You practically kill Shadow then you storm off on one of your drinking sprees, no doubt with your friend Baggers, staying away all night, and then you wander in and tell me to be nice to you? Don't you realize this upset could have brought on a miscarriage? We have a child to think about now, not just you and me.'

Simon shrank back, his eyes wild and confused looking. Then he covered his face with his hands as great sobs racked his shoulders. 'I'm sorry. I didn't mean it. I promise you it won't happen again.'

Alexia walked briskly past him and, taking a seat at her dressing table, picked up one of her new silver-backed brushes embossed with the Clifton crest, and started brushing her hair.

'I also think you must stop seeing Baggers once and for all. That man's like a poison in your system. I suppose you spent yesterday in London with him? No doubt he agreed with you that you've got a middle-class wife with middle-class values? Well, let me tell you this.' She swung round on her chair to look at him. Her cheeks were flushed, and her dark eyes sparked with anger. 'I'd rather be a common working-class washer woman than a corrupt debauched person like him.'

She turned back and gazed at her reflection in the triple dressing-table mirror. 'Meanwhile, I'd prefer it if you slept in your dressing room because I have to get up in the night to see to Shadow, and I don't want her disturbed at the moment. Your family and all the servants think she had an accident by falling off my bed. I won't be loyal to you if anything like this ever happens again, though.'

As he left the room he paused in the doorway and looked back at her. 'You know I love you, don't you? You mean more to me than anyone else in the world and I'd be lost without you.'

She smiled sadly. 'Yes, I believe you would.'

\*   \*   \*

Because of the shooting season the family remained at Marley. There were endless parties, but Alexia avoided these by saying her pregnancy was making her feel tired.

In truth this was the third shooting season she'd experienced and she'd had enough of the slaughter of the beautiful ducks and pheasants that their gamekeeper bred, purely so that they could be shot down again.

At least the shoot kept Simon out of trouble. He invited some of his old school friends to stay and whilst she found them shallow, with a brittle bonhomie that jarred, she was at least grateful that they were not decadent like Baggers. Without his insidious influence Simon was drinking less and there'd been no more mad dashes up to London for nights of debauchery.

With Shadow recovering and her pregnancy going smoothly, Alexia began to feel more confident about the future. Tempting fate, she allowed herself to hope that the worst of their troubles were over.

That was when she made a discovery that was to shatter her illusions and completely change her perceptions of the people she cared for most.

# Six

Having always loved books, Alexia decided that while the family were at the shoot one Saturday, she'd thoroughly acquaint herself with the contents of the library. The high-ceilinged room, sixty feet long and fitted out with heavy period furniture, its shelves packed with over three thousand books, was like an Aladdin's cave to her. The majority of volumes were gilt tooled and leather bound, exquisite to the touch and with some of the pages still uncut.

Her eyes scanned the oak shelves. There were seventeenth-century bibles, historical biographies, the plays of Shakespeare and Christopher Marlowe, the works of Chaucer, and the poems of Byron and Shelley. With growing excitement she slid her hand along the spines of the books, marvelling at the titles and authors, wishing she could lock herself into this room for ever, submerged in this world of fine literature.

Then she spotted a copy of John Milton's *Paradise Lost* on a higher shelf. Standing on the library steps she reached up and took it down carefully. Settling herself in an armchair beside the glowing logs she opened the volume with reverence.

A moment later she was staring at a dozen or so letters which had been tucked within the pages and had fallen on to her lap. How long they'd been there she had no idea, but with shock she recognized the handwriting.

They were love letters to Leonora, raw passionate letters which she knew she should return to their hiding place but which, gripped by a horrible kind of fascination, she felt compelled to read.

With shaking hands she saw they had been written between September 1898 and March 1901, over twenty years ago. The first ones, signed merely M, expressed wonderment at

the discovery of falling in love. Then the writer moved on
to urge the need for secrecy as the affair blossomed. *Whatever*
*happens Ian mustn't find out about our affair*, after they'd
apparently spent a night together in London. *Please, my*
*beloved darling, tell him that you need to pay your 'dentist'*
*for many more appointments! I can't bear it when you're*
*not with me.*

The wording was so intimate, the emotions so deeply
felt she knew she should stop reading them, but the compul-
sion to continue was overwhelming because of the timing.
In the next letter she read Leonora had become pregnant.
The writer's tone was panic-stricken. Ian must be made to
believe the child was his. There was both joy and fear in
the hastily scribbled notes.

Feeling sick, Alexia knew what was coming next. It was
the end of the affair. Leonora's lover wrote that his girlfriend
had also become pregnant and he must now marry her for
the sake of the child.

The last letter ended with the words:

> *You are, my own beloved darling, and always will be,*
> *the love of my life no matter what happens in the future.*
> *This is breaking my heart and I would give my soul to*
> *be by your side for the rest of my life, but you are right;*
> *we mustn't see each other again. You have Ian to*
> *consider, though you no longer love him, and little*
> *Simon. I will respect your wishes, painful though they*
> *are, and I know I must stand by this young woman, but*
> *you will always be in my heart, and when the baby*
> *arrives, you'll know you have a part of me who will*
> *love you for ever and will stay close to you, as I wish*
> *I could.*
> *Yours for ever, M.*

The M that stood for Malcolm Erskine.

Alexia sat staring into space, overwhelmed with shock.
The implications were enormous, and paramount was the
realization that Virginia was her half-sister. But what if her
mother hadn't become pregnant? Would Leonora have left
Ian and eventually married her father and settled down with

their baby daughter? Would her mother have married someone else and perhaps been happy?

It was all too much to take in, but one thing was certain. These letters must be destroyed. It was too dangerous to put them back between the pages of a book: although she realized no one in the Clifton family ever read, a cleaner might discover them, or even a house guest perusing the bookshelves.

Carefully replacing *Paradise Lost*, she slipped the letters into her pocket and hurried back to the North Wing. The family would be returning for tea in a few minutes, so she hid them at the back of a drawer in her dressing table which she kept locked. At the first opportunity she would destroy them on a bonfire in her secret garden, reducing their explosive contents to mere ashes.

Then she sat down and tried to compose herself, but her thoughts were racing feverishly. Much of what she hadn't understood in the past was becoming clearer by the moment.

A flurry of questions bubbled and frothed in her mind like a whirlpool. Had her mother known about Leonora? Had Ian ever found out Virginia wasn't his daughter? And what if Virginia ever realized she was illegitimate?

Everything was falling into place, including why she'd received the invitation to the ball at Marley two years ago. Her father had explained at the time that he'd bumped into the wife of his old friend, Ian Clifton, and that it was she who'd suggested his daughter might like to meet some other 'young people'. Obviously, out of fondness for Malcolm, Leonora had made sure his daughter had the coming-out season he couldn't afford to give her. Perhaps they'd even rekindled their affair in recent years?

As the appalling ramifications of her discovery sank in, Alexia felt overwhelmed with humiliation. She'd been a pawn, manipulated even into marrying the son of her father's ex-mistress. What twisted sort of mind wanted Malcolm's two daughters to become sisters-in-law? What perversion had made Leonora encourage her son to marry her ex-lover's daughter? And why had she left these letters tucked into a book in the library where anyone could have discovered them?

Alexia buried her face in her hands, reeling with confusion and mortification.

The two of them, her father and Leonora, had taken complete control of her life and manoeuvred her into her present situation. And she'd been fool enough to think she'd got to where she was all by herself.

That evening, while the shooting party was gathered for dinner in the main house, she pleaded a headache and said she'd have supper in bed. Once alone, and desperate to unburden herself, she slipped into her private sitting room and telephoned her grandmother, the only person she could trust.

'I can hardly believe it,' Helen said in a low, stricken voice. 'Under the circumstances, it was very wrong of your father to let you become friends with the Cliftons.'

'Do you think Mummy knew about Leonora?'

There was a pause before she answered. 'No, but I always had the feeling that there was something in his background he hadn't mentioned.'

'What shall I do, Granny? This puts me in a terrible situation. I don't get on with Virginia as it is, and now I realize she's my half-sister it's really horrible.'

'I think you should try to forget all about those letters. Destroy them and try to carry on as usual, darling. There's nothing you can do. This can never be allowed to get out. At least it's Virginia we're talking about, not Simon,' she added pointedly.

'Oh God, that thought's too hideous for words. I don't think I'll be able to look Daddy in the face the next time I see him.'

'Give it time, sweetheart. The past is the past. You're still deeply shocked, so why don't you stay at Marley for a bit? Take it easy until the baby arrives.'

'Oh dear, my birth did cause a lot of complications, didn't it? Even more than I'd thought,' Alexia said sadly. 'There's nothing like an unwanted baby to upset the apple cart.'

'You were wanted, darling girl, and more loved than you realize. Where would I be, for a start, if you hadn't been born? Looking after you has been the greatest blessing I could have wished for.'

'I think I was the lucky one to have you, Granny. And you're right about one thing. The affair is history and has nothing to do with Simon and me.'

*They've gone! Vanished! The drawer has been forced open and the letters are gone! This is a nightmare. Who could have stolen them? Let me think. Let me think.*

*After church on Sunday we'd all had lunch in the main house with Simon's parents and their house guests, then they all departed during the afternoon. It was raining so I put off having the bonfire until today and now . . . ? I can't believe it! It was an absolute disaster. Those damned letters! How I wish I'd never found them . . .*

'Are you OK, darling?' Simon whispered tenderly, leaning over Alexia as she lay in their four-poster bed.

Her eyes flew open, and reaching up she put her arms around his neck.

'Just a bit tired,' she murmured, kissing him. The emotional turmoil she'd suffered for the past few days made her feel grateful to Simon, who at that moment represented security and safety.

'They always say the first few months of pregnancy are the worst.' She looked to where Shadow slept, curled up by her feet. 'It's nice to be tucked up in bed.' She'd nearly said 'safe' by mistake.

Kicking off his shoes he lay down beside her and stroked her stomach.

'Did the doctor say everything was all right?'

'Everything's fine.'

'Will you be allowed to get up soon? This place isn't the same without you.'

She rolled on to her side to face him. 'It's going to be wonderful, isn't it? Just you and me and our baby? We must make sure he realizes how much we want him, mustn't we?'

Simon grinned quizzically. 'Aren't all babies wanted? Ma always says having babies was the best part of getting married.'

Alexia closed her eyes, as if to blot out a picture in her mind of Leonora, pregnant by her father. 'It's one of the best parts,' she agreed. Then she snuggled closer. 'And this is the other best part,' she murmured, grateful for the material comforts being married to Simon had provided.

'Funny girl,' he chuckled, kissing her, 'but I do love you to bits. You know that, don't you? It's only the drink that gets in the way.'

Soon, Alexia and Simon joined the rest of high society in flocking back to London for another round of parties. There had been no repercussions about the missing letters, no servants threatening to blackmail the family over their contents, so it seemed that whoever had taken them wasn't planning to damage the Cliftons by exposing the scandal. And yet Alexia felt deeply uneasy.

Someone, God knows who, had the power to cause terrible trouble for them all. She felt very guilty at having removed the letters from where they'd lain, undetected, for over twenty years.

'You're looking very washed out,' Simon remarked critically as they set out for yet another night of revelry.

'Am I?' Alexia looked at herself in the mirror. Perhaps he was right. She patted her face with a sheet of ricepaper before rubbing a little rouge into her cheeks. Then she took a cork she'd saved from a wine bottle and, having burnt the edge of it on a candle flame, drew it carefully around her eyes, making them look larger and more defined. As a final touch she painted her lips scarlet.

'That's more like it!' Simon told her as they set off. They were meeting friends for dinner at the Café de Paris, which was frequented by the Prince of Wales and his current mistress. Simon thrived on the throbbing life of nightclubs and cocktail bars and his endless craving for excitement never seemed quenched.

Tonight he seemed especially restless, and as soon as they were seated at their table with his usual gang of friends, he started ordering the most expensive wines and dishes on the menu. Then he sent a waiter out to get sprays of orchids for all the girls in the party and gardenias for the men's button-holes.

'Can't have you looking drab!' he declared loudly.

When the dashing Prince of Wales arrived, with his aura of

rampant sexuality and headstrong selfishness, it struck Alexia that it was the future King Edward VIII Simon was trying to emulate. They were both extremely charming and attractive when they wanted to be, but they also shared the same hard-drinking, self-destructive streak. And like the Prince, Simon had an edge of instability. She'd once found this attractive and exciting, but she now regarded it with wariness. She'd come to realize that the balance between high spirits and stormy tempestuousness was as fragile as a spider's web, suspended in sunshine one moment and torn to shreds by a storm the next.

Baggers and a hard-faced girl joined their table. It was the first time she'd seen him since her refusal to have him as a godparent.

'And how is the divine Alex-*zeeia*?' he exclaimed, flourishing his hands and kissing her cold cheek. 'My darling, it's been an *age*!'

Alexia's smile was fixed as Simon ordered more caviar and champagne for the late arrivals.

It was a long evening. Her head ached at the noise and the clatter of the place, her back ached at having to sit on a hard chair and the effort of being bright and polite to Simon's friends began to make her feel quite ill.

When the coffee was served she signalled to Simon that she wanted to go home. To her surprised delight he nodded in agreement. After saying goodbye to everyone, he put his arm around her waist and guided her to their waiting car.

'How wonderful to be going home,' she exclaimed, sighing with relief as she sank on to the leather upholstery of the Rolls-Royce.

Simon gave her a quick smile, and without replying tapped their chauffeur on the shoulder.

'I'd like you to drop me off at the Regency Club in Soho, and then take her Ladyship home, please.'

'Very well, m'lord.'

Ten minutes later the car drew up outside a dark doorway with a shabby striped awning.

Simon gave her a quick peck on the cheek. 'Sleep well. See you in the morning,' he said cheerfully as he clambered out of the car, before entering the building with a tall man who had just arrived in a taxi. It was Baggers.

Alexia managed to hang on to her self-control until the chauffeur saw her into their house. A footman was awaiting her return, but she hurried past him, her head down as she rushed up the stairs to her bedroom.

Once inside she dismissed her lady's maid. Then she flung herself on to the bed and let a river of tears flow like a flash flood, stopping only when exhaustion and nausea over-whelmed her. To be humiliated in front of the servants was one thing. To be so profoundly and cruelly hurt was another.

Throwing her jewellery down on the dressing table, she undressed, letting her clothes fall to the floor, and crawled into bed.

Her loss of innocence was complete.

# Seven

It was only to be expected that the Cliftons would celebrate the christening of the Hon. Frederick Ian Stanhope
in grand style.

Thirty-five house guests were invited to stay at Marley
Court, with a further hundred friends and neighbours
attending the lavish luncheon and dinner parties that were
being held from Friday until Monday.

Twenty extra footmen were taken on, the gardeners were
asked to check if there'd be enough flowers in the glass-
houses to decorate the chapel and the main reception rooms,
caterers were brought in to assist the kitchen staff, and a
band was hired to play for dancing each evening. The guest
list, naturally, read like a section from Debrett's Peerage.

This was Ian and Leonora Clifton's most lavish extravaganza
since 1913, and Leonora was determined to re-establish herself
as society's leading hostess. Four years after the end of the
Great War, the King and Queen had at last reinstated Court
presentations, and in May she was presenting Virginia as a
former debutante and Alexia on her marriage to Simon.

'I want Freddie's christening to be a grown-up event,' she
explained to Alexia in a perfectly serious voice. 'No dizzy
little debs, and no drunken young men. Apart from Simon's
closest friends, I suppose,' she added uncertainly.

Alexia, still feeling weak and tired from her confinement
two months earlier, was appalled.

'It's going to take such a lot of organizing,' she told Simon,
when she first heard about the grandiose plans.

'Don't worry. Ma's taking care of everything,' he replied
breezily. 'You just relax and give yourself a pat on the back

for producing a son and heir. All you have to do now is look beautiful, as you always do,' he added flatteringly.

Obviously not as beautiful as the tarts of Soho, she reflected grimly. Something had hardened in her since that dreadful night six months ago when she thought her heart would break. He was a serial adulterer and he always would be. No matter how many times he promised it would never happen again, Alexia realized he was psychologically unable to keep that promise. She either had to shut up and put up, as her grandmother described it, or leave the marriage altogether.

She'd married Simon because she'd been in love with him, though most people she knew thought she was a gold-digger from nowhere, whose determination to bag an eligible bachelor and make a brilliant marriage was her *raison d'être*. Now, however, she could no longer afford the luxury of being in love; it caused her too much pain. The agony of being betrayed and the loss of self-confidence had devastated her, and it had taken her months to come to terms with a marriage that would forever be a performance from now on. She was determined to regard her role as the Viscountess Stanhope as a job she'd taken on for life, in the way men regarded what they did as a career.

It was not what she'd planned, she reflected in the small hours of the morning when her pillow was damp with her tears, but what were the alternatives? To leave Simon and become a social outcast, which was the lot of divorced women? To deprive her son of a father, always supposing she was given custody of Freddie in the first place? To be poor once again and living on her own in reduced circumstances?

In the circles in which she'd moved since her marriage, she'd observed that many women turned a blind eye to their husbands' philandering. Some of them thought they were being 'sophisticated'. In Alexia's book, it was a case of refusing to cut off her nose to spite her face.

'You have a beautiful son now,' her grandmother told her. 'For his sake, you must be strong.'

'Oh, I will, Granny.' She gave a deep sigh. 'You were right, weren't you? Now I've got what I wanted, it isn't what I want after all.'

'You've got most of what you wished for, and you have a very privileged life, but nothing in this world is perfect. It's learning to take the rough with the smooth that matters, darling.'

'I wish you lived with us, Granny.'

Helen smiled, shaking her head gently. 'Two's company, three's a crowd.'

Roderick, putting the finishing touches to his portraits of Leonora and Ian, looked over his shoulder at Alexia who sat curled up on a sofa in the morning room, watching him as he worked.

'What's the matter, Alexia? Why are you worried about the christening next week? What could go wrong?'

She shot him a dark look, wishing she could confide in him about both Simon's behaviour and her father's love letters to Leonora.

'My parents are coming and they're staying in the North Wing,' she replied gloomily. 'And Mummy's going to make Granny's life hell because she's so jealous of her and how often she comes to stay with us.'

'Surely they won't quarrel on an occasion like this?' He leaned forward and with his long paintbrush added a detail to the background of the painting.

'Mummy will be icily polite, which creates a bad atmosphere in itself. Then Kenneth Ponsonby will no doubt stir things up by asking awkward questions about my mother's background as a dancer.' She looked fretfully. 'I can't imagine why Leonora insisted on all this fuss. We could so easily have had a nice little service in the chapel, with just a few close friends.'

'She has a reason for filling the house to the rafters, just as you do,' Roderick said quietly, turning to look at her as if he wanted to commit every nuance of her changing expression to memory.

Her dark eyes looked startled as she returned his gaze. 'What do you mean?' she asked sharply.

'Oh, come on, Alexia, both you and Leonora are unhappy, not to mention exhausted by keeping up appearances, wanting everyone to think that this is a happy family. Filling the house with people and endless entertaining is a great distraction.'

'Not for me it isn't,' she retorted, wondering how much he knew. 'I know she doesn't find Ian easy, but I don't believe she's that unhappy.'

Roderick smiled, his eyes drilling into hers intimately. 'You want me to believe that you're happily married too? Alexia, I've known Simon all his life and he's as incapable as his father is of making a woman happy.'

She flushed. 'I don't know what you mean. Of course we all get on each other's nerves from time to time, but that happens to all married couples.'

He shrugged, turning away abruptly, making her wonder if he knew more than he was letting on. 'So how is my godson today?' he continued easily, as he squeezed a blob of burnt umber on to his palette. 'I must do some sketches of him; babies are notoriously difficult to paint because their features are so soft.' He turned to look at her again, his eye sweeping from her face downwards to her breasts and her long slim thighs. 'I'd like to paint you, too, Alexia. A full-length portrait in one of your evening dresses.'

'Oh, I don't know about that,' she laughed, suddenly flustered. 'I'll have to get my figure back first.'

'You look radiant, as all new mothers should,' he said approvingly, 'and there's nothing wrong with your figure. I think I'll paint you in the orangery where the light is beautifully diffused and the lawns and the lake can be seen shimmering through the glass panes.'

'A formal painting?'

Roderick shook his head. 'No, you're far too young for that sort of portrait.' He waved his brush at the pictures of the Cliftons. 'I want to capture your youth and freshness and paint you in a pretty, floaty dress.'

'I could wear the long ropes of pearls Simon gave me when Freddie was born.'

'Definitely no jewellery and no make-up.' He spoke firmly. 'No doubt Simon would like you dressed up like a Christmas tree, but that's not what I want. Your loveliness lies in yourself, not in being all got up like a thousand other rich young women.'

She laughed, amused. 'You're being very commanding, Roderick. Do you tell all your sitters exactly what to wear?'

He didn't reply immediately. Then he said softly, 'Only the ones I care about enough to want to bring out their inner beauty.'

Malcolm and Margaret Erskine arrived with Helen McNaughten early on the Friday afternoon, declaring they wanted to see as much of Freddie as possible before everyone else appeared.

With her heart thumping nervously – for this was the first time she'd seen her father since she'd found his letters – Alexia greeted them in the hallway of the North Wing, before taking them up to their rooms. No one would have guessed she was hiding tumultuous emotions as she prattled lightly about Freddie and his nice new nanny, and who else was coming to stay.

Dismayed, she inwardly flinched when her father casually remarked that it had been a long time since he'd been to Marley Court, adding that nothing seemed to have changed much.

It had never occurred to her that he might have slept here with Leonora, when Ian had been away. Could Virginia even have been conceived at Marley? So prominent in her mind were these thoughts that she became worried in case she let slip that she knew about the affair.

For the first time in her life she felt awkward in her father's presence. Her remarks became stilted and clichéd as she chattered on about anything that seemed like a safe topic of conversation. She also studiously avoided eye contact with her grandmother, in case a shared look between them was intercepted by her mother.

Soon, she began to feel a pressure that threatened to explode. Why should she suffer the burden of keeping other people's secrets? None of it was her fault. She hadn't asked to be born. At that moment her awkwardness turned to seething anger towards her father.

It was as if he'd betrayed her by loving Leonora before she'd even been born. Had he ever loved her mother? Had he ever *belonged* to either of them?

Jealousy, like poison, coursed through her body, making her feel sick with envy. He was no longer the father she'd adored since she'd been a baby, but a stranger with a past she'd known nothing about until a few weeks ago. A past that posed a dangerous threat to her future with her husband's family and a past she had to keep secret.

The atmosphere became more strained as the day passed. From time to time Malcolm glanced at her with a puzzled expression, as if he couldn't fathom why she suddenly seemed so stiff and cold towards him.

Guests kept arriving in a constant stream, and the house became noisy with loud greetings as Simon's usual gang of friends burst into the rooms, full of enthusiasm and vibrant with life.

'Good to see you, old chap!' Simon greeted Boysie, who was followed by Porgie, Hoots and Plummy. The girls followed more sedately, Primrose, Zoe and Nona in low-waisted silk afternoon dresses, wearing hats with large brims decorated with flowers. Their high-pitched voices tinkled like silver drops of rain, punctuating the young men's booming tones.

'Alexia darling, you look too marvellous for words!' Zoe shrilled. 'You've practically got your figure back! Was it terribly, terribly painful? Mummy said she nearly died when I was born? Tell all!'

The other girls clustered around. Eyes were cast to heaven, hands were clasped and fingers wrung, and there were wails of 'I'll never be able to bear it!' and 'My dear, you're *so* brave!'

'One quickly forgets the pain,' she assured them lightly. At that moment some instinct made her turn to glance through the open drawing-room door. In that heart-stabbing moment she saw her father talking to Virginia. They were standing in the hall, laughing and joking as if they'd always known each other and been close.

Daddy's other daughter, Alexia reflected with shock. Daddy's other little girl, conceived in a moment of passion with the woman he'd really loved.

Virginia's rich chestnut hair was rippling down her back, and her dark red crepe dress clung to her slim body, so that she resembled a Rossetti Pre-Raphaelite painting. Malcolm, his head inclined to one side in an affectionate gesture Alexia knew so well, was smiling down at Virginia with an expression that could only be described as pride.

She's so much prettier than me, Alexia reflected. I hadn't realized how pale her skin is, and how fine are her features. Does she look like him? Does my father think she's beautiful? Does he wish he'd spent the past twenty years with her? Does he long for her to know he's her real father? Does he regret that I was born . . .?

Virginia looks vulnerable and sensitive. Unlike me, she thought critically, who appears to be strong and independent. But I learned as a child how to hide my pain. Now it's become a habit. That's the only way if you want to prevent being hurt again and again.

Malcolm glanced up and saw Alexia's stricken expression. Their eyes locked, hers accusing, his guilty. Excusing himself he left Virginia's side and hurried over.

'Everything all right, darling?'

In that moment she knew she couldn't lie to him. 'I found your letters to Leonora,' she murmured in a low voice.

The silence thundered between them.

'How?' he croaked at last. He involuntarily turned to look to where Virginia had stood with him a moment before, but she had gone.

'Does it matter how?'

'Oh God! Who else knows?' There was anger and a flicker of panic in his eyes.

'Only Granny. I had to tell someone.' Her tone was defiant.

'Oh, darling. I'm so sorry,' he said wretchedly. 'I'd have given anything for you not to know. Where the hell did you find them?'

She explained, determined not to cry.

'How could Leonora have been so stupid?' he muttered.

Alexia felt a sudden surge of fury. She longed to lash out and punish him.

'I'm sorry I got in the way of your affair with my unplanned arrival.' Her voice was brittle. 'Most inconvenient of me, I'm afraid. It obviously wrecked your plans with Leonora but there's nothing either of us can do about it now.'

He looked aghast and, taking her arm, propelled her into the private chapel, which was dimly lit by candles that Alexia had requested Spencer to keep alight on the altar over the weekend.

'You mustn't talk like that,' he whispered urgently, as he pulled her down beside him in one of the carved oak pews. 'I was thrilled when I knew you were expected. You know how much I've always loved you. Virginia is Leonora's daughter, and I didn't even see her until the day you married Simon. You're *mine*. That's what you must remember. *My* daughter, who I love and have always loved.'

Alexia stared at him, wanting to believe what he said. But the memory of the anguish in his last letter to Leonora still filled her with pain.

Malcolm gripped her shoulder. 'Please don't let this come between us, sweetheart. I realize you've had an enormous shock, but this doesn't alter anything between us.'

Her eyes were bleak and the skin around them looked bruised. 'How can you say that? Virginia is my half-sister. Every time I look at Leonora I think of you . . . and her. Why in God's name did she invite me to their ball? Was I meant to pave the way for you to continue your liaison?'

'It wasn't like that at all. I told you the truth. She invited you out of kindness. Don't let this spoil what you've got here, Alexia.'

'Are you sure Ian never suspected anything?'

'Why should he?' he demanded. 'Not a soul knows, apart from you now.'

'Someone else does know.'

The panic flickered in his eyes again. 'Who?'

'I don't know. I hid the letters, planning to burn them at the first opportunity, but they were stolen from—'

'*Stolen?*'

She nodded.

'Bloody hell!' He'd turned pale and he started pacing up and down the narrow aisle. 'Have you any idea who took them?'

'No. I suspect one of the servants but I can't be sure.'

Malcolm thrust his hands into his trouser pockets. 'Christ! This is a nightmare,' he muttered, turning to leave the chapel.

Alexia rose to follow him but a movement in the shadows to one side of the altar stopped her in her tracks.

'Who's there?' she called out in alarm. Then she heard a scraping shuffle and a small figure in black emerged from the darkness. It was Mrs Quinn.

*God! That old witch scares me! Simon says I'm making a fuss over nothing and she's just a mad old widow so I shouldn't be afraid. But what was she doing lurking in our chapel? Why didn't one of the servants see her enter the North Wing in the first place? Simon says she'd probably only wanted to say a few prayers, but what frightens me is how much did she hear of my conversation with Daddy? What does she want? Stupidly I mentioned it to Simon and he told his father, saying jokingly that a Bad Fairy was already on hand to attend Freddie's Christening. I didn't think it was at all funny and neither did Ian. The next moment I heard Ian bellowing with rage, saying the old bitch should be locked up. For once, Kenneth Ponsonby's presence was useful. He calmed Ian down and averted Simon and his father from having one of their usual rows.*

*For some reason, probably because he's been staying here to paint the Cliftons, Roderick is constantly in my thoughts and I find myself seeking him out. His presence is like a warm guardian angel hovering at my side and I trust him completely. Perhaps I'll confide in him about the letters?*

Dozens of white candles lit the medieval chapel as Alexia carried Freddie over to the font, in the long lace robe that generations of Stanhopes had worn for their christenings. Gathered around were the godparents, Roderick Davenport, Sir Michael McVean, normally known as Hoots, Lady Zoe Middleton and Robert, Duke of Garnock. Everyone else was crammed into the pews, the Cliftons on one side of the aisle, the Erskines on the other, eager to watch the new grandson and heir being baptized.

Simon moved to Alexia's side a moment later and she could smell brandy on his breath. He was not alone. With outraged astonishment she watched as Baggers Mortimer-Smythe stepped from Simon's shadow to join the other godparents, whispering jovially something about the last noggin taking a fraction longer than he'd expected.

She turned to Simon to protest, but it was too late. He flashed her an impish smile as the Reverend Peter Cranbrook started the service, while Roderick as chief godfather took Freddie gently from her arms.

Gritting her teeth Alexia decided it would be undignified to make a scene. Instead she would ignore Baggers' presence as if he didn't exist. As far as she was concerned she hadn't invited him to Marley, so she would cut him dead, making it plain that she did not want him there.

Prayers were being said and she glanced at Roderick, who was holding Freddie with such tender ease it made her heart contract with emotion. Then he turned and smiled at her, and his steady gaze suddenly overwhelmed her with a strange desperate longing for Freddie to have been his son.

Flushing scarlet and consumed with a feeling of heat, she wondered why such a thought had entered her head. Roderick was a friend, Simon's cousin, and the one person in the whole family to whom she could turn. And there perhaps, she reflected with a jolt of shock as she bit her bottom lip, lay the reason for her feelings.

Her back damp with sweat and the long ropes of pearls Simon had given her sticking to her neck, she tried to breathe deeply to calm her tumultuous emotions. It was impossible, of course. Nothing could come of it. She was married to Simon. But why had she never thought of Roderick in this way before? Or had she? On that very first visit to Marley?

At that moment Freddie gave a little wail as the holy water was sprinkled on his head, and started crying. When the priest handed him back to Roderick he stopped and once more lay still and content.

'What's your trick, Rodders?' Baggers jested in a loud whisper. 'Did you give the little blighter a strong gin-and-it beforehand?'

With the ceremony over the guests began to drift into the large square hall of the North Wing. Alexia turned to Simon, her eyes blazing with anger.

'You know I didn't want that disreputable bounder to be

a godfather,' she whispered fiercely. 'Why did you ask him?'

'Oh, shut up, you silly bitch!' Simon retorted drunkenly. 'I'll have who I bloody well want as godparents.'

Then he stormed off, charging through the guests who were congregating in the drawing room where the footmen stood to attention holding trays of champagne. Alexia had just handed Freddie to his nanny when Roderick came up to her.

'Are you all right, Alexia?'

'I'm fine, thanks,' she said abruptly, avoiding eye contact in case he was able to read her thoughts.

'What a beautiful christening,' her grandmother remarked, joining them. 'Wasn't Freddie good?' She turned to Roderick. 'I hear you're going to paint Alexia? That's very exciting.'

Roderick grinned. 'Well, I think so.'

Alexia remained silent, not wanting to appear too enthusiastic. Her grandmother was very perceptive and might try to stop her sitting for Roderick if she knew Alexia had feelings for him.

At that moment Virginia rushed up looking agitated. 'What's the matter with Simon?' she demanded. 'He's gone off somewhere with Baggers, and he was clutching a couple of bottles of champagne.'

'Gone off?' Roderick queried.

Virginia nodded. 'He was in one of his rages. They jumped into Baggers' car and roared off down the drive. I have a feeling we won't see him for the next couple of days.'

'For the next . . .? Oh my God!' Alexia's face fell with horror. 'He can't have gone. We've got all these guests staying. How am I supposed to entertain all his friends for the weekend?'

Roderick and Virginia exchanged knowing looks.

'Alexia, shall I go after them?' he offered.

Virginia spoke. 'What's the point? Even if you did catch up with them, Simon won't come back now. He never does when he and Baggers decide to paint the town red.'

'What's happening?' Leonora enquired, coming over to them. She looked anxiously at Alexia, before turning to Helen McNaughten. 'What's going on?'

Helen raised her eyebrows. 'I'm afraid I have no idea, Lady Clifton,' she said diplomatically.

While Virginia explained what had happened, and Leonora gasped with chagrin, Alexia glanced around the room, hoping no one else had noticed Simon's abrupt departure. Why did he have to humiliate her by running off today of all days, just because she'd voiced her objection to Baggers being a godfather?

A lot of their guests had strolled on to the terrace to take advantage of the April sunshine, while others had drifted off to the dining room where the buffet luncheon was being served. Before long people were going to ask where Simon was. What was she going to say?

Kenneth Ponsonby passed at that moment, sipping his champagne. 'So where's your beloved husband?' he asked slyly. Then, without waiting for a reply, he looked in the direction of Margaret Erskine, who was talking to the Duke of Garnock. 'I must go and say hello to your mother,' he told Alexia. 'The poor thing has had to put up with so much, hasn't she?'

Simon didn't return that evening. Leonora, her white face carefully composed into an expression of serenity, rearranged the *placement* for the formal dinner party in the main house that night.

'Such a pity Simon developed a migraine,' she informed everyone in clipped tones. 'He sends his love but I fear he'll be in bed for a couple of days.' She turned to Alexia, asking sweetly, 'Can I have a tiny word with you, my darling? About the arrangements?'

Alexia followed her mother-in-law up to her over-furnished pink damask and ornate gilt bedroom, which was fragrant with the scent of lavender.

Leonora shut the door and her mask immediately slipped, her eyes glinting like steel daggers. 'You stupid, *stupid* girl!' she raged venomously. 'How could you do this to me? Your father tells me you read all his letters to me. You had no right to poke your nose into my business. It's unforgivable! And I gather they've now been stolen? Have you any idea what this could mean?'

Alexia's heart was pounding nervously. She'd never seen

Leonora lose her temper and it was an ugly sight. Her fine face had become contorted and she looked spiteful in her fury.

'Well?' she continued aggressively. 'What have you got to say for yourself?'

'I locked the letters away in a safe place,' Alexia protested defensively. 'I apologize for reading them but I was actually trying to prevent their being found. I'd planned to burn them, which if I may say so, you should have done twenty years ago instead of leaving them in a book in the library.'

Leonora started pacing around the room, her fists clenched, her expression panic-stricken. 'Have you thought how this will affect Virginia if she finds out? You've put the whole family in danger. How could you be so careless and stupid after all I've done for you? If it wasn't for me you'd be working in a shop! A penniless young woman with no future, and you repay my kindness by prying into my private life and then you leave the evidence lying around, almost as if you wanted to ruin me!' Her voice rose hysterically and broke on a sob. 'If this gets out our good name will be ruined. No decent man will want to marry Virginia and my reputation will be in tatters.'

'Wait a moment . . .!' Alexia burst out in protest.

'Your father is deeply upset and—'

'I realize that, but—'

'We must find out who took those letters, and I'll pay whatever they want to get them back. I'll never forgive you for this.'

Alexia looked at her mother-in-law defiantly. 'Before you start blaming me for everything, whose fault is it that you, a married woman, had an affair with my father in the first place? Why weren't *you* more careful?'

Leonora seemed to crumble. Her knees sagged and, looking pale and haggard, she collapsed on to the side of her massively canopied bed.

'You don't seem to understand how serious this is,' she moaned, holding a lace-edged handkerchief to her trembling lips. 'I'm frightened. Really frightened. If Ian finds out he'll divorce me, and Virginia and I will become social pariahs. I don't know how, but we've got to get those letters back.'

\*     \*     \*

Alexia tapped quietly on her grandmother's door. 'Can I come in?'

'I was expecting you, darling.' Helen came forward, looking elegant in a long pale grey lace dress with a matching chiffon scarf wound fashionably around her neck.

'Something awful has happened,' Alexia whispered, closing the door softly behind her.

'It's Simon, isn't it?' There was deep compassion in the old lady's voice and her eyes were over-bright.

'No, at least . . . yes, he's run off to London with that dreadful friend of his, but I've become used to his antics,' Alexia said dismissively.

'Oh, my dear, I'd no idea your marriage was in such a bad way,' Helen said sadly. She sat down on a sofa at the end of the bed and indicated Alexia should sit beside her.

'Granny, it's not my marriage I'm worried about, it's those letters I found. Leonora is going crazy because they've been stolen.'

Helen tut-tutted in aggravation. 'How stupid of your father to tell her you'd found them in the first place! If only people kept their mouths shut, life would be so much simpler.'

'I know.'

'You've no idea who took them?'

Alexia shook her head, her fingers twiddling nervously with her long ropes of pearls. 'There's a staff of over a hundred people working here, not to mention the lady's maids and valets that the guests bring with them.'

'Do the Cliftons have any enemies?'

Alexia thought instantly of Mrs Quinn. 'Yes, they do.' She looked thoughtful. 'Maybe I'll pay her a visit tomorrow.'

Early the next morning Alexia set off with Shadow to walk across the park, to where she knew Mrs Quinn lived on the far side of the woods. As she approached she could see the stone building was well maintained, the window frames and front door freshly painted, the brass knocker shining, and the surrounding flowerbeds well tended. Intriguingly, money was obviously being lavished on the upkeep of this modest little cottage.

At first there was no response to her knocking, so she

stepped back to look up at the windows, wondering if the curtains were drawn and the old woman still asleep. Then Shadow started barking. Turning swiftly, Alexia realized with a start that Mrs Quinn was standing in the garden watching her.

'Oh, Mrs Quinn!' Her heart was pounding so hard she could hardly breathe. 'I've come to pay you a visit.'

The old woman's malevolent expression and the pure venom in her eyes sent a chill through Alexia. Picking up Shadow she forced herself to smile, and her tone was conciliatory. 'What a lovely house you have! And such a pretty garden. Do you get lonely, though, living here on your own?'

As if galvanized into action, Mrs Quinn raised her fists and shook them as if to strike her.

'Lonely?' she screeched. 'Lonely? I've never had a moment's happiness since that bastard crossed my path! You're all rotten! The whole lot of you! This house was bought with blood and conceived in blood. May you all die in blood!'

Alexia stood her ground, staring at Mrs Quinn who was shaking alarmingly as if suffering from an ague. Alarmed that she might collapse, Alexia asked urgently, 'Can I help you? Shall I call the doctor?'

By now Mrs Quinn had reached her front door, staggering and clutching at her chest. 'How can a doctor cure a broken heart?' she moaned. 'That bastard destroyed my life. He should be hung for what he did.'

'For what who did, Mrs Quinn?'

The enraged, bloodshot eyes turned on her with renewed fury. 'You know as well as I do. You're all in it together.' Her mouth worked convulsively and she spat at Alexia. 'Trust the ruling classes to stick up for each other. I'd like to see you all dead.'

Then she pushed her front door open and went inside, slamming it shut behind her.

Simon returned to Marley the next day, apologetic and remorseful as usual, just in time to bid his departing house guests goodbye as they headed off home.

'It's been a spiffing weekend, old boy,' Hoots exclaimed, ignoring the fact that Simon had been absent for most of it.

'Yes, thanks a million,' the Duke of Garnock remarked as he departed hand-in-hand with Lady Zoe Middleton, who was blushing prettily and giving Alexia knowing looks.

'I thought he already had a girlfriend,' Alexia remarked in surprise as she watched them speed off down the drive in his elegant Bugatti Royale, which had the Garnock crest painted on the passenger doors.

'Oh, I think he has,' Simon replied blandly.

She caught Roderick's eye as he supervised the loading of the Cliftons' portraits into a Carter Patterson van, bound for London.

'I wonder if Zoe knows that . . .' Roderick speculated dryly. 'She looked to me like the cat that thinks it's caught a large fat mouse.'

Simon chuckled. 'Not a chance in hell. He's always got a few girlfriends on the go, sensible fellow.' Then he strolled off, hands deep in the pockets of his checked Oxford bags, leaving behind a whiff of brandy and cigarettes in the air.

Alexia looked after him, her brow puckered.

'He doesn't mean it,' Roderick said comfortingly.

She directed her gaze at him. 'Oh, but he does,' she affirmed, without a trace of self-pity. 'It's exactly what he means.'

*It wasn't supposed to be like this. I feel I'm in someone else's shoes and that this isn't really my life at all. Sometimes I don't even know what's happening, because this family never talk to each other and Simon doesn't really talk to me. Not properly. It's all superficial chat like 'Let's go riding' or 'Whose party are we going to tonight?' I still don't know what he's thinking and then it strikes me that he's probably not thinking at all. He's just cruising along in a blur of alcohol and I sometimes wonder if he'd even notice if I wasn't here.*

*I thought being married to Simon would be different. Where did my bright beautiful young man go? He seemed to drift away when we returned from our honeymoon.*

*Maybe our destiny really is carved in stone from the moment of our conception? Maybe in life we don't really have a choice. We might think we do, but what impulse makes us choose a path that we know will lead to disaster?*

# Eight

R oderick glanced at the six evening dresses as Alexia held them up one by one for his inspection.

'Which do you think?' she asked. They were in his Chelsea studio where he'd decided to paint her portrait rather than at Marley, and today was her first sitting.

His eyes swept swiftly over the array of taffeta, satin, lace and georgette gowns, all in delicate pastel shades, before saying firmly, 'That one.'

She raised her dark eyebrows in surprise. 'Really? I was afraid it might be a bit insipid. I hardly ever wear pale pink.'

'Nothing you wear could ever look insipid,' he said, fixing on to his easel a canvas that measured six feet by four. 'The dress is perfect because it enhances your colouring, and I'm going to paint you against a plain grey background.'

'And you still don't want me to wear any jewellery?' she asked wistfully.

He smiled. 'It's you I want to paint, Alexia. Not your jewellery. And not some eye-catching ball gown, either. The changing room is through that door over there. Go and get ready, then we can start.'

When she emerged a few minutes later he looked up sharply, appraising the soft folds of the pink chiffon as it clung to her body, and her simple court shoes which had been dyed to match.

'Perch there, will you?' he commanded with a wave of his hand, indicating a plain high stool which he'd set in front of a grey backcloth. 'I'd like you to keep your right foot on the ground and put your other foot on the bar of the stool. Now relax your arms so you feel comfortable and look at me.'

Alexia felt suddenly shy. This was a different Roderick

from the quiet man she knew. His brow gleamed with sweat and he seemed in the grip of a creative exuberance, his eyes ablaze with energy as he gave her darting, penetrating looks every few moments.

The brittle scratching of the charcoal on the canvas was the only sound that broke the heavy silence in the large, high room, with its floor-to-ceiling window that overlooked the Thames. After half an hour of intense concentration, he wiped his hands on a damp cloth and his face broke into a smile.

'I think we've got something here,' he said softly.

'Can I see?'

'Yes, of course you can. Is your back aching?'

'No, not at all.' She slid down from the stool and walked over to him.

He stood close beside her as they looked at the canvas. 'Like it?'

She gazed, entranced. He'd only done a rough outline but it was almost as if she'd caught sight of herself in a mirror when she knew no one was watching. 'It's me, isn't it?'

'Yes, Alexia.' His tone was serious. 'It's the real you. Not an ex-debutante, and not Simon's wife, and not the future chatelaine of Marley Court, but the real Alexia.'

She frowned, perplexed. 'But how do you know the real me? How do you know what I feel?' she asked.

'That's what artists do. What's the point of a superficial likeness? One that shows you have your hair done every week and that your husband buys you valuable jewellery? If that's what you want you might as well be photographed. A portrait isn't worth doing,' he continued vigorously, 'unless it reveals the sitter's *soul*.'

She was silent, disconcerted. Then she turned to look at him. 'Supposing someone doesn't want their soul exposed?'

His eyes studied her face intently and his voice was low and intimate. 'It's up to you if you want to fool the world into believing you're happily married to Simon, but you can't fool me. You and I both know something's going on at Marley. Why is Kenneth Ponsonby always there? What drives Simon to drink? What is Ian afraid of? Both you and Leonora carry on as if everything was all right but it's not. I can see the anxiety in your face at times, and the pain. You're very brave, Alexia. Do you realize that?'

She shook her head. 'I have no alternative.'

'There are always alternatives.'

'I have to think of Freddie now.'

He gazed out thoughtfully through the giant window at the river where boats were passing to and fro at a leisurely pace. She could tell his thoughts were miles away.

'Are you going to do any more work on it today, Roderick? Or shall I come back another time?'

'What?' He started, as if he'd forgotten she was there. Then he gave her a quick smile. 'Come back next week. How about Tuesday morning?'

For the next few weeks, Alexia went to Roderick's studio. The sittings sometimes lasted two or three hours as he got carried away with enthusiasm, forgetting that her back and legs might be aching and that it was exhausting for her to hold the pose for such long stretches. Then he'd be very apologetic and insist she lie down on the chaise longue under the window, while he brought her cups of hot chocolate.

'You're pleased with the way it's going, aren't you?' she asked during one of their breaks. He'd forbidden her to look at the portrait since that first day but she could tell by his flushed face that he was excited by his creation.

He nodded silently.

'When will it be finished?'

'In another couple of weeks.'

'So soon?' She felt a pang of disappointment. His studio was a haven of peace and she looked forward to coming here, away from her frenetic life as society's darling. Away from the endless *thés dansants* and cocktail parties, dinners and balls, followed by nightclubs or casinos as Simon craved more and more excitement and wasted money wantonly.

'Haven't you found it boring, sitting still for hours?' Roderick enquired.

'I've loved it,' she replied simply. 'It's been so restful.'

His gaze was direct. 'I've liked having you here, too. You

inspire me. This is the best painting I've ever done, thanks to you.'

'Really?' She looked into his eyes and knew in that moment she was on the very edge of something dangerous. One step in the wrong direction and she'd be undone. And yet she knew that if she took that step she'd also find something she'd never completely known before: pure happiness.

'Do you regret marrying Simon?' he asked suddenly.

The question shocked her. They had skirted around the state of her marriage many times but he'd never been so blunt before.

'There's no point in regretting what was meant to be,' she replied quietly.

'What do you mean? You didn't have to marry him. There were other young men who would have loved to have married you.'

'I don't know about that,' she retorted with a self-deprecating little laugh. 'All I know is that I fell in love with him and it seemed inevitable that we should marry. Leonora was keen on the idea . . .' Her voice drifted off.

'She thought you'd keep Simon on the straight and narrow.'

'There is more to it than that.' She studied the polished floor at her feet.

'What is it?'

Alexia took a deep breath, raised her chin and looked straight into his eyes. 'I've discovered she had an affair with my father. He made her pregnant and at the same time my mother became pregnant with me.'

'Then you and Virginia . . .?' Roderick stood still, his face a study. 'You didn't know this when you married Simon?'

'Of course I didn't.' She told him about the letters. 'I'm on tenterhooks in case the person who stole them reveals the contents. It's such a strain pretending everything's all right when in reality our lives are all just smoke and mirrors. I feel as if I'm in a permanent state of siege, waiting for a storm to break at any minute.'

He came and sat down beside her. 'I had no idea you had all this on your plate. You're even braver than I thought. What are you going to do? You can't live your life like this for ever.'

'I took my wedding vows very seriously.' She looked down at her wedding ring. 'I'm Simon's wife now and that's the end of it.'

'She can't be allowed to throw herself away like this!' Leonora's voice was loud and shrill.

'Don't worry. I'll soon put a stop to it,' Ian roared menacingly. 'He should be horsewhipped for coming within a mile of her.'

Alexia was halted by her in-laws' angry altercation as she crossed the great hall of Marley with Freddie in her arms. She'd been about to let him spend a little time with his grandparents but now she lingered in the window overlooking the front drive, where she could hear what was going on.

'How can she want to marry a man who's in *trade!*' Leonora wailed. 'What will people think? How can she do this to us?'

At that moment Alexia heard a muffled sob. Turning sharply, she saw Virginia slumped on the staircase, her arms wrapped around her knees, in a huddled mass of despair.

They'd never been close, the half-sisters and sisters-in-law, but Alexia recognized someone in acute distress. Tucking Freddie under one arm she hurried to Virginia's side.

'What's going on?' she whispered.

'I want to marry William Spall but they won't let me.' Virginia wiped her eyes with a sodden handkerchief, humbled by her misery, all arrogance and conceit vanished.

Alexia looked around and spied the butler, ostensibly straightening an oil painting with great gravitas from a vantage point conveniently near the library door.

'We can't talk here,' she said. 'Let's go into the orangery.'

Once away from prying eyes and ears she looked at Virginia with compassion. 'Who is William Spall?'

'He's a young man I met in London. He's so sweet and kind and we love each other so much. They want me to marry someone titled like the Duke of Garnock, who owns half Scotland,' she explained bitterly.

'So what's wrong with this young man, in their eyes?'

Virginia raised her chin defiantly. 'He works for his father. They own a pottery that makes bricks. Half the houses in the South-East are built of bricks made by Spall and Son. It's a huge company.'

'Perhaps when they get to know him they'll realize he's very nice,' Alexia suggested hopefully, although knowing the Cliftons' snobbish views she privately doubted it. 'Why don't you invite him to stay?'

'They won't let me. They're trying to stop us meeting altogether. How can they be so heartless? I don't care about all this aristocratic stuff. I've never felt I really belong in it, anyway. William has just bought Lord Langford's old home, Thorpe Hall in Yorkshire, and he's planning to do it up for us . . . but now Mummy won't let me see him again.' Her words came out in a tearful torrent and her shoulders shook with sobs.

Alexia looked at her thoughtfully. Maybe Lady Virginia Stanhope, daughter of the Earl of Clifton, should marry into the nobility, but plain Virginia Erskine surely wouldn't expect to?

'Why don't you let me talk to your mother?' she suggested. 'After all, they didn't mind Simon marrying me and I'm from a fairly ordinary background.'

'Your background is OK, it's just that your family have no money,' Virginia pointed out plaintively. 'I simply can't bear the thought of never seeing William again. He's the only young man I've ever fallen for and we're made for each other. Anyway, I'm twenty-one now. I can marry who I like.'

Later that day Alexia cornered Leonora by the kennels, as she prepared to take the Great Danes for a walk.

'I gather you're unhappy about Virginia's choice of husband?' she asked directly as soon as they were alone. 'She's absolutely heartbroken, you know.'

Leonora stopped dead in her tracks. 'Has she told you what this young man does? He's a tradesman. He sells bricks! Not even fine porcelain or silver, but bricks. It's out of the question, Alexia. You should realize that. Please don't encourage her in this madness. Ian and I will not stand by and see her ruin her life.'

Alexia looked at her mother-in-law squarely. 'I don't know this William Spall, but the fact that he makes his money manufacturing and selling bricks should not make him ineligible.

It's an honest profession, and she tells me he's bought Thorpe Hall . . .'

'That is beside the point,' Leonora snapped, striding ahead with the Great Danes at her heels. 'I didn't bring Virginia out with a grand ball and everything, to have her run off and marry a common man. Ian and I won't allow it.'

'She told me that she's never felt a part of the aristocracy. And in fact she isn't, is she?'

The silence between them was laden with innuendo. Leonora shot her a dark, haunted look. 'Ian's name is on her birth certificate.'

'But my father's blood runs through her veins. My father would have approved of any young man I'd wanted to marry as long as he was decent and honest, and if William Spall has those qualities I don't think you've got the right to stop her marrying him if she really wants to.'

'You wouldn't tell?' Leonora croaked in a stricken voice.

'Of course I wouldn't, but if he's found to be honourable, I'll certainly help her to run away with him, if needs be. She is twenty-one now, and there's always Gretna Green, you know.'

Leonora put a trembling hand to her mouth. 'What are people going to think if we allow this marriage to go ahead? I've worked so hard to ensure she has a wonderful future; look at the guests we invited to stay for Freddie's christening. It will be too shameful if we have to announce her engagement to a *Mr* William Spall, of Spall Potteries, Essex.'

Alexia's mouth twitched at Leonora's snobbishness.

'Look,' she said coaxingly. 'This is 1922, and we're not living in the age of Jane Austen. If he makes Virginia happy and he's all she says he is, then I think people will respect you for letting the marriage go ahead. You don't want to be seen as class conscious in this day and age, do you? If you rise above it and welcome the young man into the family, no one will be able to accuse you of being snobbish.'

'But people are class conscious,' Leonora insisted. 'There were raised eyebrows when Simon married you, you know.'

'How strange, I never noticed,' Alexia replied serenely.

\*   \*   \*

Two weeks later the engagement was announced, William having spent a week at Marley. Apart from his background he was liked by everyone and the Cliftons realized that if they forbade the marriage, it was they who would appear insufferably snobbish.

Virginia was ecstatic, especially when he produced a large sapphire and diamond engagement ring, and photographs of Thorpe Hall with plans for its refurbishment.

Only Simon soured the atmosphere with a cruel play on words, urging people 'not to drop a spall' when talking, and referring to Thorpe Hall being 'a large spall house'. He laughed uproariously at his own wit and told Virginia that talking to her was 'like talking to a spall wall'.

Ignoring his juvenile behaviour, Alexia returned to London for her last sitting with Roderick. For once they hardly talked at all and the atmosphere in his light airy studio was charged with sadness. She'd delighted in the quiet hours they'd spent together, sometimes talking, sometimes companionably silent while opera music played in the background on his wind-up gramophone. She loved to watch the passionate dedication he applied to his work, never satisfied until he got exactly what he wanted down on canvas.

The end was in sight though, and she felt an acute sense of loss. She'd treasured these hours when she was the focus of Roderick's attention, aware of his eyes darting to her face, her throat, her breasts and her slim bare arms as he painted with feverish intensity. She felt exposed before him in a way that made her feel special and she wished she could stay in the studio for ever.

A tear slid down her cheek and plopped softly on to the pink chiffon of her bodice.

Roderick immediately put down his brush and palette and strode over to where she sat, reaching out to stroke her wet cheek with his thumb.

'Would you like to see it now?' he asked softly, as if he understood how she felt.

'Is it really finished?'

'I'm afraid it is. Come and have a look.'

'Are you pleased with it?'

'Tell me what you think first.'

She stood in front of the life-size portrait and gazed, shocked. It seemed as if Roderick had captured her inner self. The painting was so vibrantly alive she almost expected it to speak, to move, to smile. Her deepest thoughts and feelings were exposed in the depths of her dark eyes.

'That's how I feel,' she breathed in awe. 'How do you know so much about me and what I'm like?'

'It's what an artist should do.' He stood close by her side and she had a strong sense of the intimacy that existed between them, a deep emotional empathy she'd never shared with Simon.

'I believe I've got the very essence of you in this portrait,' he continued. 'I'm going to call it *Alexia in the Pink Dress* and I'm going to submit it to the Royal Academy for their 1923 Summer Exhibition. I think it'll create quite a stir.'

'It's even better than your portraits of Leonora and Ian.'

There was a pause and then he said in his deep voice, 'That's because it's of you.'

She glanced up at his strong-featured face and steady eyes. 'Why because it's of me?'

He gave her a wintry smile. 'That would be too difficult to explain. But I'm glad you like it.'

In contrast to Alexia and Simon's wedding, Virginia and William were to be married in the private chapel in the North Wing, followed by a modest reception at Marley Court – modest, that is, by Clifton standards.

'Are you happy about this, Virginia?' Alexia asked anxiously. They'd become surprisingly close since she'd supported Virginia in her desire to marry, and she felt guilty that the Cliftons, having given her a splendid wedding, were doing the minimum for their own daughter.

'I'm so happy to be marrying William that I wouldn't care if it was in a register office,' Virginia replied frankly. She was a changed person since her engagement, radiant, warm and friendly. 'I don't know how you made Mama and Papa change their mind but thank God you did.' She shook her head in horror at the thought of a life without William. 'If they'd forbidden me I'd have run away and never spoken to them again. You're so lucky, Alexia, especially with your father. He's one of the nicest men I've ever met.'

Alexia picked up one of Freddie's teddy bears which had been left on the floor and studied it intently, stroking its ears as if it was a real animal. 'Yes, Daddy's lovely,' she said lightly. 'Now, tell me about your wedding dress.'

*If it wasn't for my own private garden where I can potter undisturbed, I think this place would drive me mad. I've installed a large shed, screened by a pergola covered with climbing roses. Here I keep my gardening clothes and tools and I've recently bought some chairs and big cushions and fluffy rugs for Freddie to lie on. There are shelves for books and toys and picnic things, and this is my little haven. A secret place where I can go and tend all the plants I've put in, with the help of Birchall, the head gardener. He's the only person I've allowed in here, but even he doesn't have a key to the door in the wall. I lend him mine when I'm in London, so he can make sure the plants are watered and fed, and pruned where necessary.*

*Freddie will take his first steps on my little lawn, away from Nanny and all the servants. He'll learn the names of all the flowers and we'll play ball games, just he and I. At the moment his darling little hands reach out for me lest he should fall, and his deep milky chuckle harmonizes with the song thrush who perches on the wall and will, I hope, nest in the oak tree that over-looks my secret garden.*

*Only in this place can I blot out what is happening in Marley Court at the moment.*

*Ian is in a permanent, almost apoplectic rage these days, and it's not about Virginia's wedding next week. Leonora, suffering as usual, doesn't know what it's about either.*

*Kenneth Ponsonby has driven down from London several times; not to stay but to have 'meetings' with Ian. What does the wretched little man want? He certainly holds a grudge against the Cliftons. Apparently he was very jealous when they were all up at Oxford because he wasn't admitted to an exclusive dining club founded by a coterie of ten rich young men, which*

*according to an ancient copy of the* Sketch *magazine
included the 'dashing young Earl of Clifton, his cousin
Sir Edmund Davenport and Malcolm Erskine'.*

*I find it hard to think of my father as 'rich' but even
more astonishing to hear that Ian was once 'dashing'.
I wonder what happened to them. Those aristocratic
young men who had the world at their feet in 1883?*

Alexia trotted Dancer into the stable yard, with Shadow
following, and she saw Simon, his face chalk white, giving
orders to the head groom. He looked up as soon as he heard
the clop-clop of hooves on the cobbles, and dashing over,
practically pulled her down from the saddle.

'For God's sake come quickly,' he gasped.

'What's happened?'

Simon's expressive eyes were filled with panic as he
grabbed her arm tightly and almost dragged her towards the
house.

'Papa's dead,' he said breathlessly.

'How can he be . . .?' She saw the bleak look in his eyes.
'Oh my God, Simon. I'm so sorry.' She was running with
him now, round the side of the house to where, outside the
main entrance, an ambulance stood waiting.

At that moment, four ambulance men emerged through
the great portals of Marley Court bearing a stretcher, the
body lying on it covered in a white sheet.

Alexia stopped, stunned with shock, her hand to her mouth,
her eyes unbelieving.

'Come *on*,' Simon urged, frantically tugging at her hand.
'Mama's in a dreadful state.'

Leonora was standing in the middle of the hall, surrounded
by dozens of servants, all agape and trembling.

Alexia rushed up to her, but she was looking blindly
through the open door to the ambulance beyond, too stunned
to speak.

'Come and sit down,' Alexia told her gently.

'Fetch some brandy,' Simon commanded the butler.

Together they guided Leonora into the red salon where
she collapsed on to a sofa.

'I can't believe it,' she murmured through stiff white lips.

'One minute he was . . . then . . .' She covered her face with her hands. 'And he was only sixty-one.'

Alexia looked at Simon, who was swigging brandy straight from the bottle.

'How can we get hold of Virginia?' she asked in a practical voice.

'I'll have to wire them.' He looked agitated. 'They'll still be on a yacht in the Mediterranean. Oh Christ, do you know what this means?' His eyes were wide and scared looking. 'I've come into my inheritance.'

She nodded slowly. From now on he'd have the responsibility of running the vast estate as the Ninth Earl of Clifton and all that it entailed, including taking his seat in the House of Lords.

In a rush of compassion she rose from her seat and, putting her arms around him, held him close in the way she held Freddie when he was upset.

'It'll be all right, darling,' she said softly. 'I'm here to help you.'

'But how am I going to do it all?' he asked, stricken.

It flashed through Alexia's mind that it wasn't only Simon who would be burdened by his new position. She too would have to take on the charities and good works and formal occasions that her mother-in-law had carried out for the past thirty years.

'We'll do it together,' she promised, feeling protective towards a husband who seemed at that moment to be no more than a lost youth, incapable of stepping into his late father's shoes.

For the next twenty-four hours, as hundreds of letters of condolence poured in, and the chapel in the North Wing almost disappeared under a mountain of flowers, Leonora remained in a state of shock, not eating or sleeping but wandering around the house in a daze.

Then Alexia was awakened one night by sounds of terrible moaning and sobbing, coming from the hall of the North Wing. Sliding out of bed so as not to awaken Simon, she pulled on a wrap and hurried down the stairs. Leonora was on her knees at the entrance to the chapel, weeping as if her heart was broken.

Alexia managed to lead her into the drawing room. 'Drink this, Leonora.'

Her mother-in-law accepted the glass of brandy with a shaking hand.

Alexia put her arm around her shoulders. 'I know this is a terrible time for you,' she began sympathetically. 'Simon and I will—'

'You've done enough damage already!' Leonora wailed hysterically. 'This is all your fault. Ian would still be alive and I'd still be chatelaine of Marley if it wasn't for you and your meddling. You've robbed me of my position and you've probably ruined my reputation.'

Alexia drew back sharply. 'What do you mean?'

Leonora, her face ravaged with shock and anger, turned on her daughter-in-law with venom. 'Ian told me that he'd found out about my affair with your father. He'd discovered Virginia wasn't his daughter. He was ranting and raving, saying the most terrible things, calling me whore and demanding I leave Marley – and then he had a sudden seizure and collapsed.'

Alexia felt the blood drain from her head, leaving her as cold as ice. Her heart started hammering.

'So it was him who took the letters? So why did he wait until now . . .?' she began.

Leonora cut in savagely. 'He didn't find them, you fool! Someone else did, and they told him. It's your fault he's dead.'

*Leonora is trying to make me feel guilty as if I'd deliberately set out to cause trouble. What's going to happen when she tells Simon she holds me responsible for his father's death? And how will Virginia feel at being my half-sister?*

Simon gazed at Alexia in wonder, his blue eyes wide with astonishment.

'Is it true?' he asked doubtfully. 'Is Virginia really your half-sister?'

She nodded. 'Have you been able to get hold of her? Are she and William on their way back?'

'I've had a wire to say they're getting a train to Paris and they should be here the day after tomorrow.' He sank into a chair near her desk as if he was exhausted.

'So she doesn't know . . .?'

'No. It's a bit of a shocker, isn't it? I mean your pa and my mama? And you and Virginia were born only weeks apart? It makes everything seem a bit incestuous really.'

Alexia stared at one of the dozens of letters she was having to write in reply to the notes of condolence that still poured in. 'I know your mother's furious with me . . .' she began.

'Oh, my darling darling, don't get upset about it. It was a chance in a million that you happened to find the letters. It's just a shame someone else stole them before you could destroy them. But Ma's not heartbroken because Pa's died. She's having the vapours because he found out and she feels she's disgraced the family. It was obviously a shock for Papa but it's his own fault. They've had separate bedrooms for years and he's had his mistresses along the way and so . . .'

'Your father?'

'That's right.' He looked away, and she sensed he feared she was going to ask him awkward questions about what he did when he went off with Baggers to Soho.

Instead she said, 'We're going to have to pull together, Simon. There's the funeral to get through. Virginia is going to need our support even though she's got William.' A worried line furrowed her brow as she started ticking off her thoughts on her fingers. 'Do you want to move back into the main house now or stay here in the North Wing? And where will your mother want to live? What about Grosvenor Square? Is it going to remain our town house or will we take over Pa's house in Belgrave Square?'

'Hang on a minute.' He clasped his head in his hands and leaned forward, his elbows resting on his knees. 'I can't take it all in yet. I still can't believe Papa's gone. Can we leave all these details until after the funeral?'

Touched because he sounded so like a bewildered little boy, Alexia went over and put her arms around him. 'Of course we can, dearest. There's no hurry. Just let me know what you want to do and I'll see it's done.'

'Oh, Alexia . . .' He clasped her around the waist and rested his head against her body. 'What would I do without you? I've never needed you more than at this moment.'

'I'm here, Simon.' She stroked his blond hair.

'What if I'm not up to being the new Earl? So much is expected of me now and I'm frightened I'll fail.'

'You? Fail? Never in a million years. We'll get through this together. For better, for worse – remember?'

He rose and, taking her into his arms, kissed her. 'I love you so much.' His piercing pale blue eyes searched her face for reassurance. 'You do still love me, don't you?'

She stroked his face tenderly. 'Of course I do.' His need of her had rekindled those first tender feelings of love she'd experienced when she'd first known him, obliterating the misgivings and hurt she'd suffered since. Things had changed with his father's death. They were no longer a young couple enjoying a flighty existence, but the Earl and Countess of Clifton, with serious responsibilities.

Simon, Freddie, and Marley itself needed her support now as never before, and in that moment she relished the feeling of being in control of her life, as she'd always wanted. There was no turning back now. No room in her heart to have a secret longing for a romantic liaison, or another life in a studio which was still and peaceful.

*Alexia in the Pink Dress* existed only on canvas. Alexia Clifton must now be a pragmatic, sensible young woman who would give her husband more children and help to run Marley as superbly as her mother-in-law had done.

'Thank God for you,' Simon spoke profoundly as he buried his face in her pale slender neck. 'You're the best thing in my life.'

> *Oh God, I'm so confused. Yesterday when I held Simon in my arms I felt deep love for him, a protective maternal love perhaps, but I believed that I was capable of giving him the constant devotion he seems to need now his father is dead. I felt a stirring of emotions towards him that I hadn't felt for a long time and I went to sleep thinking the future would be straightforward; Simon and I fulfilling our roles at the head of the family, having more children and bringing light and laughter to Marley Court.*
>
> *And then I had a dream last night that changed everything and this morning I'm scared yet excited, shocked*

*at my discovery but at the same time appalled because my dream depicted the undeniable truth.*

*I was standing on a hilltop, looking at the view of the countryside, when the light seemed to change and I was surrounded by rainbows, glorious blues and pinks and purples illuminating the sky. The view had vanished, and I was in the centre of this brilliant yet soft light that was above me and below me and all around me.*

*At that moment I heard the voice of a man standing quite near me. I didn't recognize the rich dark voice but his words are now engraved upon my heart for ever.*

*'Turn around, Alexia, and you will find real happiness,' he said.*

*So I turned and Roderick was standing there, smiling at me. He reached out for me and as I went into his embrace I awoke overwhelmed with desire, leaving me breathless and spent.*

*How have I been blind to what was there all along? I look back now and realize that from the beginning I was attracted to Roderick, so why did I think I'd fallen in love with Simon? Was I so dazzled by him, the golden young man with the hot sexy eyes who was heir to a title and a property worth millions, that I lost all sense of reality? Was I so desperate to get away from home that I set my sights on a man who I thought was the most likely to want to marry me, and that man happened to be Simon?*

*Dear God, help me to hide and suppress this passion that devours me now. I feel I'm on a slippery slope, endeavouring to remain in control of my feelings, but I fear a slip – one slip – could send me crashing down to my ruination.*

Ian's funeral was held the following week in the local parish church of St Olaf. Six of the estate's foresters carried his massive oak coffin at the head of the procession which included his favourite hunter Firewheel, with his riding boots facing backwards in the stirrups, and his six Great Danes with black ribbons round their collars, led by two kennel maids. The hundred and fifteen members of staff, from chefs to grooms, gardeners to housemaids, watermen to footmen, lined the drive on both sides, standing stiffly to attention as the family cortège passed slowly by; Leonora was in the first car with Alexia and Simon, and Virginia, William and Roderick were in the second.

'I've cancelled the house party for the shoot next weekend,' Leonora announced, hiding her emotions with chilling efficiency. Veiled in black and with ropes of pearls and silver fox furs draped over her shoulders, she looked formidable beside Alexia, whose simple black silk coat and wide-brimmed black straw hat gave her a look of youthful dignity.

'Right,' Simon replied tersely. His fists were clenched and his breath smelled of brandy.

In the car behind, Virginia sat weeping. 'Poor Papa. Why did he have to die when I was away and I couldn't say goodbye to him? It's so unfair.'

Roderick averted his face, leaving William to comfort her. No one had yet dared tell Virginia that Ian wasn't her father.

'At least he saw you happily married,' her new husband pointed out.

This brought on a fresh wave of grief. 'But he wasn't happy about my marriage,' she sobbed undiplomatically.

William looked crestfallen and Roderick quickly intervened. 'Ian was perfectly happy about it once he got to know William. At first he just thought you were too young to settle down, but he soon realized he was wrong.'

'Really?' William asked anxiously.

'Absolutely,' Roderick replied firmly.

Alexia started to tremble when they arrived at the church, where crowds had gathered to watch the proceedings. Although she had not cared for her father-in-law she'd found the past few days and the funeral that lay ahead a very emotional experience and she longed to have Roderick stand close to her to give her courage and support. This was the first time she'd appeared in public as the Countess of Clifton and everyone was looking at her, wondering how she'd conduct herself.

Instead she had Simon, who was nervous and fidgety and looked ill at ease.

\* \* \*

The final prayers had been said, the eulogy delivered, the hymns sung, and at seemly intervals Leonora had dabbed her dry eyes with a dainty white handkerchief, while Virginia's sobs could be heard by everyone in the congregation.

There was only the coffin to be placed in the family vault now. Ian Henry Giles Stanhope, Eighth Earl of Clifton, would lie beside his ancestors, who had been laid to rest there since 1562. Alexia watched as the coffin was shouldered carefully and turned around to be borne back down the aisle.

Suddenly, the main doors of the church were flung wide. A small malevolent figure in black stood there, blocking the way.

'May his soul never know a moment's peace!' screamed Mrs Quinn, shaking her fists as the coffin approached. Tears were pouring down her pale wrinkled cheeks and she looked crazed with grief. 'God will punish him now! If I never know another day's peace then neither will that bastard!'

# Nine

'The police have taken her off and are charging her with disorderly behaviour,' Simon announced, joining the immediate family as they sat huddled, deeply shaken, in the library.

'The woman should be in a straitjacket,' Leonora stormed. 'How dare she make a scene like that in front of everyone!'

They could hear the animated hum of speculation coming from the ballroom where two hundred guests were enjoying the lavish refreshments being offered at the wake.

'But what was it all about?' Virginia wailed.

'I tell you she's mad,' her mother snapped. 'Don't pay attention to anything she said.'

'Could she have been referring to, you know, something in those letters?' Simon suggested, his voice slurred.

Alexia, Roderick and Leonora turned on him with warning looks.

'Absolutely not,' Roderick said dismissively. 'For some godforsaken reason Mrs Quinn has always had it in for Ian. Now, don't you think we should make an appearance? It's going to look very odd if we all stay in here.'

Ignoring him, Virginia looked at her brother. 'What letters?'

'It's nothing, darling,' Leonora said hurriedly. 'Roderick's right, we should go and mingle for a few minutes.' She rose, gathering her silver fox furs around her shoulders.

'Wait a minute, Mama. I can tell something's going on. What is it, Simon?'

He looked embarrassed. 'We found some letters . . .' he began hesitatingly.

Roderick cut in, 'Now is not the time, Simon . . .'

'*Alexia* found some letters,' Leonora said harshly, 'and she had the cheek not only to read them, but to leave them where they could be found . . .'

'That's not true!' Alexia sprang to her feet. 'I locked them away . . .'

'That's not the point.' Simon turned angrily on his mother. 'And stop laying the blame at Alexia's door.'

He took a deep breath and faced Virginia squarely. 'It seems our mother had an affair with Alexia's father some twenty-two years ago.'

Virginia looked at him blankly. The silence in the library was almost palpable.

'Don't you get it, sweetie?' Simon looked at her pityingly. 'Malcolm Erskine is your real father. Not Papa. Alexia is your half-sister. And I'm only your half-brother.'

William Spall gave a loud gasp of surprise and Roderick shuffled his feet uneasily, as if waiting for a bomb to explode.

He didn't have long to wait.

Virginia looked at her mother and then at the others as she broke into loud rasping sobs. 'You buggers! You rotten filthy buggers!' she shrieked, and then she turned and ran out of the library. Her high heels could be heard clicking across the marble hall floor as she ran into the garden.

They all looked at each other. Then Roderick spoke to William, whose jaw had dropped leaving his mouth gaping.

'I think you'd better go after her, old fella,' he said gently. 'She's obviously very cut up.'

'Oh my God, my parents are in the next room,' Alexia remembered. 'I don't think my mother knows any of this. What shall we do?'

'Nothing,' Roderick said firmly. 'The whole county will know in seconds if we don't try and contain this situation. Go after Virginia, William. Quickly.'

Leonora marched towards the door. 'You can do as you like. I'm going up to my bed. This whole thing is too much for me. And as for *you*,' she swung on Alexia, 'I brought you, a penniless girl, into this family as a kindness because I was fond of your father, and all you've done is ruined my life, killed my husband and now alienated me from my daughter. I hope you're pleased with yourself.'

Her heavy, rose-scented perfume lingered sickeningly in the air after she'd slammed the door behind her.

White-faced, Alexia swayed and looked faint.

'Don't take it to heart, darling.' Simon grabbed her arm and led her to a sofa. 'Mama's upset and she doesn't mean it. It's been a wretched day for us all and she's overwrought. Here, let me get you a drink.'

Getting drinks was what Simon was good at, and he continued to ply everyone with brandy, whisky or champagne for the rest of the day. To Alexia's relief it was decided that her own parents would not be involved in the fracas over the letters and what they revealed, but told privately and quietly at a later date. It was enough that Mrs Quinn had set the whole county agog with her hysterical outburst, put down to madness by the locals who were accustomed to her eccentric behaviour, but devastating to the Clifton family.

Later that afternoon, thinking all the guests had left, Alexia took Shadow on to the terrace. As she strolled in the August sunshine, deep in thought, she was aware of footsteps coming up behind her.

'What a busy day you've had, haven't you?' sneered the well-oiled tones of Kenneth Ponsonby.

She spun round, rattled. 'I didn't know you were here.'

'I've been very much here, my dear Alexia . . . or do you want to be addressed as Lady Clifton now you've achieved your ambition?' he sniggered. 'Who would think it? You, a girl with no money and a father disgraced by his gambling debts, the new Countess of Clifton of Marley Court? My, my! I look forward to your being the hostess here and I'm sure you'll be brilliant at it. People from nowhere always succeed at that sort of thing much better than those born to it.'

He raised his camera and took a quick snapshot of her.

She stood her ground, a slender figure in a simple black dress, her youthful face set in determined lines. 'Let us get one thing straight, Mr Ponsonby. You may have been a friend of my late father-in-law but you are not a friend of either my husband or myself. We will not be extending invitations to you in the future and I'd be grateful if you'd leave Marley now.'

The curl of his lip was impish. 'Now, little lady, it's unwise for an upstart like yourself to start throwing your weight around, while your father-in-law is barely cold. He and I—'

'How dare you talk to me like that,' she shot back hotly. Her dark eyes flashed with anger at his impudence. 'Simon and I live here now. I shall have the staff remove you unless you leave at once.'

His small hazel eyes bore malevolently into hers and his voice was deadly soft. 'That would be a really unwise move. You seem unaware that I have the power to bring this family to its knees. Why do you think Ian allowed me to come here whenever I wanted? Why do you think Mrs Quinn is deranged with grief?'

Alexia felt herself grow cold with unease. Kenneth Ponsonby wasn't just a social-climbing sponger, hanging on to a rich family like a sucking leech as she'd at first suspected, but a serious troublemaker.

'My husband will deal with you and see that you leave,' she said coldly, turning her back and walking away.

'Your husband?' he scoffed in mock disbelief. 'My dear Lady Clifton, your husband's always so drunk he couldn't deal with a badly behaved child. If he wants proof of what I'm saying, tell him to look in his father's desk.'

Alexia hurried in through the French windows of the drawing room, where Roderick was sitting.

'Are you all right?' he asked anxiously, seeing her face.

She dropped on to the sofa beside him, happy it was him and no one else. It was easier to keep her feelings for him in check if they had practical things to talk about, and so she said at once, 'Am I crazy or is it this family? What's going on, Roderick?' She told him about her meeting with Kenneth Ponsonby. 'How are we going to get rid of him? He's not going to leave us alone unless we take serious measures. Apart from free weekends in the lap of luxury, what does he actually *want*?'

'I think he was blackmailing Ian.'

Her eyes widened and she looked at him incredulously. 'Why do you think that?'

Roderick shrugged. 'Why else would Ian have let him use this place like a hotel?'

'Because he was sorry for Kenneth?'

'Ian was a ruthless man and he didn't have a charitable bone in his body.'

'Well, Simon and I are not going to allow it to continue.'

Roderick looked at her closely. 'So what does the future hold for you now? Everything's changed, hasn't it?' he added almost sadly.

She swallowed hard and gazed at the Persian rug at her feet. When she was with Simon she felt a tender fondness for him, a protectiveness as if he were a difficult child. If she hung on to that thought the future would be all right. She'd manage to be a good wife, a good mother, a good chatelaine.

But the moment she was with Roderick her feelings changed as swiftly as the sun suddenly breaking through rain clouds. She felt drawn to him in a way she'd never felt about anyone before.

'I suppose things are different now,' she admitted.

'If you ever need me I'll still be around, you know,' he said softly.

A feeling, part desire and part alarm, shot through her, and she couldn't help being thrilled by his unexpected boldness.

'Don't forget.'

'I won't.' Her eyes brimmed with sudden tears and she turned abruptly to look out through the windows to the garden beyond.

Then she felt his warm strong hand close tightly over hers. 'I still wish I'd got there first,' he murmured.

She glanced back and flashed him an agonized look before turning away again. 'I wish you had.' Her voice was filled with despair, and so low she barely heard it herself.

Virginia and William stayed in their suite of guest rooms that night, refusing to join the others for dinner. Alexia felt relieved. It was enough of a strain to sit at the long table in the formal dining room with Simon, Roderick and her mother-in-law, without having to deal with the obvious shock and pain that she knew Virginia must be suffering.

'You're looking very flushed, darling,' Simon mumbled,

as he staggered drunkenly to the table. 'What have you been up to?'

Alexia's cheeks flamed and she kept her eyes down, not daring to look at Roderick. 'Too much whisky, I imagine,' she retorted with irony, managing to keep her voice level.

He turned to his cousin. 'And what have you been doing with yourself all afternoon, Rodders?'

'Mostly reading the newspapers,' Roderick replied lazily. 'The only amusing story is that Queen Alexandra's car broke down in the middle of Holborn, and she had to sit in it for over half an hour, surrounded by crowds of hundreds all gawping at her, while the wheel was changed.'

'Ha! She should have had our new Bugatti Royale. Now there's a car that never goes wrong,' Simon slurred, before taking another gulp of his burgundy.

'You and your cars,' Leonora said wearily. The day's events had taken their toll. After a lifetime of pretending her life was perfect, all energy had been drained from her so that her eyes looked dully upon an unkind world. Now she was the Dowager Countess of Clifton she was no doubt about to be relegated to the Dower House on the estate, where she would live alone apart from her staff. Without the husband whom she'd never loved, she wouldn't even have the social status she'd enjoyed for nearly thirty years. After a life given to duty and keeping up appearances there were few compensations now; only a sense of freedom, but no one to share it with.

At last the evening came to an end. Everyone wished each other a cordial good night. Simon stayed in the library with a decanter of whisky but Alexia, exhausted, slowly made her way up to bed, with Shadow trotting at her heels.

As she turned into the dimly lit corridor on the first landing she almost bumped into Roderick, who'd gone ahead. He was waiting for her in the semi-darkness.

'Roderick?' she whispered.

He came forward, so tall and broad-shouldered, his dark eyes fixed on her face as if he wanted to commit it to memory.

Taking both her hands in his, he spoke in a low voice. 'I wanted to say goodbye, Alexia. I'm leaving very early tomorrow morning and I . . .'

'You're leaving?' Her mouth drooped and her eyes were glazed with sudden unshed tears.

He nodded. 'It's for the best,' he whispered. 'You have your place here, married to Simon and with Freddie. I've got to get on with some commissions in London, and . . .' he paused and took a deep breath, 'it's probably better if we don't see each other for a while.'

Alexia hung her head, knowing what he said was right, and true. The more she saw of him, the harder it was becoming not to slip into a world of exciting fantasies where they could be together.

Her voice was choked. 'I'll miss you terribly.'

'I'll miss you too, but I shall comfort myself by looking at *Alexia in the Pink Dress* every day, and when it's exhibited at the Royal Academy next May, I'm going to be so proud that my best painting is of you.'

A sob broke from her throat. 'I don't think I can bear this.'

'We've both got to bear it, darling.' He leaned forward and kissed her tenderly on the cheek. A moment later he'd turned and hurried off down the corridor to his own room.

*My God! My God! My God! I never in a million years thought this would happen. I'm so in love with him I can't think of anything else. I can't eat, I feel sick and I don't sleep. Hour after hour I lie awake, recalling every moment of when I was in his studio. How I treasure those memories. How I repeat in my mind every conversation we had, and how I dream about those conversations we never had. I feel as if my brain is on a wheel going round and round until I'm exhausted. Sometimes my heart suddenly springs to life as if it was asleep and has suddenly been awakened by some magical clarion call. One moment I'm elated because I know he loves me then I plunge into despair because there can be no future for us. Sometimes I feel enraged as if I'd been cheated. Why didn't he tell me he loved me at the beginning? Why didn't He ask me to marry him?*

*Then I have to ask myself . . . was it the thought of Marley Court and the money that made me fall for Simon so that I never considered anyone else? Was it*

*Simon, dazzling with his ruffled blond hair and hot sexy
blue eyes, galloping up the hill on Prancer that caused
me to fall under his hypnotic spell?*

*How, how, HOW am I going to live the rest of my
life without Roderick?*

'And all along . . .?' Virginia said accusingly, glaring at Alexia
the next morning after Simon had told her all about the
letters. 'You must have known he was my father, too.'

'No,' Alexia insisted. 'I had no idea until I found the
letters – and now I wish to God I hadn't.'

Virginia was walking up and down the morning room
while Simon sat smoking one cigarette after another.

Suddenly she spun round and faced Alexia defiantly. 'I've
done my sums. You're only three months younger than me.
That means your father left my mother because his girlfriend found she was pregnant with you. Do you realize
what that means?' Tears sprang to her eyes and her hands
were bunched into fists. 'If it hadn't been for you my mother
might have got a divorce and then they could have married!
And I'd have had parents who loved each other, instead of
which . . .' Her voice trailed away and she wiped her cheeks
with her fingertips.

'Stop talking bunkum,' Simon snapped. 'Our mother would
have been ruined if she'd got a divorce, not to mention the
small fact that if she'd done that she'd have had to abandon
me and Pa would have got custody. And you still wouldn't
have been legitimate because they'd never have had time to
marry before you were born.'

Virginia stopped her pacing and looked aghast. 'You mean
I'm illegitimate?'

'Of course you are.'

'Oh-h-h-h!' Virginia wailed. 'What is William going to
say?'

'He's probably already grasped the fact in the past few
hours that nothing in this family is as it seems. No one else
need know. You're listed in the Peerage as Pa's daughter, so
you'll always be Lady Virginia, er . . . umm – Spall,' he
concluded, trying to suppress his amusement.

She looked venomously at Alexia. 'I wish you'd never

been born! You've brought bad luck to this family and ruined my happiness,' she exclaimed venomously.

'There's no point in blaming me,' Alexia retorted hotly, 'and please don't go rushing up to London to see my father, because I don't think my mother knows about this yet. Their marriage isn't happy and this could be the last straw.'

'Why are you suddenly trying to protect her?' Virginia exclaimed. 'I thought you didn't get on? Anyway she's going to know, sooner or later, whether you want it or not.'

Simon rose to his feet. 'You're the most spoilt little brat I've ever come across, Virginia. Alexia might not be close to her mother but she's got the decency not to want to hurt her.'

She shrugged carelessly. 'I've just lost the man I thought was my father and now you're saying I shouldn't get to know the man who is?'

'Simon's not saying that, but let my father be the one to tell her about you,' Alexia begged. 'It's bound to be a shock. It's been a shock for us all.'

Virginia dropped into a chair and covered her face with her hands. 'I'm the one who has had the worst shock. Thank God I found a husband before all this came out. No one would have wanted me if they'd known I was a bastard,' she added bitterly.

'William loves you for yourself, Virginia.'

'It's all very well for you to sit there looking smug. If you'd been in my shoes Simon wouldn't have married you. Would you, Simon?'

He scowled. 'Perhaps not.'

'There! You see?'

Alexia rose, thinking Roderick wouldn't have minded because she knew he at least really loved her.

'Where are you going, darling?'

'I'm taking Shadow for a walk. Why don't you go through your father's papers? Remember what Kenneth Ponsonby said? You might find why he thinks he has power over us. And why he was always turning up to stay here.'

Simon shrugged. 'He was bluffing. Any excuse to be a freeloader. Have you given orders that he's not to be admitted to the house if he turns up?'

'Of course, but you'll have to tackle your father's papers sooner or later.'

'There's no hurry.' He yawned and lay back in his chair. 'The will's OK, everything comes to me and he's set up trust funds for Virginia and my mother, so everything else can wait until I feel like it. Ring the bell, will you, darling? I feel like a pick-me-up.'

'You're just hungover,' Virginia said accusingly. 'William says you drink too much.'

Simon shot her a filthy look. 'Tell William to mind his own bloody business.'

A week later Kenneth Ponsonby arrived by taxi at Marley Court. Alexia and Simon returned from their morning ride to find him in confrontation on the front steps with the butler who, with meticulous good manners, was barring him from entering.

'If Sir would be good enough to return to his car . . .' Thompson was saying patiently as Simon turned Prancer towards the house and trotted up to them.

'I thought we'd made it clear you are not welcome here, Ponsonby,' Simon shouted, his voice harsh.

Kenneth switched on his smarmy smile. 'I think you should reconsider, Simon,' he said without flinching. 'I'd hate to harm you and your family and it can easily be avoided if you'd just cooperate, old chap.'

Alexia reined in Dancer beside Simon's horse. 'You're intruding, Mr Ponsonby. If you don't leave at once we shall call the police.'

He blinked as if astonished. 'Isn't that a trifle heavy-handed? I've been coming to stay in this house for over forty-five years, before my friend Ian was even married, and I've always been warmly welcomed; is this the way to treat an old family friend?'

Simon spoke pompously. 'I don't know what you're up to, Ponsonby, but you're not a friend of mine and I have not invited you to stay. Kindly leave immediately.'

Kenneth smoothed his brilliantined strands of dark hair over his balding crown and frowned as if perplexed. 'You're forcing me to speak in front of the servants; we have some business to conduct and this is hardly the place.' He spread his arms in a gesture that took in the drive and the massive entrance to Marley. 'Could we not be more civilized and talk in the study?'

Simon, looking dubious, glanced at Alexia. Then he dismounted and signalled for her to do the same. Handing the reins to the butler he turned to Kenneth, and raised his chin.

'Five minutes, Ponsonby. That's all. Then I want you to leave.'

Grabbing Alexia's hand he strode ahead, his riding boots clattering across the hall, with Kenneth Ponsonby trailing behind.

Alexia darted Simon a questioning look.

'I want to hear what he has to say,' Simon muttered out of the corner of his mouth.

Once in the study he sat down behind his father's desk. 'So? Speak up, man!'

Kenneth lowered himself carefully on to the chair as if his joints hurt. 'I've come to collect my monthly allowance, that's all,' he said blandly.

There was a stunned silence. 'Your – *what*?'

'Every month your late father gave me twenty pounds. In cash. And of course he welcomed my presence whenever I felt like a little break in the country. Now that he's sadly gone I shall come to collect it from you in future.'

Simon's jaw hung slack. 'He gave you . . . why, for God's sake?'

Kenneth's expression was positively prim, like a young girl asked if she is still a virgin. 'It was an arrangement we had.'

'Since when?'

'Ever since we came down from Oxford.'

Simon jumped to his feet, infuriated. 'I don't believe this! You're trying it on.'

Alexia watched Kenneth carefully. She was sure he was telling the truth.

'Blackmail is a punishable offence, Mr Ponsonby,' she said quietly.

Kenneth looked triumphant. 'But what he did is a much more serious offence than blackmail.'

Simon suddenly looked hot and cross, like a youth who
has been outwitted by an adult and doesn't understand what's
going on. 'I don't believe a word you're saying. What could
my father have possibly done to warrant him giving you
twenty pounds a month for ... for thirty-seven years!' he
asked incredulously.

'Plus ten pounds a month and a cottage for life for Mrs
Quinn,' Kenneth added with relish.

Simon gave a helpless yelp and sank back on to his chair.

'So you and Mrs Quinn are in this together,' Alexia
observed thoughtfully, looking straight at Kenneth.

'What do you know about it?' Simon asked sharply.

'No more than you. But haven't you wondered why she
lived on the estate, without any obvious means of support?'

'Well,' Simon glowered, thumping the desk with his fist,
'neither you, Ponsonby, nor that wretched maniac Mrs Quinn
are getting a penny out of me in future, and that's final.'

'I rather thought you'd react in this rash way,' Kenneth
said calmly. 'I'll leave you to think it over. I have a feeling
you'll change your mind.' He rose majestically. 'Don't under-
estimate me, young man. This family has been sitting on an
unexploded bomb for the past thirty-seven years and it's
thanks to me that no one knows. At least not yet. I have the
evidence to ruin you all. Do you want me to expose what I
know? It would be a tragedy for your little son and heir,
wouldn't it? To have everyone know the details of a scandal
that would rock society to its very core.'

Simon looked shaken. 'I don't believe you.'

'You would if you saw the evidence. And believe me, I have
the evidence.'

Alexia's mind worked fast. 'Mr Ponsonby, surely if my
late father-in-law had done something wrong nothing can be
done about it now he's dead?'

Beside her she could feel Simon relax and she put her
hand reassuringly on his shoulder.

Kenneth Ponsonby's laugh was sardonic. 'Oh, I grant you
he can't be punished! No doubt his Maker is undertaking
that task right now. But it's beyond your power to "atone
for the sins of your father", Simon. A stain on the family
name is a stain for ever.'

'Let us be the judge of that,' Alexia said, determined to try and break this parasite. 'If we knew what you were talking about we might be able to judge the situation more clearly.' She spoke bravely but she had serious misgivings; what was it Mrs Quinn had said about Ian?

'You'll find out quicker than you think unless you give me what is owed to me,' Kenneth retorted nastily as his eyes glanced in the direction of the safe, which was built into the wall near Ian's desk, hidden behind two false shelves of imitation books.

Simon seemed to wake up suddenly, like a rabbit who has decided not to be transfixed by oncoming headlights after all. With one bound he came around the desk and, grabbing the lapels of Kenneth's suit, yanked him roughly to his feet.

'You filthy little toad!' he yelled, scarlet in the face. With a violent push he slammed the older man up against the wall. 'If you ever show your face here again, I'll set the dogs on you! You're a blood-sucking leech who's been preying on my father like a vampire! I'll never give you a penny. Never, as long as I live.' He crashed his fist into Kenneth's jaw with a howl of fury.

Appalled, Alexia rushed into the hall, summoning a footman. 'Quick! Get the others.'

As if by magic four strong young footmen appeared, and a moment later Kenneth was being bundled out of Marley and pushed into the waiting taxi.

'You'll regret this!' he screamed. 'Don't think I've finished with you, Simon. I'll see you all cursed before I'm done.'

Watching from the doorstep, Alexia felt an icy sensation sweep through her, like a sudden Arctic breeze. She shivered and glanced at Simon; his eyes had a wild look.

If things were bad at this moment, a voice in her head told her they were going to get much, much worse.

Later that day she decided to see for herself if there was anything to prove Kenneth Ponsonby's staggering claim that he'd received a total of nearly nine thousand pounds since they'd come down from university, and that Mrs Quinn had received four and a half thousand. It seemed unbelievable. These were enormous sums of money for doing nothing. She thought of her father, working in the accounts department

of the London County Council, earning a hundred and twenty
pounds a year, which was more than the average wage.
Freddie's nanny, who was given full board and keep, received
forty pounds a year with only one day off each week.

The family solicitors were dealing with the matter of
probate and death duties and they'd taken all the recent
accounts and papers to do with the estate in order to examine
them, but what she was looking for were old bank statements. If, as Kenneth claimed, Ian had given him and Mrs
Quinn monthly sums in cash it should be easy to check if
he was telling the truth or not.

An hour later her search was rewarded. Neatly filed in a
Coutts Bank folder were bank statements dating back to
1886. It was all she needed. There, in black and white, were
regular cash withdrawals of thirty pounds on the first of every
month.

'Look at these, Simon,' she said, seeking him out in the
garden, where he was lazing in a deck chair on the terrace,
a glass of wine in one hand and a cigarette in the other. On
the nearby table stood an almost empty bottle of Chablis.

'Kenneth Ponsonby wasn't lying,' she continued, sitting
down beside him. 'Your father really was giving regular
payments to him and Mrs Quinn.'

Simon waved the bank statements away with a dismissive
gesture. 'So? That's history, Alexia. Ponsonby is finished.
I've got rid of the bastard and he'll lie doggo and not dare
show his face now. It was a whiz-bang idea of yours to
remind him blackmail is illegal.'

'But he could still reveal whatever your father desperately
wanted kept secret.'

Simon sat upright, looking indignant. 'Are you suggesting
there's any foundation to Ponsonby's blackmail?' He reached
for the bottle and topped up his glass. 'My father's never
done anything to be ashamed of, so I don't know what you're
fussing about.'

Alexia spoke carefully. 'But why was he giving so much
money to Kenneth and Mrs Quinn?'

'Obviously because he felt sorry for them,' Simon retorted.
'Now that the golden goose has died, Ponsonby has lost his
benefactor. He's just trying to frighten me into treating him

as a charity case, but charity begins at home. He's not getting a penny from me.'

'Do you suppose Mrs Quinn is a relative of his?'

'Who the hell cares? As far as I'm concerned she can go into an old people's home. Or a mental institution.'

Alexia winced at his callous attitude. It also worried her that he seemed determined to ignore what she saw as a potential threat to the family. She was sure they hadn't heard the last of Kenneth Ponsonby. Ian Clifton was a mean-spirited man, and he'd never have lavished money on an old woman and a friend from his university days without a very good reason.

By November Simon was itching to return to Grosvenor Square. The family were still in mourning, and would be for another eight months, but that wasn't going to stop him returning to a hedonistic existence. Alexia went with him in an effort to prevent him carousing with Baggers. As long as she was there, she believed, she could curb his excesses and restrict their social life to a discreet level, merely going to the theatre or opera and having small supper parties.

'You've got a position to keep up now,' she said encouragingly, as if she were talking to a wilful child.

'You're talking as if we were in our forties!' he retorted breezily. 'Do you have to wear black all the time? It doesn't suit you.'

'Of course I have to wear black.'

He looked sulky. 'You're no fun any more. You've turned into a dull middle-aged woman who is desperate to do the right thing all the time.'

'What would you have me do?' she asked crossly. 'I wish you'd realize I'm trying to save you from yourself, Simon. You have responsibilities now and Freddie to think of. Life isn't just one long party, you know.'

'As far as I'm concerned life is what you make it and I intend to enjoy myself.' He leapt up from the breakfast table, suddenly furious. 'I've come into my inheritance now and I'll do as I damn well like.'

Within weeks of being back in London he'd established a coterie of people around him who succeeded in gradually pushing her to the outskirts of his life. There were 'advisors' and 'organizers', 'assistants' and 'secretaries', 'fixers' and 'negotiators', and in her opinion spongers and toadies as well. Simon seemed to attract decadent types like moths to a flame. His dazzling blond looks, flair for entertaining and recently acquired title and wealth made him more popular than he'd ever been, and he loved every moment of it.

He started to shun the elegant dinner parties Alexia organized, giving weak excuses at the last moment to explain his absence before rushing off to seek excitement in the shady, seedy life of Soho. The novelty of having a baby son had worn off too, and he barely saw Freddie. He spent as little time as possible with Alexia and when he did he was quiet and sullen. Even frantic letters from his mother, who had moved into the North Wing, preferring it to the Dower House, were thrown aside and dismissed as 'boring'.

'He's out of control,' Alexia confided to her grandmother one day when they were lunching together. 'He goes off on wild tangents and spending sprees. He's bought another car, a new hunter, more clothes and now he's talking about buying a yacht.'

'What about Roderick Davenport?' Helen asked.

Alexia started guiltily. 'What about him?'

Her grandmother gave her a strange look. 'I was wondering if he could talk to Simon. He might listen to a man of his own generation.'

'Oh!' Alexia had flushed a deep red. 'I don't know. We haven't seen anything of Roderick since Ian died.'

Helen raised her eyebrows but said no more.

Alexia continued hurriedly, 'Virginia's coming to London next week and she's staying with us. I've invited Daddy to luncheon so they can – they can talk,' she said with difficulty. 'He hasn't told Mummy yet, has he?'

Helen gave a wry smile. 'There's no one more reticent than a guilty husband. I've told him it will be worse for him if your mother finds out, but he seems to be waiting for the right moment.'

'There's no such thing as the right moment.'

'Maybe he's waiting for her to make the first move. She

wants a separation, you know. She feels there's no point in their staying together now you're grown up and married.'

Alexia looked shocked. 'A separation? What will she do? What will *you* do, Granny?'

'I'm not sure, darling. I think your mother wants to go and live with her old friend, Hilary Martin. They've known each other all their lives and she's got a nice house in Bournemouth. As for your father, he's always said I would have a home with him.'

'Oh Granny, come and live with us. It would be so wonderful to have you around, and so good for Freddie, too. I'd love you to do the things with him that you did with me, like go to all the museums and take trips to the zoo.'

Helen laughed, pushing her white curls back from her face. 'It's a sweet idea, darling, but I don't approve of a young couple having their relatives with them. I only stayed with your parents because your mother wanted me to look after you.'

'But this would be different! We wouldn't be on top of each other. God knows there's plenty of room both here and at Marley, and it would be such a comfort to have you around. After all, Simon's parents have always lived with us.'

'No, you've lived with them. There's a big difference. I shall be fine, looking after your father.'

'I'm feeling terribly sick but I'm so excited,' Virginia announced when she arrived at Grosvenor Square. 'Isn't having a baby the most wonderful thing in the world?'

Alexia hugged her half-sister, sharing her delight. 'I'm thrilled for you. I don't know what I'd do without Freddie, and the bigger they grow the better it gets.'

'Where's Simon?'

Alexia's tone was clipped. 'Out somewhere.'

Virginia shot her a knowing look. 'Oh God! Poor you. How do you bear it? If William behaved like that I'd want to kill him.'

'What's the point? Simon will never change. He's ruining his health but he won't listen. He's spending money like water, encouraged by Baggers, and God knows what else he gets up to.'

'I never thought I'd feel sorry for you,' Virginia said bluntly, 'but now I do and I think you're being really noble to put up with him. It's a shame we weren't friends at the beginning; I'd have begged you not to marry him if I'd liked you then.'

Alexia smiled. 'If I'd liked *you* then, I might have listened. Actually, Roderick tried to warn me but I refused to listen. Thought I knew best. How arrogant one was at eighteen!'

'You'll stick by him, then?'

'I have no option. We're married and there's Freddie, and I think I'm pregnant again. Actually,' she paused thoughtfully, 'I don't believe I ever had a choice. Some things are meant to be and my marriage to Simon is one of them.'

Virginia looked at her with renewed respect. 'But what would happen if you met someone else and fell in love with them?'

Alexia averted her eyes and forced her voice to sound light and jocular. 'First of all I'd have to find someone brave enough to fall in love with me, and that's not likely. Now,' she continued swiftly, 'Daddy's coming to lunch tomorrow. There'll just be the three of us and he's terribly nervous. He's desperate for you to like him but I told him not to worry.'

'Oh, I'll like him all right. Actually, I've always rather envied you having him as a father. What about your mother? Does she know about me yet?'

Alexia shook her head. 'Not as far as I know.' She refrained from repeating what her grandmother had told her about their impending separation.

Virginia sounded excited. 'I'm longing to tell him he's going to have another grandchild. Won't he be thrilled?'

*I'd no idea I was capable of such jealousy. He's always been* my *father and mine only. Having to share him is much worse than I anticipated. When he arrived for luncheon yesterday I wished I hadn't arranged for them to meet as father and daughter. I could just about bear it when they saw each other at Marley because she didn't know then. Yesterday she rushed past me to greet him, kissing him on both cheeks, chattering on about*

*how thrilled she was to know he was her real father –
and I hated her at that moment. Hated her so much
I wish I'd never met the Clifton family because then
she'd never have known him.*

*He knew how I felt because he kept looking at me
anxiously, trying to be nice to me and flatter me, but
I felt overwhelmed by a childish desire to burst into
tears and throw myself into his arms and beg him to
tell me he loved me the most.*

*God, how it hurt to see this pretty girl glowing with
happiness, hanging possessively on to his arm as she
gazed up at his face.*

*Never again can I bear to have them under my roof
at the same time, and when they meet in future I don't
even want to know about it. I know it's infantile of me
but I feel betrayed; how dare he be so sweet to this
hateful creature who is usurping my position? I feel
even more hurt and angry than when I found out Simon
had been cavorting with prostitutes. Now I'm older I've
learned that men can be unfaithful to their wives, but
it's for lust not love and that is the difference.*

*My father's affection for Virginia is based on love.
After all she is his child, conceived in a moment of
passion that he's never been able to reveal.*

*For the first time I realized I feel sorry for my mother.*

*'Isn't this fun?' Virginia chirruped as the three of us
drank cocktails before lunch. Her words fell like bright
raindrops on an arid desert and I couldn't bear to look
at her, I hated her so.*

# Ten

*May 1923*

As soon as Alexia and Simon arrived at the private view of the Summer Exhibition at the Royal Academy in Piccadilly, people clustered around them as if they were celebrities. There was a babble of upper-class voices, sparkling with admiration.

'My dear Alexia, I've just seen your portrait, I couldn't adore it more!'

'It's blissful, darling.'

'Too *too* divine, Alexia,' simpered a debutante.

'You must be over the moon, my dear!'

'I'd give anything to have Roderick Davenport paint me like that,' shrilled an elderly dowager.

Simon turned to Alexia in wonder as they struggled through the crowds to the gallery, where her life-size portrait dominated every other painting in the room.

'I say, old girl, Rodders has done it this time, hasn't he? He's famous at last,' Simon chortled.

Alexia blushed as she searched the room for Roderick, whom she hadn't seen for months. Trembling at the thought of seeing him again and at being the centre of such intense attention, she managed to smile politely and murmur something about him being very talented.

A packed gathering stood before her portrait, gazing up at her likeness and chattering to each other animatedly.

'He's got you to a T, hasn't he, Alexia?' someone beside her remarked. It was the Duke of Garnock, accompanied by her old friend, Lady Zoe Middleton.

'Not that I've ever seen that expression on your face before,' Zoe giggled suggestively.

Alexia glanced up at the painting and felt a stab of shock. How come she hadn't noticed that the expression in her eyes betrayed her? Roderick had asked her to look at him as he'd worked on her face, and now she realized her intense look was one of naked desire, her dark eyes filled with longing and her full mouth tipping up seductively at the corners as if she were smiling at a lover.

Had her expression really been like that as she'd sat for Roderick? Or was it wishful thinking on his part because he'd wanted her to be in love with him?

Her heart lurched painfully in her ribcage, reminding her how deeply she loved him and wanted him, something she usually forced to the back of her mind. Oh God, the painting said it all. Her passion, her longing, and the unrequited love that would never know fulfilment.

Her chest felt tight as she grappled with her emotions, aware of the crowds who kept glancing at the painting and then back at her.

At that moment Roderick bore down on them, emerging through the throng who parted to make way for his charismatic figure. He shook Simon's hand then bestowed a social kiss on Alexia's cheek.

'Well, there it is!' he said, waving his hand towards the painting with a flourish. 'What do you think?'

Simon spoke immediately. 'Bloody marvellous, old chap. Bloody marvellous. You've captured her perfectly! This will lead to a lot of commissions, won't it?'

Roderick grinned. 'You haven't seen the newspapers today, then?'

Alexia cleared her throat, unable to meet his steady, direct gaze. 'Why? What's in them?'

'Your portrait has stolen the show,' Roderick replied triumphantly. 'It's been reproduced in every newspaper. You've been hailed as "the beautiful young Countess of Clifton".'

She looked astonished. 'I'd no idea, but the credit goes to you, not me.' Her words tumbled out impulsively because she was so glad for him.

'There have been a few quite nice things said about my work, too,' he admitted modestly.

'I should think so, old chap.' Simon slapped him on the back. 'Congratulations. You deserve to be the tops. Look, we must celebrate! Let's all go to the Savoy for dinner tonight. Bring your girlfriend, Rodders, and we'll make a night of it. Meet in the bar at eight o'clock. OK?'

Roderick caught Alexia's eye and then looked swiftly past her. 'That would be great, Simon. I'll look forward to it.'

'What a great chap he is,' Simon remarked, as he and Alexia drifted off to look at the rest of the exhibits. 'I'm so glad we've contributed to his success today.'

But she wasn't listening. Shards of ice were piercing her heart and she didn't think she could bear the pain. A girlfriend? Did Roderick have a girlfriend now? She'd always pictured him alone, working hard and not even having much of a social life. But a *girlfriend*? How was she going to bear seeing him with someone else?

A sob of despair broke from her throat.

'Are you all right, sweetie?' Simon asked, amused. 'A bit overpowered by all this attention, I expect,' he continued confidently, as he steered her through the crowded galleries where people were turning to look at her and point her out to their friends.

'It is a bit much,' she murmured, her voice wobbling dangerously.

'I know what you want.' He strode over to a waiter who was holding a tray of champagne. He came back with two glasses. 'Knock this back, darling, then you'll feel better.'

She took the glass gratefully but doubted if she'd ever feel better. *Alexia in the Pink Dress* would hang on the wall, a reminder of a young woman who was madly in love with the artist. The real Alexia would plod on doing her duty, being a good wife, a good mother and a leading light in society, but all the time the bright flame inside her would be slowly extinguished until there was nothing left but darkness.

The group of friends Simon had invited to join them for dinner were already drinking in the bar when they arrived. She scanned the faces, bracing herself to see a girl she'd probably never met; would she be blonde or brunette? One thing she was sure of: whoever it was would be very beautiful.

'Good-o!' Simon greeted everyone. 'What are we all having? Champagne?'

'Orange juice for me, please,' Alexia said, seating herself at one of the little glass-topped tables. She patted her swollen stomach. 'I've already had my ration for the day,' she said with forced jollity.

'Yes,' Simon exclaimed unfeelingly. 'Alexia was in tears at the Academy today because she was overwhelmed by all the fuss over her portrait! There's no pleasing women, is there? If they're ignored they sulk and if they're the centre of attention they burst into tears!' He laughed uproariously.

Alexia looked up, her mouth set in hard lines, and saw Roderick standing at the entrance to the bar watching Simon with distaste. Then his eyes met hers and his expression was filled with sympathy.

'Ah! Here's the Rubens of the twentieth century,' Simon exclaimed, clapping his hands. 'Or is it Joshua Reynolds?'

Some of Simon's friends tittered foolishly.

'Anyway, come along, man. What are you drinking? And where's your girlfriend? Preening herself in the cloakroom?'

Alexia took a deep breath as she looked up into Roderick's face. He was looking into her eyes.

'I don't have a girlfriend, Simon. I hope I haven't dropped a social faux pas and done something unforgivable like making the numbers odd,' he continued sarcastically, 'but I've come on my own. Does that upset you?'

Simon looked dashed. 'No. Not at all, but I've always had you down as quite a ladies' man. You're not a pansy by any chance, are you?'

Roderick suddenly laughed at the stupidity of his cousin and Alexia started breathing again. 'No, Simon, I'm not a pansy, as you so charmingly put it.'

'Well, let's have another drink before we have dinner.'

'So how is everything at Marley?' Roderick asked her as they sat down to dinner in the restaurant, where a dance orchestra played softly in the background.

She felt quite light-headed with relief. 'Fine. It's much more peaceful without Ian, too,' she confided in a low voice.

'Leonora seems happy and she enjoys seeing Freddie when we return at the end of the week.'

'How is my godson? I really want to paint him, how old is he now?'

'He had his first birthday last month.'

Roderick looked thoughtful. 'I might bring my stuff round to Grosvenor Square one day. Children are more relaxed in their own home and if I came when he's in his high-chair having lunch, I could do a preliminary sketch whilst he's distracted by food.'

'That would be lovely,' she said quietly.

'Perhaps I could do one of you together?' His eyes swept over her features. 'I'd love to paint you again. You're growing more beautiful all the time.'

Alexia's insides seemed to melt at the way he was looking at her. 'Perhaps in the autumn? After I've had the baby?'

He smiled. 'Whenever you like, Alexia.'

They were interrupted by Simon and his rowdy friends, who were laughing loudly and making jokes she didn't understand. Vast quantities of wine were being consumed and she could see it was going to be a long night.

When the coffee had been served, Roderick asked her to dance.

She hesitated. 'I don't think so, thank you. I'm quite tired.'

'It's the only way I can hold you in my arms,' he said softly.

She looked back at him, flushed and weak with desire. 'All right.'

As he led her on to the dance floor Simon raised his glass to them, shouting 'Bravo!' in a loud drunken voice. Then he added, 'She's the size of a house, old chap, so steer her carefully back to port when you've had enough.'

Alexia could feel Roderick's body and arms go rigid with anger as he swept her away to the far side of the room, and his grip on her hand was fierce.

'Pay no attention to him,' she whispered.

He held her close and looked down into her face. 'How do you stand it, Alexia?'

She smiled. 'I ignore him when he's drunk.'

'Which is most of the time,' he said wretchedly. 'For God's sake, you deserve so much more.'

She shrugged and moved closer into the circle of his arms and her silence conveyed more than any words could. He rested his cheek against hers, and she closed her eyes and let herself believe for a few bittersweet seconds that they belonged together.

'She's gone! Mrs Quinn has left! The cottage is empty and everything's been cleared out,' Simon shouted, leaping off Prancer's back as he trotted into the stable yard, where Alexia had taken Freddie to see the horses.

'Gone?' Alexia asked, stunned. The old woman had been seen prowling around Marley recently, peering in through windows and trying to enter the chapel. Only the previous week she'd given Alexia a terrible shock by lying in wait for her when she'd come down the stairs. 'I wonder where she's gone.'

Simon threw the reins to a stable lad. 'No one seems to know. I've asked the foresters but they hadn't even realized she'd left.'

'Someone must have helped her move out,' Alexia remarked, holding Freddie in one arm while she offered Dancer a piece of apple.

'Probably Ponsonby. I told you he'd leave us alone when I refused to give him a penny. Now we've got rid of them both. Isn't that marvellous?' he added as he strolled off to look to his latest hunter, Orlando. 'Papa had no idea how to manage things, or people for that matter.'

He swaggered around the yard, proud of the new horseflesh he'd purchased. Then he turned back to her again. 'I wish you still went riding. It's so boring of you to stay at home.'

'I will as soon as I've had the baby,' she pointed out mildly.

'Couldn't you ride side-saddle or something?'

She could tell he was edging towards one of his irascible moods. 'The doctor would have a fit,' she said lightly. 'Supposing I was thrown?'

'You wouldn't get thrown if you weren't so bloody feeble,' he snapped. Then he turned and marched off, heading towards the house and, she knew, the nearest decanter of brandy. Determined to ignore the pitying looks from the head groom and the stable lads she held her head high and talked brightly as she told Freddie the names of all the horses.

By the time she got back to the house and had taken Freddie up to the nursery for his lunch, Simon was already drunk. She found him sprawled in a chair behind Ian's old desk, talking on the telephone. As soon as he saw her he said a hurried goodbye and hung up.

'What d'you want?' he asked nastily.

She eyed the empty brandy balloon by his side. 'Simon, it's not even noon yet,' she expostulated, knowing she was nagging, but she hated to see him destroying himself like this.

'God damn you!' he yelled, picking up a glass paperweight and throwing it at her with all his strength. She gave a cry of pain as it hit her shoulder then bounced off and thudded to the ground. 'Why can't you mind your own bloody business, you stupid bitch,' he raged. 'I'll drink when I like and you can't stop me.'

She rubbed her shoulder and glared coldly at him. Shadow nervously moved in close behind her legs. 'We can't go on like this, Simon. Your rudeness to me in front of the servants is unforgivable and . . .'

'I don't see any servants in the room,' he jeered.

'You're sick and you need treatment,' she told him bluntly. 'If you don't see a doctor I'm going to leave you, Simon. I can't stand it any longer. I can't bear Freddie seeing you like this either.'

'Stop interfering in my life, damn it! I'll drink what I like when I like. Who wouldn't want a drink? Married to a dullard like you?'

Alexia stood her ground. 'Can't you see what you're doing to yourself? At this rate you'll be dead by the time you're forty.'

He laughed mirthlessly. 'You'd like that, wouldn't you? Then you could reign supreme here, with your precious Freddie, the wonder child who will never be allowed to be like his father,' he added bitterly.

'That's not true. I want him to be like you, but like the person you were when I fell in love with you,' she said more gently, going over to the desk and putting her arms around his hunched shoulders. 'I married one of the most handsome and dashing young men in England, full of energy and promise, and I want Freddie to be like that, too. And I want you to live long enough to share Freddie's future with me.'

Simon suddenly started crying, clutching her hands as sobs wracked his bony frame. Already his drinking had caused his face to be bleached white, while his eyes were sunken into hollows of darkened skin and his blond hair was beginning to thin.

'I c-can't help it,' he wept. 'Everything's such a bloody mess.'

'What's wrong?'

'I'm being bombarded by the lawyers. They're writing to me all the time and that was one of them on the telephone now. We're broke, Alexia. Stony broke.'

She frowned, horrified. 'What do you mean? How can we be broke?'

'Apparently Pa's been living way beyond his means for years and years. Most of the money he inherited has gone, and now we've got to pay death duties on the estate. We're going to have to sell most of the land to pay a huge bank overdraft he's incurred, too. We're on the edge of ruin . . .' His voice broke and he covered his face with his hands.

A cold hand clutched her heart; how often had she heard the word 'debts' when she'd lived at home and her father had lost still more money at the races?

'But you've got your own inheritance, haven't you? The money you came into when you were twenty-five?' she asked, trying to sound calm.

'I've spent near all of it,' he said in a small voice. 'I've had to cancel getting the yacht and some of the cars must go. My tailor's bill needs to be paid, too. The lawyers keep telling me to economize, and they think we should cut back on the number of staff we have. But how can we? Marley Court won't run itself. I'm going to have to raise some money to pay off my overdraft as it is, or the bank will foreclose.'

She didn't dare ask him how much he owed the bank. Nor how much the house in Grosvenor Square was costing, not to mention Ian's house in Belgrave Square which Leonora wanted to keep on.

'Then we must cut back,' she told him sturdily. 'Why don't we get a much smaller house in town? And entertain at home instead of going out every night? There are all sorts of things we can do to economize.'

Simon blew his nose on a large snowy handkerchief and looked sulky. 'But I like going out. Where's the fun in staying at home? And I enjoy shopping, looking at the lovely things I've bought. Which reminds me . . .' He unlocked one of the drawers in the desk and took out a flat leather jewel box.

Alexia's heart sank. More jewellery. She'd already inspected the family jewels which were kept in the vaults of Coutts Bank. Four diamond tiaras, six diamond necklaces, some set with large emeralds, more than a dozen pairs of earrings, boxes of bracelets, rings, brooches, and ropes of pearls; all of it worth a fortune. Yet he kept buying her more baubles and became angry if she didn't show her delight.

'Take it,' Simon was saying, thrusting the case into her hands.

Reluctantly Alexia opened it. On the midnight-blue velvet lining lay an exquisite gold art nouveau powder compact, inlaid with her initials, AC, in diamonds and sapphires. It was a work of art, worthy of Fabergé.

'Simon! It's exquisite. I've never seen anything so beautiful.'

'It was made in 1892, so it is quite special,' he remarked proudly. 'I was going to give it to you when you had the baby.'

She leaned down and kissed him. 'Thank you very much. I love it and I shall always treasure it, but this is the last expensive present you must give me.'

As his face fell, so she continued hurriedly, 'You're spoiling me with kindness, but we've got to be careful with money until we get the present situation sorted out.'

As she went slowly up to her room, followed by Shadow, she realized that Simon's way of getting out of trouble was to give her a present, knowing she'd accept it with pleasure. He'd just done it again. It always worked. Like a manipulative child who picks wild flowers to appease an angry mother, Simon did it with diamonds, rubies, sapphires . . .

Alexia sighed, feeling trapped. She hadn't the heart to

reject his gifts. It would be crass and ungracious, but on the other hand every time she did she was digging herself deeper and deeper into conspiring with him to overspend. His talk of debts frightened her. She'd never known quite how rich the Cliftons were but from appearances it had seemed their coffers were bottomless. Now she wasn't so sure.

As May gave way to June, the weather became hot and balmy with a gentle cooling breeze. Nearing the end of her pregnancy, Alexia spent more and more time sitting in her secret garden, which flourished around her as she sat reading in the shade of a trellised pergola.

With the help of Birchall, the head gardener, to whom she'd now given a spare key because she trusted him totally, she'd worked hard to create this little paradise of peace. The borders bloomed with Canterbury bells, lupins and delphiniums, and in the four stone urns placed at each corner of the lawn, a mixture of lobelia and pink petunias overflowed. Roses grew in profusion along the ancient brick walls and there were beds of lavender and sweet-scented stock.

This was a place where she could relax away from everyone and she loved walking around it with Shadow, admiring her handiwork.

Then one afternoon Birchall appeared, apologizing for disturbing her.

'That's all right,' Alexia replied, putting down her book, while Shadow jumped up in welcome. 'Have you got any special plants for me?'

Birchall leaned towards her and spoke in a low voice. 'You have a visitor, m'lady. He stopped his car halfway up the drive to speak to me. He asked if you were at home, and I told him you were here but that his Lordship was out. The gentleman would like to speak to you alone.'

'Who is it?' she asked, with a frisson of alarm. Surely Kenneth Ponsonby didn't have the gall to turn up at Marley now?

'It's Mr Roderick Davenport, m'lady.'

Alexia got slowly to her feet, her face lit up with pleasure.

'Bring him here, Birchall.' Her hands shook with excitement. She hadn't seen Roderick since the night they had danced together at the Savoy and she wished she was wearing a prettier maternity dress. Pinning up her hair which had grown long again, she stood waiting for him to appear through the doorway in the wall, while her heart pounded with exquisite pain.

'Alexia.' He looked more striking than ever, with his dark eyes that regarded her steadily and a warm smile on his face.

'Roderick,' she said, opening her arms without thinking as he strode across the lawn towards her. 'Are you all right?'

He closed his arms around her and held her close, his face buried in her shoulder. 'I had to come and see you,' he whispered.

'What a lovely surprise.'

He pulled back and looked searchingly into her face. 'How are you? Is everything all right? When's the baby due?'

'In three weeks.' She patted her stomach as she sat down again.

'I've got something to tell you. That's why I'm here.'

A shaft of fear made her go cold. She'd always dreaded the moment when he'd come and tell her he was getting married, for surely that would happen one day? They had no future together and there must come a time when he'd want a wife and a family. Her hands trembled but she took a deep breath, determined to control her emotions.

'What is it?' she asked carefully.

His smile drained away and he looked bleak. 'My father has just died.'

It was the last thing she'd expected and she immediately felt guilty at the rush of relief that flowed through her.

'Oh, I'm so sorry,' she exclaimed. 'How awful for you. Was he very old?'

Roderick gazed around at the profusion of flowers as he spoke, his thoughts far away. 'He was nearly seventy and he'd been ill for a long time, so it wasn't entirely unexpected.'

'That doesn't make it any better though, does it?'

'It's still a shock. He never really got over the death of my mother when I was ten. They'd been so happy together and he missed her dreadfully.'

'My God, how awful for you.' She reached for his hand and held it in both of hers. 'Is there anything I can do?'

He turned to look at her, his dark eyes over-bright. 'You're here for me now and that's all that matters.'

'I'll always be here for you,' she said quietly. 'You know that.'

He nodded. 'I wouldn't have burdened you right now by coming here if it hadn't been for something else.'

'What?'

'He left a sealed letter with his solicitors addressed to me. I only received it yesterday. Simon can look after himself, but if there's any trouble . . .'

'Roderick, you're scaring me. What does the letter say?'

He fished a folded sheet of paper from his inner pocket. 'You know my father was at Oxford at the same time as Ian Clifton?'

She nodded. 'So were my father and the dreaded Kenneth Ponsonby.'

'Exactly. That's what I mean. I think this proves that Ponsonby had a reason for blackmailing Ian. My father used to tell me that Ian formed an elite dining club where outsiders were banned and their loyalty to each other was unquestionable. Father once admitted to me that they were all quite spoilt and badly behaved, but not in a malicious way. They were young and rich and high-spirited and they used to play silly pranks, and drink too much, and I suppose they were rather snobbish in those days, too.'

Alexia nodded. 'And I imagine Kenneth wanted to join the group and Ian wouldn't let him?'

'I think that's probably what did happen, and there's no doubt Ponsonby was very jealous of these young men with their money and social position. Then one day something happened.' He glanced down at his father's neat handwriting and then looked up at Alexia again. 'Ian apparently went to my father and he was in a terrible state, according to this letter. Because my father was a cousin as well as one of the group, Ian asked him to provide him with an alibi for the previous afternoon and evening.'

'And?'

'Father writes here that he's spent a lifetime feeling guilty about being party to a cover-up of something too dreadful to write about, even now. At the time, apparently, he thought

Ian had got into some stupid scrape and so he gave his word. It was only afterwards that he realized what Ian had done.'

Alexia frowned in bewilderment. 'So what does this mean? That your father lied to the police to save Ian's skin?'

Roderick nodded. 'This is my father's confession of having made a false statement.'

'But this was – what? in 1882, '83?'

Roderick's voice was rough with sadness. 'It obviously preyed on the poor old fellow's mind all these years. He was a really good man but he must have been torn between loyalty to his cousin and wanting to do the right thing.'

'But what had Ian done?' she asked, appalled.

'Father doesn't say.' Roderick glanced at the letter once again. He read aloud, '"Something too dreadful to write about even now". The only person who can answer that, I suspect, is Kenneth Ponsonby, and that's the hold he had over Ian. That's why he blackmailed him. To get money and have his revenge for being excluded from their elite dining club.'

Alexia covered her face with her hands. 'That's ghastly, Roderick. Ian must have done something terrible to be willing to shell out thousands of pounds to prevent the truth coming out.'

'I know.'

'But now that Ian's dead there's nothing Kenneth Ponsonby can do, is there? That's why he hasn't been near us when Simon refused to give him any money; he's lost his power over the Cliftons.'

'Maybe or maybe not. Who else did my father tell? He was a great letter writer, especially when he knew his days were numbered. And I think it preyed on his conscience that he'd lied.'

Alexia's hand flew to her mouth. 'Is that possible?'

'His housekeeper told me he wrote a lot of letters in the past few weeks which he got her to post. Obviously she didn't look to see who he was writing to. If the case were to be reopened there's nothing the police could do about Ian, but what about your father? Did he also give a false statement to protect Ian?'

'Oh God, I hadn't thought of that.' Her face turned ashen.

'That's why I wanted to see you. To warn you, in case there's trouble.'

'I could ask him,' she said doubtfully. 'They were very good friends, that is until my father disgraced himself with his gambling debts. That mad old woman, Mrs Quinn, has vanished, you know. We don't know where she's gone.'

'Good riddance, I'd say.' Roderick rose, stretching his back as if he was tired. 'I don't think there's any point in mentioning Father's letter to Simon, do you? It would only upset him, and what can he do about it anyway?'

'I agree,' she said, imagining how he'd rave and rant and swear his father would never have done anything wrong and it was all Kenneth Ponsonby's fault. 'Let's hope that's the end of it.'

'I'd better be off. I'm driving back to Penhalt to see to a few things and make some arrangements with the house-keeper.'

'Will you live there eventually?' She rose also, hating to see him go as they walked slowly towards the door in the wall.

'Oh, yes.' He smiled almost dreamily. 'It's a lovely old house overlooking the sea. There's a path from the garden that leads right down to the beach. I was born there and I love every stick and stone of the place.' He paused to look down into her face with a tender smile. 'One day I'll move back there and try to do something with the garden, which is a wilderness compared to all this.' He glanced around appre-ciatively. 'You have green fingers, don't you?'

She focused on a rose bush, heavy with dark crimson blooms, as she tried to quell the pain of parting from him. Her eyes pricked with unshed tears. Would she ever get used to the acute sense of bereavement she felt when he left her side, even if they had only been together for a short while?

He noticed her expression and reached for her hand. 'Oh, Alexia darling . . .'

The next moment she was in his arms, sobbing. 'I'm sorry . . .'

His lips were pressed against her dark hair. 'Don't be sorry, darling. If it were possible I'd stay with you for ever and we'd live in Cornwall and you'd make my garden look beautiful.'

When Simon returned to Marley in the late afternoon, Spencer informed him that her Ladyship had retired to bed and had asked not to be disturbed because she had a very bad headache.

'Thanks, Spencer,' Simon said breezily. 'I had a mind to meet up with some friends anyway, so I'll be out for dinner.'

'Yes, m'lord.'

The following day Alexia gave birth to a baby girl, the delivery brought on early, according to the local doctor who was called in the middle of the night, by a sudden and serious rise in Alexia's blood pressure. She was ordered to stay in bed for several weeks, and the doctor warned Simon there were to be no celebrations until her blood pressure was normal again.

'The baby's OK, though?' Simon queried, looking at the tiny creature who lay in her cot, swaddled in a white Shetland shawl.

The doctor beamed. 'She's a fine healthy little girl, but I'll drop in each day to check on both of them for the time being.'

Bouquets of flowers started arriving and Alexia's bedroom quickly came to resemble a florist's shop. Accompanying notes spoke of the joy of a new birth in the family after the tragic death of Ian, 'who would have been so proud and happy to have a granddaughter'.

But Alexia, resting in her grand four-poster bed and feeling appallingly burdened by the secrets she had to keep, thought only of Roderick and his old stone house in Cornwall. What a farce her life had become. Everyone thought the Clifton family a perfect example of nobility and morality, a rich family who had never put a foot wrong, never told a lie, who loved each other and cared for the people on their land.

'We must present a united front in public and uphold the good name of the family even if we have our little ups and downs,' her mother-in-law had stipulated when she'd married Simon. 'Once we lose our good reputation we lose every-thing. Remember, my dear, we belong to the ruling class and we must set a good example to the working class, as the royal family do.'

Lying in her bed now, Alexia felt certain that the royal family had never had as many secrets to keep as the Cliftons. The thought of having to perform the role of a happy and devoted wife to a drunken and philandering husband for the rest of her life was now more than she could bear.

Gazing down at the adorable face of her new baby, whom she'd decided to call Emma, she dreamed of a garden with stone walls warmed by the sun, surrounding a wild and windswept garden; in the background there would always be the hushing sound of the sea as the waves uncurled on to the sandy shore while seagulls, calling to each other, wheeled overhead.

# Eleven

*We seem to be on a crazy merry-go-round of social-izing, and if I thought Simon's behaviour was wild a couple of years ago it's nothing compared to the frenetic life we lead now. I'm so tired I could lie on the floor and go to sleep, and I've lost so much weight I've had to order new clothes for the winter.*

*The newspapers are talking about this being the 'Roaring Twenties', whatever that means. It feels as if we're caught up in a cyclone, being violently whirled around and around, unable to stop. The mood in London could have been invented just for Simon; he's in his element. I've worn out five pairs of evening shoes because we go to* thés dansants *every afternoon and then dash home to change to go dancing every night. Jazz music blares through every open doorway, cocktails are* de rigueur *and I even wear rouge and bright lipstick these days. If this is what it takes to be the Countess of Clifton, trying to contain my husband's debauchery from becoming public know-ledge, then it's what I've got to do. If I stick by his side I hope to keep him out of trouble, but still he slips away some nights and doesn't creep back until dawn.*

*As well as heavy drinking he's taking cocaine; he says Baggers gets it for him and I should try it too.*

*Who am I? What am I doing? I feel I'm no longer the person Roderick loved. I think he'd be shocked if he saw me now. When I look in the mirror I'm startled to see a hard-faced woman who is slim and chic and sharp with watchful eyes, clinging on to a lecherous man who is doomed.*

*Maybe we shall end up destroying ourselves? And each other?*

*Dear God, what have I got into? I sometimes worry I'm not spending enough time with Freddie and Emma, although they're well looked after by Nanny, but I feel that as long as I keep this marriage going it will be better for them. Simon has bought Freddie a Shetland pony and he's teaching him to ride. He's not a bad father when he gives his mind to it, and they adore him – and that's what matters.*

Alexia and Simon returned to London in October after a two-week trip on a yacht sailing around the Greek islands as the guests of his old friend, Porgie Hargreaves-Webb. For once there had been a halt to their rackety life, as they swam and sunbathed, stopped to explore Corfu, Crete and the Cyclades, and relaxed in the pleasant company of one of Simon's nicer friends.

The trip had given Alexia time to regain her health after Emma's birth, and even Simon, deeply tanned and with his hair more golden than ever, seemed to have regained the youthful exuberance that had so attracted her at first.

They went straight to Grosvenor Square. That night they were expected at a drinks party given by Robert Garnock to celebrate his engagement to Zoe Middleton, from whom he'd been inseparable since they'd met at Freddie's christening.

Looking beautiful in an ankle-length cream silk dress with her long ropes of pearls, Alexia waited in the hall while Simon fussed over the stack of mail which had arrived in their absence.

'Leave those letters, darling,' she told him. 'We'll be late if we don't leave now.'

'What's the hurry?' he replied languidly, sauntering out of his study several minutes later, while she tapped her foot impatiently.

'I hate being late.'

'It's fearfully middle class to be on time. One should always be a few minutes late.' He stopped to adjust the gardenia in his buttonhole, before following her into the Rolls-Royce. 'Where's the party being held?'

'The House of Lords.'

'Let's not stay long.'

Alexia glanced at Simon in surprise. 'We've got to stay a little while,' she pointed out.

'Plummy and Hoots said they'd be at the Savoy at six thirty, so I thought we might have a quick drink with them when we get away from this shindig.'

Alexia suppressed a sigh. 'You haven't forgotten we're going to the Stirlings' ball tonight, have you?'

'Why should I forget? You've been droning on all week about which bloody tiara to wear. God, you take everything so seriously, Alexia. Why can't you float freely around as I do?'

She ignored his taunts, wishing they were still in the Mediterranean. He'd been in such good form while they'd been away, light-hearted and happy all the time, and now within hours of their return he was obviously trying to pick a fight.

They drove on in silence.

'Damned lot of post has arrived while we've been away,' he complained after a few minutes.

'Anything important?'

'How should I know? You didn't give me time to look at it.'

'Well, we have been away for two weeks. It's probably just mounted up.'

But it was more than that, and the moment they entered the crowded room she sensed a distinct oddness in the atmosphere. People stopped talking for a moment, followed swiftly by the low hum of whispered chatter, the nudging of elbows, and stares of intense curiosity.

'Hello there!' Robert Garnock greeted them, without making eye contact.

'How lovely to see you,' Zoe remarked, flashing them both a sympathetic and rather embarrassed look.

Simon immediately spotted Baggers and shot off to greet him as if they hadn't seen each other for months, leaving Alexia to stand alone. For once she felt isolated. What was so strange was that instead of a rush of people coming up to say hello as they usually did, she had the distinct feeling that the other guests were moving away as if no one knew quite what to say to her.

She looked around in puzzlement when Simon came hurrying back, bringing Baggers with him. His eyes were ablaze with anger.

'Tell her, Baggers. Tell her,' he said urgently.

'Tell her yourself,' Baggers drawled. She looked into the depraved face of the man she held responsible for so much of Simon's wild behaviour. He was sniggering.

She frowned and spoke sharply. 'What is it, Simon?'

Baggers cut in with malicious relish. 'Kenneth Ponsonby has written a novel and it's the talk of the town. It's caused a sensation – as you can see,' he continued, looking around the crowded room where everyone was giving them furtive looks or else staring at them. 'It's called *Hubris and Hell* and it's selling in the shops like hot cakes.'

She frowned and looked at Simon. For the first time she saw fear in his eyes.

'It's about us,' he whispered, stricken.

'How do you mean – us?'

Baggers took it upon himself to enlighten her. 'It's a fictional account of what's happened in the Clifton family. You obviously don't know the half of it, or if you do you've made a great job of keeping it secret,' he laughed jeeringly.

'But nothing's happened in the family,' Alexia retorted with loyal dismissiveness.

Baggers raised his eyebrows and let his jaw drop in an expression of mock astonishment.

'Really? I call betrayal, adultery, illegitimacy, murder and blackmail quite a lot to have happened in any family, my dear.'

Alexia gave a mirthless laugh. 'You said Kenneth Ponsonby has written a novel? That's the sort of thing that happens in *novels*, or perhaps you don't read much?'

'It's a *roman-à-clef* if ever I read one. The stately home is even called "Farleigh Court"! There's not a shadow of a doubt it's based on fact. I can tell you it makes gripping reading. You're the talk of the town. It's only called a novel so you won't be able to sue the publishers.' Baggers rolled his eyes theatrically. 'And Kenneth Ponsonby is making a fortune! He'll end up as rich as Croesus!'

Simon looked panicked. 'Let's get the hell out of here.'

'That's exactly what we won't do,' she said firmly. 'Brace up, Simon. Kenneth's undoubtedly written a work of fiction, although your friend here seems only too happy to believe some trashy pot-boiler is based on your family history, but it's up to us to show people it's a load of nonsense.'

Simon hovered, unsure of himself. 'What did you say it was called, Baggers?'

'*Hubris and Hell.*'

'Then it can't be about us,' Simon said with relief. 'There's no one in our family called Hubris.'

Alexia looked away, aware of Baggers sniggering. 'We've got to stay calm,' she whispered. 'We don't even know what's in the book and if we rush off now it will look as if we can't face anyone.'

'Well, I don't think I can,' he admitted feverishly.

'Let's stay for a short while,' she continued, 'and on the way home we'll get the chauffeur to buy us a copy so that we can see what it's really about.'

There was fear in Simon's voice. 'I don't like it. This is Ponsonby's revenge because I refused to give him money. God damn it!' he swore under his breath. 'I wish I'd shot the bugger when he came crawling for cash.'

Alexia hid her fear behind a smiling face. She'd never told Simon about the letter Roderick's father had left. Did Kenneth Ponsonby's book reveal 'something too dreadful to write about' that had caused Ian to ask his friends to give him an alibi? All this time Kenneth Ponsonby must have known what it was. And because Ian was no longer alive to silence him with money, he'd decided to reveal everything in *Hubris and Hell* instead.

'Bloody hell, we're ruined, aren't we?' Simon spoke in a low voice as he closed his copy of the book.

It was six o'clock in the morning and they were lying on sofas in their drawing room, having been up all night. As soon as Alexia had glanced at the first few pages of her copy, she sent her apologies to the Stirlings, saying they were unwell and couldn't attend their ball. Then, ordering supper to be served on trays, they sat, each with their own copy, and started reading through the night.

A chilly blue dawn was stealing over the trees in Grosvenor Square now, and the distant clip-clop of horses' hooves made Alexia wish they were in the country, far away from the gossip and scandal that was enveloping the family like a malodorous cloud. They might not be financially ruined, and Marley Court would always be there, but the name of Clifton would be forever tainted now; and it was the name Freddie would inherit one day. And his son, and all the eldest sons for generations of Cliftons to come.

The quote . . . *The sins of the fathers* . . . kept going through her head. Simon was surely paying the price for his father's sins. Even as she laid down her copy of *Hubris and Hell* she heard the chink of glass on glass; during the night Simon had consumed a bottle of brandy, and she was sure his drinking had begun in order to blot out the angry shouting of his father when he'd been a child.

Had her mother-in-law known all along? Did the terrible knowledge drive her into the arms of another man, as a temporary means of escape from her pain? That other man being Malcolm Erskine?

Alexia rose from the sofa and threw more logs on to the fire, and it sparked and spluttered. She went over to Simon, who had pulled back the heavy damask curtains and was gazing out of the window.

Putting her arms around his waist she spoke softly. 'We'll deny there's any truth in this book,' she said softly.

Simon shook his head. 'I'm finding it hard to believe my father would do such a thing, but why else would he give Ponsonby so much money? Where's the evidence? The proof?' He turned to look at her. 'Isn't it possible that Ponsonby's invented this horror story to get his revenge on us for not giving him money in future? Can he prove his book is based on fact? The real problem will be can we prove it isn't? Mud sticks.'

He moved away from her to pick another cigarette out of the silver-crested box that stood on the side table. 'What do we do, Alexia?'

She remained silent, having no ready answer.

'Do we ignore the book as absurd?' he continued. 'Or get a lawyer to look into it for us? Surely it's against the law to invent a terrible incident and then write a novel based on a recognizable family?'

'One would have thought so.'

'As a family we're done for. Don't you see? I think it must all be true.' He spoke with growing horror, his eyes widening in alarm. 'Everything fits into place, when you think about it. I've always known there was something terribly wrong. Remember the fight Mama and Papa had at luncheon one day? About Mrs Quinn living in that cottage?'

Alexia nodded. Simon had got terribly drunk and that had been the first time since they'd married that he'd driven off to London, not returning until the next morning.

'I remember,' she said hollowly.

'And do you remember I told you that the argument over Mrs Quinn had triggered something in my mind? When I'd been a small child? I can't exactly remember the details but Papa didn't know I was in the room and he had this argument with Kenneth Ponsonby and it was about Mrs Quinn. I remember him threatening Papa.' Simon's voice dropped to a hoarse whisper. 'And Papa was terrified about something.'

Alexia felt cold and nauseous and there was a deep trembling sensation in the pit of her stomach. The truth was going to ruin Simon. She could see it happening before her eyes.

'The book has to be true!' he exclaimed wildly. 'Oh, dear God, what are we going to do?' He ran his fingers through his hair before reaching for another drink.

'Are you saying we should take it lying down?' she asked. 'Make no comment? Remain dignified?'

He turned round to look at her and she saw defeat in his blue eyes. 'We don't have a case to go to law. Look at the second page. "*All the characters in this book are fictitious and any resemblance to real people, living or dead, is purely coincidental.*" We'd be fools to try and sue Ponsonby.'

'But I think we'd have a case for defamation of character,' she argued, picking up the book again. 'He's changed the family name to Clevedon, and Freddie is Viscount Stamford instead of Stanhope. Do you realize he's used our initials throughout? Leonora is called Laura, Ian is Ivor, and Virginia becomes Lady Veronica. I've become Anthea Egerton and my father Miles Egerton. Do you see? He's deliberately written it so that everyone will know it's about us. And this is rich! The so-called hero, based on himself, is called Keith Pritchard, but of course he hasn't depicted himself as a black-mailer, but a "family friend who was always supportive". He's even quoted passages from my father's letters to your mother. I remember them exactly! That means it was him who stole them from my room when he was staying at Marley that weekend—'

In sudden fury, Simon grabbed the book from her hands and threw it forcefully across the room.

'The bastard!' he yelled. 'The goddamn bastard.' Then he covered his face with his hands and broke down sobbing.

Alexia led him to a chair, but he staggered and nearly fell as the full impact of what had happened, coupled with copious amounts of brandy, hit him hard. If life had been difficult in the past, she knew it was going to get much, much worse.

Leonora faced them squarely. 'I knew Kenneth Ponsonby was getting money out of your father but I didn't know why. I didn't know how much he was giving him either. Ian said something about a student prank that went wrong, and . . .' she paused painfully, 'because I was his wife I chose to believe him.'

Alexia and Simon had driven down to Marley, unable to bear the curious looks they attracted whenever they went out. There was even a newspaper reporter with a grubby notebook lurking near their front door accompanied by a photographer, his camera mounted on a tripod, ready to take their picture when they emerged.

Simon had decided a family meeting was required and he'd summonsed Virginia and William, as well as Roderick, to stay for a few days so they could decide what to do.

'What about Mrs Quinn? Weren't you curious about her?' Alexia asked Leonora. She felt genuinely sorry for her mother-in-law who, like herself, had spent her life trying to put on a good front so everyone would think they were just one big happy family.

Leonora fiddled with her rings, twisting them round and round her bony fingers. 'I truly believed Ian when he said she was the widow of one of our tenants and that his father, Henry Clifton, had given her the cottage for life. Why should I doubt it? If I'd known . . . Oh my God, I'm not surprised Mrs Quinn made that scene at Ian's funeral,' she added, shuddering.

'So she's the mother of the girl who died?' Virginia asked in a shocked voice, not having yet read *Hubris and Hell*, but trying to pick up what had happened as she went along.

'Ruby Quinn was her daughter. A working-class girl Papa murdered because she was an inconvenience.' Simon spoke with such harsh, brutal honesty that everyone winced. 'Murdered because she was an ordinary shop girl he'd got pregnant. Murdered because if my grandfather had found out Papa had impregnated Ruby, out of wedlock, Papa would have been disinherited. Marley Court and all the money would have gone to some distant relative because I hadn't yet been born. We all know what my grandfather was like. A martinet, a strict disciplinarian, a brimstone-and-fire Bible-basher. Papa hadn't the courage to face him,' he added in a low voice.

Virginia, looking aghast, reached for William's hand. 'When did all this happen?'

'When Papa was at Balliol. He had a wide circle of friends,' Leonora explained, 'and Kenneth Ponsonby wasn't one of them. I vaguely remember how he longed to be accepted by all the Old Etonians who made up the group. People used to tease Kenneth about hanging around, always hoping to be invited to join in whatever they were doing. It's a tragedy now that Ian didn't let him,' she added bitterly.

'Is this really true?' Virginia asked incredulously. 'I simply can't believe it.' She turned to her husband. 'Can you believe it, William? Papa a murderer? It doesn't seem possible. How did he actually . . . do it?'

There was a dreadful silence in the old library. No one was brave enough to describe what had happened.

Virginia looked at Roderick, her voice full of anguish. 'You've read the book. What happened?'

Roderick took a deep breath. 'He knew Ruby Quinn couldn't swim so he took her out in a punt. On a quiet deserted bend in the river he – he tipped her out and apparently held her down under the water with the pole until she drowned. Her body was found down river two days later.'

She gave a little scream of horror then clapped her hand over her mouth.

'Dear God!' Leonora wept. 'That's the most ghastly thing I've ever heard. I can't believe Ian really did it. He had a bad temper but otherwise he was quite . . . quite an ordinary man.'

William, looking pale, spoke for the first time. 'It seems so far fetched. Surely the police . . .?'

'At least two people knew what Ian had done,' Roderick cut in, his expression grim. 'My father – and, unfortunately, Kenneth Ponsonby.'

There was a stunned silence. Alexia looked down at the carpet, avoiding Roderick's gaze.

'Your father?' Simon exclaimed in amazement. 'You never said—'

'I only found out when Dad died a few months ago. Apparently he provided a false alibi, saying he'd been with your father all that day and into the evening. He left me a letter, a deathbed confession, saying he felt guilty about it, but he was sure Ian would have stood by him under similar circumstances.'

Leonora wiped her eyes. 'My God, your father was a truly loyal man in that case. He must have suffered though, knowing he'd helped to cover up such a terrible crime.'

'What about Kenneth Ponsonby, then? How does he know all the details?' William asked sceptically. 'Did he provide a false alibi too?'

Alexia spoke, her voice strained from tiredness, for she hadn't slept for two nights. There was something she and Simon hadn't told the others.

'No, Kenneth didn't supply a false alibi. He blackmailed Ian instead. Simon and I got an anonymous note in the post a few hours after we'd finished reading the book. It just said, "Here's the proof but the negatives are in a safe place." It was written in a spidery hand on a sheet of plain paper and I guess it was from Mrs Quinn. With it were half a dozen photographs of . . .' Alexia's voice failed for a moment. Taking a deep breath, she cleared her throat and then continued, 'The pictures were taken from the bank of the river and they showed everything, from the moment Ian and the girl appeared in the punt coming around the bend in the river, until he punted back again. Some time later. Alone.'

The single word hung poignantly in the air. A young girl drowned. A man who'd had a brilliant future forever hounded and blackmailed for the crime he'd committed. And a mother who would never recover from her grief.

Alexia looked up and realized Roderick had been watching her intently. His eyes were filled with love and something else: admiration and compassion. He stood, so tall and strong, his feet planted wide, overshadowing Simon who stood beside him.

Alexia quickly averted her face to break the spell between them before anyone noticed. At that moment she'd never wanted Roderick more.

'Kenneth Ponsonby was always taking photographs, wasn't he?' Virginia was saying in disgust. 'It used to drive me crazy. Whatever we were doing, playing tennis or going riding, or even having a picnic, there he'd be. Click, click, click.'

'Yes, he must have thousands of pictures of us all,' Leonora agreed. She looked as if she'd aged ten years in the past hour, her black clothes adding to the skeletal effect. 'When I think how we entertained him; how he must have been laughing at us behind our backs. And all the time he must have been threatening Ian with exposure unless he paid up. It's too terrible for words. Poor, poor Ian. What are we going to do now?'

No one answered. They all knew that if the family responded in any way they'd draw even more attention to themselves.

Virginia looked at her mother. 'I was very upset at first, but now I'm glad Papa wasn't my real father.'

'But he was *mine*,' Simon groaned brokenly, 'and I'm like him. I know I am. A coward, a drunk, selfish and . . .' He broke down, unable to continue.

Roderick laid a brotherly hand on his shoulder. 'Don't be so hard on yourself, old chap. None of us are responsible for our parents' actions.'

'But I can never hold up my head again,' Simon stormed in anguish. 'The family is ruined. This is a stain we can never, ever get rid of. Papa did the most terrible thing by taking the life of a young girl in order to protect himself. Now we have to live with the shame and the horror and it's never going to go away.'

Alexia knew he was right. Kenneth Ponsonby's book had stripped the Clifton family of its grand veneer. He'd laid bare their darkest secrets, revealing that Ian was a cowardly murderer, Leonora an adulteress with an illegitimate child and Simon 'a deeply flawed, promiscuous alcoholic' while Virginia, his half-sister, had married into 'trade' and was no better than she should be. And that was just the Clifton family.

Alexia found her own family truths devastatingly hurtful and damaging. Her father was portrayed as 'a member of the aristocracy who had squandered all the family money gambling on horses'. The book went on to add that he'd married beneath him, to the horror of the 'Egerton' family, as his wife's mother had been a 'dancer whose career had peaked when she'd appeared in the chorus of *Puss in Boots* in Bournemouth in 1892'. Also noted was the fact that their daughter, 'Anthea', had been born a mere four months after their marriage, but had 'wormed her way into the "Clevedon" family, through her father's previous liaison with "Laura Clevedon", in order to bag the most eligible young man of the Season'.

Even Freddie and Emma, referred to as Fergus and Elsa, were recognizable, dubbed as 'mere babies whose misfortune it was to have been born into an inheritance that was rotten to the core'.

It had to be admitted that everything in the book was factually true, showing that life in high society was one of chilly glitter and that nothing was as it seemed.

And now never would be again, Alexia reflected with a heavy heart. How could any of them go on pretending when the truth had been dug up and put on display?

'Your mother must know about me by now,' Virginia remarked. 'Have you spoken to her?'

'I spoke to Daddy. He's told her everything. Apparently she'd always suspected him of having someone else when they were first going out together.'

'So what happens now?'

'I think they're getting divorced.'

Leonora remained silent, lost in her own private memories of being with Malcolm, wishing at the time he'd whisk her away from Ian so they could marry and have their baby together. The shock of learning he'd made someone else pregnant and was going to get married was the most painful moment of her life.

'What are we going to do about Ponsonby?' Simon asked again. He resembled a lost little boy, unable to cope.

'Why don't you talk to a lawyer?' Roderick suggested.

'I think we should,' Alexia agreed. 'But the irony is that the truth seems so far-fetched, I bet ordinary people who have never heard of us are thinking it's a good yarn but couldn't possibly have happened in real life.'

'If only that were true.' Simon spoke with feeling. 'I wish I could go to sleep, and wake up and find the whole thing had been a terrible nightmare.'

'You're going back to Cornwall?' Alexia asked, as Roderick prepared to leave Marley the next morning.

'Yes, I have to go sort out some things before I begin my next commission.'

She scooped Shadow up into her arms. 'You're not selling up, are you?'

'Not in a million years. It's the only place where I can recharge my batteries and gather fresh inspiration.'

She longed to ask when he'd be returning to London, when she might see him again, but a certain finality in his manner chilled her. She peered into his car, no longer the battered old Alfa Romeo in which she'd first seen him rattling up the drive, but a new Armstrong-Siddeley four-seater sports coupé.

'Have you got everything?'

'Yes. Thanks for everything, Alexia. I wish I could have been of some help this weekend. It's a hellish situation and all you and Simon can do is to try and ride out the storm, but I'll help in any way I can. You only have to ask.'

Her eyes looked bleak. 'No one can help us, Roderick.'

'Will you be all right?'

She hesitated and then raised her chin. 'If I can protect the children I'll be all right. I'm sure we'll get through this somehow.'

'I'll be off then. Simon's gone riding, hasn't he? Say goodbye to him for me, will you?'

She nodded, unable to speak. Roderick's presence was like an emotional anchor, steady and secure, making her feel strong. Without him she feared she might drift off course and crash into the rocks, faced with Simon who'd been permanently drunk since he'd read the book, and Leonora who was on the brink of a nervous breakdown.

'Goodbye then, Alexia.' He looked into her eyes for a long moment before leaning forward to kiss her on the cheek. 'Take care of yourself.'

He turned swiftly and, getting into the car, started the engine and drove away without a backward glance. She watched as it disappeared down the drive and it seemed as if he was taking the rest of her life with him. Her heart felt as if it was being ripped out of her body, and the future had never seemed so dark. With tears running down her cheeks she headed for her secret garden with Shadow at her heels. Removing the key from its hiding place under a stone she let herself in, and there, among the autumn leaves that were fluttering down in the breeze, lying scattered on the lawn like gold coins, she sobbed inconsolably, for the loss of the man she loved and the prospect of a future of notoriety as a member of the Clifton family.

# Twelve

A girl in torn black fishnet stockings, silver shoes and a crumpled mauve lamé evening dress lurched out of the dining room of Grosvenor Square and looked around the hall. Her make-up from the previous night was smudged and streaked and her bright red hair tousled.

At that moment Alexia walked up the front steps of the house with Evans, the chauffeur, who opened the door with his key.

'I don't understand why one of the servants didn't answer when you rang the bell,' she observed as she stepped over the threshold. Normally the butler would be waiting for her arrival and there'd be a couple of footmen to carry her luggage.

At that moment the young woman turned around. Her hands clutched a cheap evening bag and Alexia noticed the chipped scarlet nail varnish.

'Oi, missus!' she asked in a cockney accent. 'Where's the bloomin' toilet?'

Alexia stood still for a moment, shocked into silence. So Simon was now bringing tarts back to the house when she stayed down at Marley with the children.

Evans stepped swiftly forward, his expression impassive as he took the girl by the elbow and propelled her swiftly towards the servants' quarters in the basement.

'A big place yer got 'ere!' she chirruped cheerfully. 'Simon's dad, are yer?'

The stink of fish, stale tobacco and cheap perfume drifted into the hall. Alexia strode into the dining room and stopped, aghast. It looked as if a hurricane had swept along the mahogany table, leaving a trail of dirty dishes and glasses, pools of spilt candle wax and lipstick-stained table napkins. There was even the debris of a buffet supper strewn around the floor. In one corner a heap of empty wine bottles, some broken, had been flung down with abandon.

'This way, Shadow,' she commanded as the little dog started trotting around licking the dirty plates. Then she hurried up to the first floor drawing room, having a gut feeling even before she entered that the furniture would have been pushed back to clear a space for dancing. Not only that, but there were red wine stains on the cream damask sofa, while her silk cushions had been piled into a makeshift bed and were surrounded by cigarette stubs ground into the Persian rugs, resembling a drift of flotsam on a beach after a storm.

Broken wine glasses lay shattered, glittering in the reflected morning light that streamed through the French windows, revealing the aftermath of a scene of sordid licentiousness.

Scooping Shadow up into her arms and with her heart pounding, she ran up the next flight, taking the steps two at a time. She was desperate to reach the sanctuary of her bedroom but was stopped in her tracks by a trail of blankets and pillows on the landing. A girl's shoe, a pink feather boa and a long pair of pink gloves lay abandoned just outside her bedroom door.

Then she heard Simon's voice and a female giggle.

For a moment she froze, trapped in the paralysis of shock, her only thought being to get away. This was her home and she'd loved it, but now it had been besmirched and she could never live here again.

Turning on her heel she retraced her steps down to the hall as she tried to blot out the hideous images that the woman's laugh had conjured up.

Evans was standing alone by the open front door as if he instinctively knew what was expected of him.

'I'm returning to Marley.'

'Yes, m'lady.'

In silence they drove away from Grosvenor Square. Alexia felt as heartbroken as if someone very close to her had died. Her beautiful house had been ruined, raped by a bunch of drunken low-lifes. Shunned by people of his own class, Simon had attached himself to those who were impressed by his title and money. Showgirls, pimps, racketeers and drug

dealers now figured in place of dukes and debutantes, baronets
and barristers, earls and Old Etonians. With nothing to lose,
marked down as the son of a murderer, he'd flung himself
into a degenerate world of promiscuous pleasure, where
cocaine and champagne were his staple diet.

He'd thrown away his golden youth and the publication
of *Hubris and Hell* was doing the rest. How sweet the taste
of revenge must be to Kenneth Ponsonby at this moment,
Alexia reflected bitterly, knowing that she too had now fallen
from grace. In society circles she was no longer the beautiful young Countess of Clifton but the opportunist daughter
of a dancer and a gambler, who had struck lucky.

As they neared Marley she felt as if a black shutter had
come crashing down, trapping her in a prison of her own
making. She should never have allowed herself to be dazzled
by charm, money and position. She should never have married
Simon.

Simon returned to Marley the next afternoon, breezily striding
into the hall whistling a cocky tune, for all the world as if
he'd been out in the garden picking flowers.

Alexia had lain awake the previous night planning what
she'd say to him when he reappeared, and now she was ready.
Following him into the library where he went straight to the
drinks tray, she opened her mouth to speak, but before she
could say anything he exclaimed enthusiastically, 'Hello,
darling darling! Isn't it a glorious day? I thought we might
go riding this afternoon. Want a drink?'

She stood gazing at him in silence.

He glanced up. 'Why are you looking at me like that?' he
asked, decanter poised aloft in his hand.

'You'd obviously forgotten I was coming up to London
yesterday.'

A flicker of confusion and fear crossed his face.
'Yesterday? Yesterday was Thursday.'

'Exactly. We were supposed to go to the opera house to
see *Madama Butterfly*.'

'I'd forgotten all about it.' He scowled, puzzled. 'What
happened?'

'What happened,' she began, her temper rising, 'was that

I arrived at Grosvenor Square during the morning to find the house in the most disgusting state and you in *my* bed with some tart. Does that ring any bells, Simon?'

His mouth fell open and his face turned ashen. 'You . . .? Oh, Jesus Christ!' He banged the decanter down on to the tray with a thump. 'Bloody hell! Why didn't you remind me you were coming up? How am I supposed to remember everything? You could have rung me the previous day to say . . .'

Her eyes flashed dangerously. 'To remind you not to hold an orgy in our home? To tell you not to give the servants the night off? Or would that have spoilt your fun? If they'd been there it would have cramped your style, wouldn't it? The scum you've let into your life wouldn't have been able to wreck the house, would they? Or trail bedding on the landing? Or end up in my bed?'

'Don't you dare talk to me like that, woman!' he shouted angrily. 'Who the hell do you think you are? You owe everything you've got to me! You used to live in a basement flat in Kensington without tuppence to your name and look at you now!' He flung his arm wide, as if to indicate that everything was hers. 'I bought the house in town, I bought everything in it, and I'll bloody well invite who I want and I'll bloody well do what I like.'

'For all I care you can turn it into a brothel, because I'm never setting foot in that place again.' Her fists were clenched and her face white with rage. 'How could you let such guttersnipes into our home? What must the servants have thought?'

'You and your bourgeois fear of what other people think,' he taunted, refilling his glass. 'You should have married someone like William Spall, who holds his knife like a fountain pen and talks about serviettes,' he added scathingly.

Alexia stared back at him defiantly. 'At least I come from a respectable family.'

'You're so damned prudish!' Simon drained his glass in one long gulp. 'Baggers was right. He always said you were a suburban prig who was never going to turn a blind eye to boys being boys. A fella's got to have a bit of fun, you know.' His speech had begun to slur, making her realize he'd probably been drinking before he arrived. 'All we had was a little party.'

'Have your fun,' she retorted furiously, 'but don't expect me to be a part of it. From now on you'll sleep in the dressing room and we'll stay married in name only.' Her voice broke and she struggled to control her emotions as she turned to walk out of the room.

'Bitch!' he yelled, grabbing a heavy glass inkwell from the desk and hurling it at her retreating figure. It smashed into her side, the brass lid flew off and black ink splashed the side of her face and all down her front, staining her tweed skirt and silk blouse.

'Get the hell out of my life . . .!' Simon roared as she turned away, determined to ignore him while the tears poured down her cheeks.

*I really wanted to be happily married and I wanted it to last for ever, and now I can't help grieving for the death of my dream. I thought . . . once I'm grown up I'll be in control of my life and I'll be married and have a family and everything will be wonderful. I really believed that and I'm finding it hard that the bubble has burst and there's no happy ever after.*

*I walked around my garden today and because it is winter all the plants and shrubs are asleep, lying dormant until next spring, their roots resting in the damp soil, their energy being stored up so they will burst into leaf and flower next year. There'll be no spring in my soul though.*

*God give me the strength to keep going and stop me thinking of Roderick and that house in Cornwall.*

'You're getting too thin,' Simon grumbled as they sat in the drawing room, waiting for Nanny to bring Freddie and Emma down from the nursery after tea.

Alexia ignored the remark, knowing full well it was true. Her clothes were hanging unbecomingly from her fragile-looking frame and her face was gaunt.

'Which story are you going to read to them?' she asked instead. This afternoon ritual was the one thing she insisted on for the benefit of the children, who adored their father.

Simon picked over the stack of books on the side table. 'Are they too young for *The Wind in the Willows*?'

'I think they're probably more likely to want "Chicken-Licken and the Day the Sky Fell on his Poor Bald Pate",' she chuckled. This was the best time of the day for her, when they at least put on a joint pretence of being a happy family.

A minute later Nanny appeared and Freddie and Emma ran into the room, flinging themselves into their parents' arms.

'Daddy's going to read you a story, so let's sit on the sofa in front of the fire where it's warm,' Alexia suggested. Emma, in a red velvet party frock with a cream lace collar, plumped herself on her mother's lap while Freddie, a miniature replica of Simon, with his startlingly pale blue eyes and blond hair, sat astride the arm of the sofa, pretending it was a horse.

As they listened enraptured to their father, Alexia studied them both, marvelling at how she and Simon had produced two such beautiful children. They were well behaved too, calm and good tempered, and Freddie was very intelligent for a three year old. Emma, just two, was all dark curls and eyes, and very feminine.

Alexia cuddled her close, hoping she'd always be able to protect both of them from the undercurrent of ugliness that pervaded Marley. As long as she could preserve their innocence and only let them see the good side of their father, then she'd be satisfied. But for how long was that going to be possible? They couldn't stay in the nursery for ever.

'Can we play hide-and-seek?' Freddie asked, when the story was finished.

Simon jumped to his feet like a boy. 'Yes! What a good idea. Why don't the three of you go and hide, I'll count to fifteen and then I'll come and find you. And don't all hide together. That's no fun!'

'Come on then,' Alexia said encouragingly, grabbing their hands and running with them into the hall. She indicated that Freddie should duck down behind a large brass dinner gong which hung from an ebony stand, while Emma hid behind one velvet curtain and she slipped behind the other.

'One . . . two . . .' Simon was shouting, then she heard the dreaded chink of the whisky decanter knocking against a glass. It was several minutes before they heard him say 'Thirteen . . . fourteen . . . . fifteen. I'm coming to get you!'

In a high state of excitement he started racing around the
hall, pretending he hadn't seen them, banging the gong,
drawing the curtains, exclaiming 'Where are you? Have you
all flown away?' so that the children were squealing with
laughter. He even ran up and down the stairs searching for
them until, with apparent astonishment, he discovered first
Emma and then Freddie.

Alexia was laughing herself when he grabbed her through
the heavy folds of the curtain, telling the children he'd found
'a big fat sausage'.

'Let's hide again,' Freddie begged, tugging at his father's
hand.

Simon was enjoying himself. 'OK. Look, I'll hide with
you this time and then Mummy can find us.'

'I'll count to twenty to give you lots of time,' Alexia promised, hurrying back to the drawing room, where she proceeded
to count loudly, amused by the scuffles and giggles coming
from the hall.

'I'm coming to get you!' she called out at last. There was
dead silence. She looked around the hall but there was no
sign of them in the obvious places. Then she glanced into
the morning room, the dining room and billiard room, the
red saloon and the ballroom, and finally the orangery. She
felt a pang of irritation. At this rate, in a house the size of
Marley, the game could last for hours and it was time for
the children to have a bath and go to bed.

Nanny appeared at that moment, to collect them.

'They're playing hide-and-seek with their father but I can't
find them anywhere,' Alexia explained. 'You don't know
where they're hiding, do you?'

'No, m'lady. I'll help you look.'

Alexia and Nanny started calling the children's names.

'It's bedtime,' Alexia shouted. 'Come along now. Game's
over.'

There was silence. The great house suddenly seemed dark
and unfriendly, as if it were harbouring yet another secret.

'Freddie! Emma! Where are you?' Nanny called out
crossly. 'Come here at once.'

There was no answer. Alexia was suddenly overwhelmed
with an inexplicable sense of apprehension, although she

told herself it was absurd to be worried. Simon would never do anything to hurt the children.

Spencer, the butler, joined in the search with several footmen, while other servants searched the kitchen and pantry quarters and even the garden.

'This is ridiculous,' Alexia exclaimed in frustration as she came running down the stairs from the bedrooms. 'They must be somewhere.'

Spencer came running up to her. 'The keys to the cellar have been taken, m'lady. Maybe his Lordship has taken the children to hide down there?'

She hurried after him as he led the way through a heavy door where steep stone steps led down to a cavernous cellar, filled with racks containing hundreds of wine bottles.

Spencer struck a match and lit a candle which he held high so they could descend into the darkness.

'Freddie? Emma?'

There was silence.

'Freddie! Emma!' she shouted again, fear making her voice sharp.

Then they heard a thin wail coming from the pitch darkness below.

'It's all right, darling. I'm coming. Don't be frightened, Mummy's here.'

When they reached the bottom of the steps Spencer strode ahead, candle aloft, between the rows of wine racks which were festooned with dusty spider's webs. The only sound was the scrabbling scuttle of a rat.

'Where are you, darlings?' Alexia called out.

A moment later Emma, followed by a silently weeping Freddie, emerged from the darkness, white-faced and terrified. They were shivering and their faces were smeared with dirt.

'It's all right, it's all right,' Alexia kept saying reassuringly, as she put her arms around them and held them close.

'Dada said you'd never find us,' Freddie quavered, rubbing his eyes with the back of his hand.

'I-I didn't like it,' Emma sobbed, hanging on to her mother.

Simon lurched forward out of the darkness holding a half filled bottle of gin. His pale eyes looked mad in the candlelight and he was grinning demonically. 'Took your time, didn't you?' he slurred. 'We've been hiding for ages.'

Ignoring him, Alexia picked up Emma, indicating to Spencer to carry Freddie up the stairs.

'Time for bath and bed,' she told the children, forcing her voice to sound cheerful and matter-of-fact, 'and a nice drink of warm milk, don't you think, Nanny?'

'Yes, definitely,' Nanny agreed in her no-nonsense way.

Simon followed them up the steps, taking the occasional swig from the gin bottle as if he'd forgotten they were there. The servants quickly dispersed in embarrassment. No one spoke.

Two hours later, having stayed with the children until they went to sleep, Alexia swept into the drawing room where Simon was mixing cocktails before dinner.

'What were you thinking of, Simon? The children were scared to death. And frozen. They're far too young to be treated like that.'

'Oh, shut up, woman. You make me sick. They were fine. Until you started screaming their names like a fishwife. That's what frightened them.'

He stood swaying with his back to the fire, his bloodshot eyes barely able to focus on her face.

'You're completely irresponsible,' she blazed. 'I can never leave you alone with them again. Nanny and I had a terrible time trying to get them to go to bed tonight. They're frightened of the dark now, which they never were before.'

'You're such a neurotic bitch!' he shouted, suddenly striding forward and raising his hand to strike her. He missed her face by inches as she managed to dodge the blow. 'Stupid, common bitch!' he screamed, punching her on the shoulder this time. She reeled back from the pain, dazed for a moment, and he stumbled, tripping over his own feet so that he made a grab at her to save himself from falling. There was a ripping sound as her chiffon dinner dress tore and he landed in a crumpled heap at her feet.

'You're a bloody bitch, always going on at me,' he seethed, trying to get to his feet but staggering before falling again.

'I can't stand this any more,' Alexia said in desperation.

'You're making my life a living hell. If I don't get away from here I'll go mad.'

Simon somehow got to his feet and flung himself against the door, blocking her way.

'You're my *creature*! You can't leave!' he yelled, his face almost black with rage.

She tried to elbow him aside. 'I've only stayed because of the children, but I can't do it—'

His fist slammed into her cheek, throwing her off balance, knocking the breath out of her body.

'You're my wife and you're staying with me.' He was in a frenzy now, wild and uncontrollable. Suddenly her anger gave way to fear.

Feeling as if she were fighting for her life, she pulled away from his grip and, streaking across the room, managed to reach the bell and press it long and hard before he came for her again, raining down blows on her body with his fists.

'You . . .! You . . .!' he gasped in a terrifying paroxysm of rage.

The library door flew open and the butler and two footmen rushed in. Without a word, they quickly surrounded him in silent condemnation, acting as a barrier so Alexia could run from the room, clutching her torn dress.

Leonora was standing in the middle of the hall, pale and wraith-like, her hand to her mouth, her eyes scared. She gazed at the torn dress. 'What happened?'

Alexia, running past her up the stairs, shouted over her shoulder, 'I've got to get away from here.'

*It's over. I can't stay in this madhouse any longer. Simon is out of his mind with drink and tonight he really hurt me. I've got to get away and the children must come with me. I don't care what anyone thinks any longer.*

*I'm sick of the endless secrets I'm expected to hide. If the rules of the game state I must keep up appearances that does not mean that in private I should have to endure the unendurable.*

*The servants' hall must be alive with gossip tonight, like a hive of active bees. The lord and master isn't only a drunken philanderer, he also beats up his wife.*

*He plays cruel pranks on his small children and
frightens them to death. The lord and master is the
biggest braggart and bully in the county. The son of a
murderer too; so what do you expect? That's what
they'll be saying, but I no longer care.*

*It's two o'clock in the morning and I still can't get
to sleep. My bruises ache and I shall have to put on a
lot of make-up tomorrow to hide the mark on my cheek.
A little while ago I crept downstairs because Shadow
needed to go out, and as I tiptoed along the corridor
I heard the most dreadful sobbing coming from Simon's
room. My heart stood still for a moment. It was the
abandoned sobbing of a small child but with the strength
and passion of a man. Then I heard Leonora's voice,
trying to calm him.*

*It changes nothing, though. I have to leave.*

Shortly after dawn, Alexia slipped out of Marley in her riding
clothes. She needed to clear her head before she could plan
her future. Meanwhile she wanted to be on her own to gather
her thoughts. It was a bright winter morning with a touch
of frost in the air and as she walked briskly round to the
stables, she took deep gulps of cold air to steady herself.

Smith, the head groom, was already up and carting bales
of hay from a storeroom into the stables when she entered
the yard.

'Good morning, m'lady,' he greeted her without surprise.
No doubt he'd heard what had happened the previous night.

'Good morning, Smith. Could you saddle up Dancer for
me, please?'

'Yes, m'lady. Beautiful morning for a ride, m'lady.'

Dancer was already peering over the door of her loose
box, ears pricked at the sound of Alexia's voice. She stroked
the mare's muzzle and gave her a sugar lump. In the adjoining
stable Prancer whinnied in greeting, stamping her hooves,
wanting to be taken out too.

Once saddled and bridled, Dancer stepped daintily into
the yard, swishing her tail. 'Come along, my lovely,' Smith
whispered to the mare as he led her to where Alexia waited
by the mounting block.

'Thank you, Smith.'

As Alexia trotted out of the yard she decided she'd ride cross-country to the hills beyond, to the spot where Simon had taken her that first day when she'd ridden Silver Stream and been so terrified. Now she and Dancer moved as one, attuned to each other and working in perfect rhythm and coordination. They trotted through the woods, and then walked quietly for a while. As Alexia looked around at the sleeping countryside, dormant for the next few months, resting peacefully before the hectic blossoming of spring, she gradually began to feel better. She patted Dancer's smooth neck, and clicked her tongue.

'Come on girl,' she urged softly. 'Let's go to the top.'

She set off across the field and Dancer flew effortlessly over the fence on the far side before cantering diagonally across the next field to a second fence. She took this one too with precision and then, gathering speed, raced on.

Alexia was smiling to herself now, feeling wonderfully free as the mare galloped on, faster and faster, hooves thundering on the frozen earth, her mane and tail streaming in the wind as Alexia gripped the saddle with her knees, balanced like a jockey. There was another fence and the wind whipped past them as the horse sailed over, but as they landed Alexia frowned, thinking she'd heard her name being called.

Turning to glance over her shoulder she saw with dismay that Simon, mounted on Prancer, was galloping flat out as he tried to catch up with her.

She urged Dancer on. She'd come out here to be alone and the last person she wanted to see was Simon.

'Come on girl, come on.' She flicked the horse with her riding crop.

Dancer, sensing Prancer was coming up behind, started to race harder than ever, intent on getting to the top of the hill first.

Alexia looked swiftly over her shoulder again. Simon was coming up to the last fence. Prancer took off, and she watched as the horse soared effortlessly over it; *Simon will catch up with me now*, she thought.

But Prancer landed awkwardly, slipping on the hard ground. Simon was thrown like a rag doll as the horse crashed down on her side and he disappeared under half a ton of dapple-grey horseflesh. Prancer rolled over, legs in the air, then got to her feet, obviously shaken, before taking a few tentative steps.

Alexia reined Dancer in sharply. Turning, she saw Simon lying still.

With a cry of horror, she cantered back and, dismounting, rushed to where he lay.

'Simon!' She flung herself down beside him and peered into his white face.

She laid a hand on his shoulder. She needed help. She must get an ambulance. She must get him to hospital. 'Simon!' she shouted in terror.

His eyes opened slowly and looked into hers. With relief she grasped his hand.

'Are you all right?' Maybe he wasn't as badly hurt as she'd feared. Maybe he'd just been stunned by the fall.

'Are you all right?' she repeated when he didn't answer.

He was still looking at her with those pale blue eyes that had so hypnotized her at first.

'I'm so sorry, Alexia,' he whispered.

Then something happened. A sudden stillness came over him as if a switch had been turned off and although he was still looking at her, there was nothing there. He was dead.

# Thirteen

'It's all my fault,' Alexia sobbed in devastation. 'I should never have said I was leaving him.'

Leonora, too shocked to take in what had happened, remained silent.

'You mustn't blame yourself,' Virginia said fiercely. 'He brought it on himself. He treated you abominably. I don't know how you put up with it for as long as you did.'

Alexia shook her head. 'He couldn't help it.'

The local doctor had been called to give Alexia something to calm her down after she'd galloped back to the stables, leading Prancer and calling out wildly for help. The only words she could utter were, 'Help me. He's dead. He's dead.'

It took Smith some time to find out where Simon lay so he could send out a party to bring the lord and master home for the last time.

Later that day Virginia and William arrived to comfort Leonora. Alexia was beyond comforting, wrenched apart with guilt, and all they could do was plead with her not to blame herself.

'I can't help it,' she stormed angrily, her tear-stained face white and pinched, the black dress her lady's maid had put out for her to wear hanging limply on her slim frame. 'I handled him so badly. I should have taken him to a doctor to help him stop drinking, instead of having rows with him.'

'He wasn't only drinking, I know for a fact he took drugs,' William said in judgemental tones.

'Then he needed help more than ever,' she lashed out angrily. 'Does nobody understand? Simon is dead and he was only thirty-one. Thirty-one,' she repeated distraught.

'We realize that, Alexia, but you couldn't have been happy

with him if you'd threatened to leave him,' William pointed
out. 'I can understand you're upset, but nevertheless . . .'

'You don't understand at all! You don't understand
*anything*, William. He was a golden youth when I first met
him, funny and wonderful and so charismatic. I fell in love
with him; I adored him. I knew he was flawed but who is
perfect? And he was Freddie and Emma's father, and they're
asking where he is all the time. They're still so small and
they loved him so much and I believe he loved them, too.'
She wiped her eyes then pressed the damp handkerchief to
her trembling lips.

Virginia looked distressed. 'You'll have to tell them he's
in Heaven,' she said. 'Poor little mites. Thankfully they're
too young to understand, but it is a tragedy.' She looked
thoughtful. 'His whole life was a tragedy.'

Leonora looked pained. 'Don't say that,' she said brokenly.
'I've lost my only son and I want to remember the happy
times. He could be so sweet and I did my best . . .'

Alexia, remembering how she'd heard Leonora talking to
Simon in the middle of the night, only a few hours before
he'd been killed, jumped to her feet and ran from the room,
unable to bear seeing the pain of her mother-in-law's anguish.
Without stopping she ran out of Marley in her thin black
dress and headed for her secret garden, where she could
grieve in private.

It was late in the afternoon now and the light was failing
but she didn't care. Letting herself into the shed she lit a
candle and, wrapping a rug around her shoulders, sat huddled
on a chair, overcome with utter despair.

Every time she closed her eyes she saw Prancer rise up
to take the fence, with Simon sitting astride, looking at her
appealingly, shouting her name and then . . . and then . . .
Would she ever get the sight of the fall out of her mind? Or
seeing Simon lying still on the chilled ground? And then his
last words: *I'm sorry*, breaking her heart, some part of her
dying with him.

Her mind kept going back to the previous day. Their last
day as a family. If only she hadn't let him play hide-and-seek
with the children; if only she hadn't been angry with him
afterwards; if only she'd walked calmly away and left him to

go on drinking by himself. And finally, if only she hadn't told him she was leaving him.

'Oh God,' she whispered in torment, running her hands through her hair. Why had she quarrelled with him? The whole thing was a terrible mess. Grief-stricken, she sat and wept, knowing she would have given anything to be able to turn the clock back twenty-four hours.

Regret and remorse, the worst of all ills, brought a sense of desolation she didn't know existed. Weeping and dozing from exhaustion, she stayed in the shed unaware of the passing time. When the door creaked open she sat upright, startled.

Roderick stood in the doorway, his expression full of sympathy.

She gave a little cry of shock, wondering for a moment if she was dreaming.

'I'm so sorry,' he said quietly.

She started sobbing wildly. 'That's what he said to me before he died. I don't think I can bear this. It was all my fault.'

With one stride he was by her side, holding her hands, talking softly but firmly to her.

'Alexia, you need to rest properly. You've had the most terrible shock and I'm more sorry than I can say, but you must remember it wasn't your fault. Prancer slipped on the frozen ground and it wasn't her fault either. Simon was a first-rate rider but accidents happen. No one is to blame.'

He half lifted her to her feet as he spoke. 'Everyone's very worried about you, wondering where you are, but I knew where I'd find you.' He took her arm and gently led her across her garden. 'Come along. You should get some proper sleep. The children are going to need you to be brave and I know you won't let them down.'

Like a child, Alexia allowed herself to be led back to the house, where her lady's maid gently coaxed her upstairs to her room, giving her a glass of warm milk and another sedative before helping her into bed.

*I'm walking around without a heart. It's four days since Simon died and I'm completely numb. I don't feel anything now as I plan his funeral and tell Freddie and Emma that*

*Daddy is happy with the angels and they'll see him again one day. It's so strange to be like this, without feelings. I find myself comforting poor Leonora, who has stayed in bed, and discussing the service with Virginia, wondering what hymns Simon would like.*

*Roderick is staying and he keeps us all sane with his calm manner and deep compassion. He sits with Leonora and reads the letters of condolence to her, and he comforts Virginia and tells William to stop being so judgemental about Simon.* ·*I don't know what I'd do without him right now and yet my feelings are frozen as far as he's concerned, too.*

*I feel nothing. I am nothing. Except perhaps a woman who has two small children to think about. A widow who must be strong. Roderick tells me ruefully when I complain about my lack of emotion that it won't last. He calls it 'delayed shock' and says it's nature's way of closing down for a while, to stop me suffering. How long will I stay like this? I ask him, hoping he will say a long time because it's so pleasant to be in this state of nothingness. He shrugs and smiles and says, 'It depends.'*

It had been nearly three years since Ian Clifton's funeral, and yet it seemed like only yesterday to the hundreds of mourners who filled St Olaf's church as they watched the same careful arrangements being carried out.

Once again the hundred and fifteen members of staff lined the route as Simon's coffin passed by, carried by six foresters and accompanied by Prancer, led by Smith, just as Firewheel had accompanied Ian's coffin to its final resting place.

Alexia sat with Freddie and Emma in the first car, while Leonora, shrouded in a thick black veil and accompanied by Virginia, William and Roderick, rode in the second car.

'Alexia's being so brave,' Robert Garnock whispered to his wife as Alexia took her place in the front pew of the church, her children on either side.

'I don't know how she does it,' Zoe replied, tearful herself.

In the row behind, Kenneth Ponsonby made a sly aside to Simon's old friend 'Hoots' McVean, who happened to be sitting next to him.

'Two lots of death duties in three years is going to finish the family off, isn't it?' Kenneth noted with relish.

'I thought you'd already done that,' Hoots retorted angrily, stepping out of the pew and stalking off down the aisle.

People were whispering in horror, 'Fancy that dreadful man turning up today.'

'Terribly bad form,' everyone agreed.

Alexia held Freddie's hand and drew Emma on to her lap. Roderick watched her with concern, wishing he could comfort her but knowing she wouldn't welcome anyone trying to get close at this time.

It seemed that in death Simon's old friends, who – mostly on the advice of their parents – had avoided him after the publication of *Hubris and Hell*, were out in force today. They were all there, looking grimly sad, a world away from the low life with whom he'd surrounded himself for the past eighteen months.

Only Baggers, a lonely, dissolute figure shunned by everyone, pushed himself to the front in order to get a good seat. Alexia turned slowly and gave him a long hard stare of loathing. Simon had been weak and he'd been flawed, but Baggers had taken advantage, getting Simon to finance their nights of debauchery. The drink, the drugs, the restaurants and the girls; she'd recently discovered that it was Simon who had paid for everything.

The service began and for the next forty minutes Alexia felt as if she were in a dream. A sense of total unreality stole over her as the congregation prayed and sang hymns and Roderick gave the eulogy.

He spoke movingly of the black thread of original sin that runs through the human condition, but added that Simon's black thread was overshadowed by the many gold and silver strands which also made him an unforgettable and loveable character. When he added that 'The most fortunate thing that ever happened to Simon was meeting Alexia', she caught her breath and sat very still, thinking *I must remember to tell Simon the nice things Roderick has said* . . . and then realized with shock that Simon was gone and she'd never see him again.

'But he will live on in Freddie and Emma and for that we

must be grateful,' Roderick concluded, looking down at the front pew where Emma sucked her thumb and Freddie sat very upright, looking up at him.

Alexia gazed back, but she was thinking of Simon as he'd been when she'd first known him, so full of laughter and enthusiasm, a golden youth with incredible expectations and his life spread before him, filled with promise.

Back at Marley Court she received the guests with the quiet dignity of someone who has everything under control.

'Everyone is being so kind,' she kept saying, smiling warmly as friends and neighbours offered their condolences. Cynically she remembered that people had thought she and Simon had had the perfect marriage, so now she would forever have to pretend they did, even if only for the sake of the children.

'Darling, you're being so brave,' her father said, drawing her to one side in the crowded red salon as footmen served tea and stiff drinks. 'You are allowed to grieve, you know. It's not good for you to bottle it all up inside.'

She looked at Malcolm squarely. 'I'm not suppressing my feelings, Daddy. I just don't feel anything. Not a thing. I wish I could, but . . .' she gave a little shrug and twisted the long rope of pearls between her fingers, 'but I can't. I feel perfectly calm now, as if nothing had happened. In fact I keep expecting Simon to come through those doors at any moment, saying he's just bought a new car or something,' she added with a little disbelieving laugh. 'Isn't that strange?'

As she continued to talk to people, smiling and thanking them for coming, she realized others were circling around her, watching her closely with puzzled expressions. Why were they looking at her like that?

Roderick came up and drew her aside. 'Are you all right, Alexia?' he asked in concern.

She looked surprised. 'Of course I am. Why? I've passed the crying stage. I suppose I cried myself out when it happened, but now I feel absolutely nothing,' she confided, lowering her voice. 'I wish I'd always felt like this; life would have been so much easier. It's like I've got nothing more inside me to give.' Her eyes looked dreamily serene.

'I felt like that after my mother died.'

'Oh my God!' she exclaimed as if she'd suddenly remembered something. 'You don't think Simon will want Baggers to stay for dinner tonight, do you ...?' Then she stopped dead and, for a second, looked confused.

'It's all right,' he whispered gently. 'Anyway, Baggers returned to London after the service. I think maybe we should have a quiet family evening, don't you? Leonora certainly isn't in any state to entertain and I think you need to rest.'

'I'm really all right, you know. I wish people wouldn't fuss. I need to keep busy, Roderick, I have a lot to do.'

His smile was almost wistful, but his eyes drilled directly into hers. 'I know you do, but I'll always be around to help you and do anything I can for you, Alexia. You know that, don't you?'

She knew how he felt about her, had always felt. There had been a time when she'd felt the same way about him. But things had changed since Simon's death and her feelings had been severed as if by an axe, leaving her devoid of all emotion.

'It wouldn't be fair on you,' she told him directly. 'I'm dead inside now. As dead as Simon. I've been through too much and I'm spent. I'm sorry, but the children are my life now.'

His eyes scanned her beautiful features, so pale and drawn these days, and he reached out to take her hand. 'When you come back to life, which you will in time, I'll be waiting,' he whispered.

'Nobody seems to understand that I don't want to come back to life,' she replied with brutal honesty. 'I've never felt as much at peace as I do now. Nothing upsets me; not sad music or memories or *anything*. I want it to stay like this for ever. I shall bring up the children here and make sure they have wonderful lives.' She turned to look out of the window, almost as if she'd forgotten Roderick's presence. 'It seems strange that Freddie at three and a half is already the Earl of Clifton and I ...' she gave a mirthless laugh, 'and I at twenty-four am already a dowager, like Leonora.'

A pained expression crossed Roderick's face. He opened his mouth to say something but stopped and averted his gaze.

'We'd better mingle,' Alexia said. 'I'd no idea so many

people would come to the funeral.' She walked off to talk to a group by the fireplace and Malcolm strolled up to Roderick.

'She'll be all right,' he told the younger man, seeing his worried expression. 'No one could maintain the intensity of grief she suffered that first day. There'll be days when she's shut off from reality like now, and days when she'll be raw with pain and unable to come to terms with Simon's death. It'll be months if not years before she really gets over this,' he confided sadly. 'It's because she feels guilty.'

Roderick's eyes were bleak. 'I know.'

The two men who loved her best looked at each other. 'Her grandmother has moved in here, permanently. Alexia needs her more than ever now. But we'll still be there to pick up the pieces when the time's right, won't we?' Malcolm observed, and it was more a statement than a question.

'Without doubt,' Roderick replied quietly.

'Simon squandered his life and now we learn he squandered his inheritance, too,' William exclaimed furiously. 'He acted as if the world was his playground! I can't believe he was so irresponsible.'

'Stop being so bloody smug!' Alexia retorted furiously. 'He had temptations you have never even known, so you're in no position to criticize him.' She sat very still and upright, glancing at her grandmother from time to time, trying to absorb what the lawyers and accountants had told them. None of it seemed to make sense.

It was two months since Simon had been killed. The family lawyers, George Leighton and his assistant, Andrew Brown, who had looked after Ian Clifton's affairs, had informed them that a second lot of death duties, coming so soon after the first, had wiped out what was left of the family fortune. As they explained, even Simon's separate inheritance, which he'd come into when he reached twenty-five, had all been spent, and he'd left large debts as well.

Leonora and Virginia sat close together, exchanging troubled glances from time to time, while William seemed to have assumed that as he was the only male member of the family, he should now take charge.

'Alexia, you can't deny Simon was—' William began in a bullying voice.

She turned on him, angry as a cat whose territory has been invaded. 'Will you please keep out of this,' she snapped. 'Simon was *my* husband and the father of *my* children, and it is up to me to decide what is to be done.'

Helen McNaughten nodded silently. The lawyers looked uncomfortable.

'But how can he have spent all the money?' Virginia queried. Alexia leaned forward, her elbows on the table.

'Let me get this straight,' she said. 'Are you saying that there's no way we can raise enough to pay the death duties?'

The two men nodded gravely.

'I very much fear every penny has gone.' Mr Leighton spoke heavily. 'And there are debts to be settled. As we now know, Simon's father had been living beyond his means for twenty years, and financially speaking, Simon's recent death has been the last straw.'

Leonora sat, too stunned to speak, unable to believe that everything had gone.

Alexia continued relentlessly, 'So the only way to get out of this mess and pay the death duties is to sell Marley Court, lock, stock and barrel?'

'That is correct,' Mr Brown agreed.

Leonora started weeping.

Mr Brown continued almost apologetically, 'If you were to sell the whole estate, the house, the contents and the land with its fourteen cottages, you could pay the death duties. And most importantly, you would have enough left over to buy a reasonably sized house, and enough to live on and educate your two children as your late husband would have wished.'

Alexia drew in a deep breath and leaned back. 'Are there any alternatives?'

Mr Leighton shook his head. 'We've gone into this very carefully, as you can imagine. If you'd had some particularly fine works of art that could have been sold, that would have helped, but everything's been listed for probate. The only solution is to sell up completely if you and the children are to have a secure future.'

'And that must include my grandmother and my mother-in-law,' Alexia pointed out firmly.

'Don't worry about me, darling,' Helen insisted. 'I have my old age pension and I can always go back to London.'

'Nonsense, you're staying with us, Granny.'

'And Mama can always live with us,' Virginia pointed out, without looking at William. 'There's plenty of room at Thorpe Hall.'

'I want to stay here. This is my home.' Leonora wailed, looking stricken. 'I don't understand . . . where can all the money have gone?'

'I'll tell you where it's gone! On wine, women and song!' William announced bluntly.

'Oh, do shut up.' Virginia spoke irritably.

'I was only saying . . .' he began peevishly.

'Well, don't. What's done is done.'

'In fairness to Simon,' Mr Brown pointed out, 'the financial situation was in a heavily depleted state when his father died three years ago.' He turned to Leonora who sat trembling, clutching Virginia's hand. 'I warned your late husband on many occasions that he was living beyond his means and if the situation continued for much longer he could face bankruptcy.'

Leonora gave a muffled groan and covered her face with her hands. 'It's Kenneth Ponsonby's fault,' she wailed. 'He was bleeding my husband dry, but Ian never said anything.'

Alexia looked at Mr Brown. 'Did you tell Simon how serious the situation was when he came into his inheritance?'

'We both did,' Mr Leighton intervened heavily. 'He instructed us to sell enough land to cover his father's death duties and at the same time raise enough for his own future needs. This we did.' He paused as if not sure whether to continue.

'So what went wrong?' Alexia asked sharply.

Mr Leighton hesitated. 'Young men are not always very good at managing their affairs,' he admitted regretfully, staring down at his feet.

'Bloody extravagant you mean,' William observed brutally. 'He was always buying cars and clothes and taking people to expensive restaurants. I never knew such a spendthrift.'

'That's because you've never known anyone of quality!' Virginia said furiously.

There was an embarrassed silence.

'What have I got to live on, in the meanwhile?' Alexia asked in a practical voice. 'We have a staff of over a hundred here; can we pay their wages? And what about the running costs of Marley? I've only recently realized how enormous they are.'

Leonora looked up, surprised. 'Are they? I've never seen a bill in my life. I've always taken it for granted that we had enough money to live as we wanted.'

'I'm sure you'll get a bank loan to tide you over,' Mr Leighton observed. 'Hopefully, whoever buys Marley will keep your staff on, so there might be no need for any redundancies.'

'Perhaps one of our rich friends will buy it?' Virginia remarked. 'Then we could all come and stay.'

Leonora looked hopeful. 'I suppose Roderick couldn't afford it? It would be nice to keep Marley in the family for Freddie.'

Alexia shook her head. 'He may be a famous artist these days but I'm sure he hasn't made that sort of money.'

'It was just an idea,' Leonora murmured dolefully.

'Poor Mama,' Virginia sympathized. 'You've been so proud of Marley, haven't you?'

'Oh, why did this have to happen?' Leonora burst out in anguish. 'It was bad enough losing Ian but I expected to stay here until I died, with Simon looking after me.' She turned to Mr Leighton, her manner accusing. 'Do you realize Marley Court has been the family seat since 1544? Henry the Eighth gave it to Thomas Stanhope for the part he played in the Reformation. We've always lived here. Queen Elizabeth stayed here when she was a young woman. And in 1716 Henry Stanhope was the Lord High Chancellor of Great Britain before being created Earl of Clifton. This is our home, steeped in history and one of the finest buildings in the land.' She looked wildly at the others and her voice rose piteously. 'We can't just sell up, as if Marley was some suburban semi-detached villa?'

Virginia broke the dismal silence. 'Simon used to say this house was cursed.'

Alexia nodded. She realized how much Marley meant to
her mother-in-law, if only in terms of prestige, but she'd
always had mixed feelings about it herself. At moments it
was the most magical place she'd ever known, where mir-
acles could happen, and on that first visit it had completely
seduced her with its grandeur and beauty. But at other times
she felt as if the occupants were doomed, trapped in a prison
with golden bars.

Undaunted, Leonora continued. 'We must fight to save it
for Freddie. It's his inheritance and he must stay here and
bring up the next heir here,' she added, her voice breaking
dangerously.

William leaned back in his chair and surveyed them all.
'And how much happiness has this place brought any of
you?' he asked bluntly. 'Surely life isn't about living in a
museum and forcing yourself to preserve every stick and
stone, so that the next generation can be unhappy here, too?'

Virginia looked at him, shocked by the truth of his words.

Leonora drew a sobbing breath. Rising to her feet, she
fled from the room, clutching a handkerchief to her mouth.

Mr Leighton cleared his throat and spoke diffidently. 'I think
the older generation care about this sort of thing more than
you young ones,' he suggested, sympathetically. 'It's under-
standable that the Dowager Lady Clifton should feel a fierce
loyalty to her husband's home. It will be traumatic for her to
have to leave here.'

The task ahead was daunting. Lying in bed that night, with
Shadow tucked up by her side, Alexia wondered how she
was going to manage.

All her life other people had made the arrangements:
where she lived and what she did as a child and as a young
girl, where she moved to and how she lived when she got
married. Now it felt as if a splendid jigsaw puzzle depicting
a beautiful picture had been flung up in the air and the
pieces scattered to the four winds, so that she was going to
have to create new pieces and try to make them fit together
into another picture.

But what sort of picture? How much money would there
be left after all the debts had been paid? Enough to buy a

nice country house, or even a cottage, for her and her grandmother and the children? Would she be able to keep Dancer
and Freddie's Shetland pony? What was going to become of
Ian's Great Danes? Would they be able to keep Nanny on?
Unable to sleep, tormented by worry over tiny trivial details
mixed up with the overwhelming prospect of moving out of
Marley and its one hundred and twenty rooms, Alexia lay
awake throughout the long black night.

The future was full of so many uncertainties, she felt as
if she'd been blindfolded and ordered to step off the top of
a cliff.

A week later Leonora came over to the North Wing, where
Alexia and Helen were having breakfast.

'I have some good news, my dear,' she announced.

'What is it?'

'I've invited Roderick to stay. He'll advise us what to do.
The lawyers are all right but we need a man, a family member,
to help us get out of this mess, and William just doesn't
understand. Roderick is Simon's cousin, after all. I hope you
don't mind?'

Everything was suddenly going too fast and Alexia felt as
if she were being swept out to sea. She hadn't yet come to
terms with the upheaval that lay ahead.

'When is he arriving?'

'On Friday. He's just finished painting the Duchess of
Sutherland so he's got a couple of weeks before he begins
his next commission. I've told Mr Leighton and Mr Brown
to explain the financial situation to him.' She paused and
looked at Alexia, puzzled. 'Aren't you pleased? I hope you
don't think I'm interfering. You have so much on your plate
and it's lovely for you having your granny here, but I thought
if someone like Roderick could help it would take some of
the burden off your shoulders. I'm sorry if I've done the
wrong thing.'

Alexia shook her head. 'Mama, you haven't. I'm most
grateful, and Roderick will be a tremendous help.'

'William was hopeless,' Leonora continued crisply.
'I shouldn't say it but I'm quite glad they've gone home.'
She looked down at her hands, her mouth working as she

strove for control. 'I didn't like the way he talked about Simon.'

'Neither did I. He was judgemental and unkind.'

Leonora looked up and her expression was beseeching. 'And we loved Simon, didn't we? We loved him, in our own way?'

'Oh, Mama!' Suddenly Alexia's frozen feelings collapsed as if a dam had burst, and a flood of emotional tears overwhelmed her. Bereft of self-control she flung her arms around her mother-in-law and sobbed as if her heart would break, while Helen watched sympathetically.

The two women who had loved Simon most clung together, united in a grief that forgave Simon his weaknesses and sins, and remembered only the dazzling young man who had been so popular and who'd had the world at his feet.

Malcolm had warned Alexia that something small would tip the balance and touch the nerve that brought her out of her numb state of shock. And so it had proved to be.

Alexia greeted Roderick when he arrived at Marley the next day. After one quick look at her puffy eyes and quenched demeanour he gave her a quick, brotherly kiss on the cheek, and then became cheerfully matter-of-fact and businesslike.

It was obvious she'd 'come back to life', as she'd described it. So he trod gently, gauging the ebb and flow of her emotional moods, answering in a practical way her endless questions about what was going to happen.

'Marley obviously doesn't mean as much to me as it does to Leonora,' she explained, as they sat by the library fire drinking cups of hot chocolate while Helen took Shadow for a walk. 'But I want to know for the children's sake, what sort of house are we going to be able to afford?'

'At a guess I'd say a decent country house with eight to ten bedrooms and a bit of land, and at least four indoor staff and probably a gardener, too.'

She stared at him in amazement. 'You really think so? That would be wonderful.'

'I've gone over the figures and you're not going to be poor by normal standards,' Roderick explained, smiling. 'Church mice poor compared to Marley Court standards, but you'll have a house similar to mine in Cornwall – if you can manage in that?'

She smiled. 'I used to live in a three-bedroom basement flat in Kensington,' she reminded him, 'where we had to keep turning off the lights to save on the electricity bill.'

He raised his eyebrows in amusement. 'Your lawyers are setting up a trust fund for the children's education and giving Leonora enough to live on, and you'll also have a private income.'

'Will I?' She frowned in concentration. 'Enough to keep a few horses and dogs? And someone to look after them?'

Roderick smiled affectionately. 'Dearest Alexia, they've really frightened you about money, haven't they?'

'Well,' she paused thoughtfully, 'when you consider what we *had* – this house and thousands of acres and fourteen cottages, the house in Grosvenor Square and my in-laws' house in Belgrave Square, not to mention a dozen cars, works of art and antiques, and enough jewellery to please a sultan – by comparison it's a terrible comedown for the Clifton family, isn't it?'

'And for you personally?' he asked searchingly.

'None of it brought me any happiness, so I don't mind at all. I'd rather live in a normal house and have a normal life, than the rackety existence Simon and I used to lead. I was always exhausted and while part of the time it was fun, there were other times I'd rather forget,' she added quietly, thinking of the remains of the orgy Simon had held in London in her absence.

'I'm free to take control of my own life now,' she continued, 'to do whatever I want to do.'

'And what will you do?' Roderick asked, watching her intently.

'First of all I have to find myself. Who is the young Dowager Countess of Clifton, widow and mother of two? I shan't know until I'm settled in my own house, a house of my choice, not an ancestral home that I now believe cast a shadow over all of us.'

There was a long silence, broken only by the disintegration of a large log in the great fireplace that crumbled in a mass of sparks and white ash, leaving an empty space in the middle. Roderick gazed at it broodingly, his mouth turned down at the corners with disappointment.

'Will it be easy to sell this place?' she asked.

With an effort Roderick rose and went to look out of the window at the formal gardens, where the light was failing and darkness was enveloping the countryside.

'I'll talk to some agents tomorrow,' he said stiffly. 'Get the ball rolling for you.' Then he turned and walked briskly out of the library.

'Have you heard, Alexia?' Leonora hurried up to the nursery, where Alexia was reading a bedtime story to Freddie and Emma. She looked flustered.

'Heard what, Mama?'

'Roderick has just told me the Duke of Garnock has agreed to buy Marley.'

'What? Robert and Zoe?'

'Yes. Apparently he's been looking for somewhere appropriate in the south of England because Garnock Castle is too far away to go to at the weekend. If we have to sell up I'd rather it went to Robert Garnock than anyone else. He was a friend of Simon's and he's Freddie's godfather, so it's perfect, isn't it?'

'Perfect,' Alexia echoed. 'That's very quick. Roderick only contacted some estate agents a few days ago.'

'Robert didn't find it through an agent. Roderick phoned him and said we were selling and it was all agreed in a matter of moments. He's buying all the contents, too, except for the things we want to keep.' Leonora's voice broke and her eyes filled with tears.

Alexia nodded sympathetically. 'Where is Roderick now?'

'Downstairs.'

'Congratulate him for me, will you? And tell him I'll be down when I've settled the children.'

She looked around the nursery where generations of Cliftons had been brought up since Elizabethan times. At first she'd felt the squandering of an enormous fortune by her father-in-law and then by Simon had deprived her children of their rightful heritage, but now it struck her that the poisonous atmosphere that pervaded the magnificent old house, always hidden from outsiders but suffered by those within, could do Freddie and Emma more harm than the robust life she now planned for them.

It was a revelation to realize that once they'd moved she and the children would be freed from all pretence and the terrible secrets of the past. And she wanted them to have a normal childhood, without being surrounded by servants as if they lived in a royal palace like a little prince and princess.

It would be a new start, and she could hardly wait.

# Fourteen

'Mummy, can we go swimming tomorrow?' Freddie asked.

'Oh, yes!' Emma squealed excitedly, as they sat cross-legged on a rug in the garden of Elmscroft Grange, having a picnic luncheon.

'It's quite a long drive to the sea,' Alexia protested mildly as she offered him an egg sandwich. 'Let's see what the weather's like.'

Elmscroft had turned out to be the perfect eighteenth-century house to move into when they left Marley. The large rooms were light and airy and the place had a cheerful atmosphere. There were stables for Dancer, Silver Stream and the children's ponies, too, and a nice sized garden to play in.

Taking the simplest furniture from the big house, she'd created warm and cosy rooms, filled with soft colours and comfortable chairs and sofas. A cook, a kitchen maid and two parlour maids kept the place clean and tidy. She also employed a part-time gardener and Smith, the groom, who in semi-retirement had moved into a flat above the stables and looked after the horses.

Best of all, her grandmother had moved in with her, her stay made permanent because Malcolm Erskine had decided to remarry. Everything, she had to admit, had also been made easier when Leonora had decided not to move to Hampshire with them.

'I hope you don't mind dreadfully, my dear,' she'd said to Alexia, 'but Robert Garnock has insisted I remain in the North Wing. I think I'm what is called a "sitting tenant". Isn't that amusing? He only wants a peppercorn rent and he's even letting me keep Ian's Great Danes, so of course I've promised to keep an eye on the place when they're in London. Isn't that absolutely splendid?'

'Mama, I'm thrilled for you,' Alexia had replied, feeling secretly relieved.

Roderick had agreed it was a perfect solution. At the same time he'd pointed out that Elmscroft should be put in Freddie's name; not only would he then have a nice inheritance, but there would be 'no death duties to pay next time'.

*Next time! That made me think about my own mortality! Next time . . . and I'm only twenty-six! But Roderick was right. Two lots of death duties in three years brought us to final ruin. If the worst happened, a third lot would be fatal.*

*I love it here in Hampshire, away from all the bad memories of Marley. The countryside is beautiful and I have a lovely garden, though not a secret one. There is no need for that now. No need to have a place where I can go and hide and be on my own.*

*Strangely, although I'm in complete control of my life, as I swore I wanted, circumstances have made me revise my views on being in control.*

*All you can really control, I realize, is how you deal with what happens in your life. In reality, we are all controlled by fate and although we appear to have choices, what makes us choose one path and not another?*

*I don't regret the past at all now. I love my house, and I love the fact that Dancer and Silver Stream are happy in the stables, and that Shadow still follows me wherever I go. I have my children and Granny is my rock.*

*This is what, in the end, was meant to happen.*

Alexia's bedroom door burst open early the next morning.

'It's a lovely day,' Emma announced.

Freddie jumped up on to her bed, crushing her feet. 'You said we could go swimming today if it was fine.'

'Why don't we go and see Uncle Roderick? He lives by

the sea,' Emma pointed out as she stroked Shadow, who was curled up by Alexia's side.

'Yes, Mummy! Why don't we go and visit him? He's always saying we can stay in his house even if he's away.'

Alexia leaned back against her pillows, deep in thought.

Freddie clapped his hands. 'We could surprise him!'

'Yes, we could surprise him,' Emma echoed excitedly.

To the children's surprise Alexia burst out laughing.

Freddie looked at her with suspicion. 'What's so funny?'

'I was thinking Uncle Roderick would be very surprised indeed if we all turned up unannounced.'

'We don't have Nanny now, we can do what we like, can't we?' Freddie wheedled.

Alexia grinned. 'Actually I think it's a good idea.'

The children gazed at her in silent amazement. Then there were squeals of delight.

Alexia leapt out of bed, her face glowing. 'Come on then. Let's throw a few things into a suitcase and set off; it's a very long drive to Cornwall.'

Emma put her head on one side. 'Are you happy, Mummy?'

'Very happy,' Alexia exclaimed, throwing her arms around both of them and hugging them close. 'Now go and tell Great-Granny we're going to be away for a few days and ask Mrs Mason if she could make us some sandwiches for the journey.'

They scuttled off while Alexia, feeling strangely elated, got dressed and packed a case with a few essentials for the three of them. This was going to be an adventure and if Roderick happened to be away it wouldn't matter, because he'd always said his housekeeper would be there to let them in.

'When will we get there?' Freddie asked for the hundredth time.

Alexia kept her eyes on the road ahead and pressed down on the accelerator, knowing the children were getting tired and fidgety. They'd had a short nap but now they were impatient, wanting to arrive.

'We'll be in Boscastle in about half an hour,' she promised, 'and Penhalt is just beyond.'

'Can we swim then?' asked Emma.

It was now late in the afternoon and there was that stillness in the air that happens just before the sun starts its
downward dip prior to setting.

'Let's see what it's like when we get there,' she hedged,
hoping she hadn't made a dreadful mistake. Supposing
Roderick was away in London for a long while? Supposing he'd
given his housekeeper time off and there was no one there to
let them in?

At last they saw the sign to Penhalt, and with her heart
racing Alexia drove swiftly, knowing by the sun that she was
driving west towards the sea.

At any minute now . . .

'There!' Freddie shouted. 'There's a big house over there.
That must be where Uncle Roderick lives.'

Silcott Manor was more imposing than she'd expected. Made
of stone and with large windows, it was set in a tropical-style
garden tucked into a hollow at the top of the cliffs, overlooking
the Atlantic.

'We're here! Can we swim now?' Emma cried excitedly.

Alexia parked the car in the drive and climbed out slowly,
stiff from the long journey. At that moment the front door
opened and a kindly looking middle-aged woman came out.

'Can I help you?' she asked politely.

'I'm Alexia Clifton. Is Mr Davenport at home by any chance?'

The woman's face lit up. 'Oh, welcome, m'lady. Mr
Davenport isn't here, I'm afraid. He's driven into Bude to
get supplies but he'll be back shortly. These must be . . .?'

'Freddie and Emma,' Alexia replied smiling.

'Come in. Come in and welcome. I expect you'd like a
cup of tea? And milk for the children? And I've got a Dundee
cake just out of the oven.'

As she talked she led them into a large bright hall, off
which led a series of reception rooms. Glancing through the
open doors Alexia realized they all overlooked the beach and
the sea beyond.

Freddie and Emma ran into one of the rooms while the
housekeeper continued, 'I'm Mrs Wilmott and I was origin-
ally employed by the late Sir Edmund Davenport.'

'So you must have known his son since he was quite
young?'

Mrs Mason's smile broadened. 'I have indeed. He was a lad of eleven when I first came here.'

Freddie came running back into the hall. 'You're in there, Mummy,' he announced.

'What do you mean?'

'Come and look.'

He grabbed her hand and she followed him into an elegant room where Emma stood, looking up at *Alexia in the Pink Dress*. The picture was hanging facing one of the windows, as if the sitter was looking out to sea.

'Mr Davenport thinks the world of that painting,' Mrs Wilmott observed with satisfaction. 'He once told me it was his most precious possession.'

Alexia blushed and felt herself grow hot, remembering those long quiet afternoons in the Chelsea studio and how close she and Roderick had felt.

At that moment she knew she'd been meant to come and find him today, the time was right for her. But although they'd spoken on the phone, she'd hardly seen him in the past eighteen months. So was the time right for him, too? Or had she left it too long?

At that moment they heard a car stop in the drive and footsteps on the gravel.

Her chest felt so tight with a mixture of fear and longing she could barely breathe. Standing in front of her portrait she braced herself, praying she was not too late.

'Mrs W?' Roderick called out. He came bounding into the room, and stopped dead in his tracks when he saw her.

Somehow Alexia found her voice. 'I was waiting for you.'

He gave her one look and then, stepping forward, put his arms around her and pulled her close.

'Not nearly as long as I've been waiting for you, my darling Alexia.'